THE LOVE DEPARTMENT

Ally Bunbury is a bestselling novelist, based in Ireland. Inspired by the TV sitcom *Absolutely Fabulous*, she embarked upon a PR career in New York, London and Dublin. During a personal sabbatical in Paris, Ally wrote the draft of her first novel, *The Inheritance*.

A frequent contributor to *The Irish Times*, Ally lives with her husband, historian Turtle Bunbury, in the countryside.

www.allybunbury.com

PREVIOUS TITLES
All Wrapped Up
Infidelity
The Inheritance

The Love Department
ALLY BUNBURY

HACHETTE
BOOKS
IRELAND

Copyright © 2023 Ally Bunbury

The right of Ally Bunbury to be identified as the author of
the work has been asserted by her in accordance with the
Copyright, Designs and Patents Act 1988.

First published in Ireland in 2023 by
HACHETTE BOOKS IRELAND
First published in paperback in 2024

1

All rights reserved. No part of this publication may be reproduced,
stored in a retrieval system, or transmitted, in any form or by
any means without the prior written permission of the publisher,
nor be otherwise circulated in any form of binding or cover other
than that in which it is published and without a similar
condition being imposed on the subsequent purchaser.

All characters in this publication are fictitious and any resemblance
to real persons, living or dead, is purely coincidental.

Cataloguing in Publication Data is available from the British Library.

ISBN 9781399713207

Typeset in Book Antiqua by Bookends Publishing Services, Dublin

Printed and bound in Great Britain by Clays Ltd, Elcograf S.p.A.

Hachette Books Ireland policy is to use papers that are natural, renewable
and recyclable products and made from wood grown in sustainable
forests. The logging and manufacturing processes are expected to
conform to the environmental regulations of the country of origin.

Hachette Books Ireland
8 Castlecourt Centre
Castleknock
Dublin 15, Ireland

A division of Hachette UK Ltd
Carmelite House, 50 Victoria Embankment, London EC4Y 0DZ

www.hachettebooksireland.ie

In memory of my father,
Archie Moore
1943–2002

'Let everything happen to you: beauty and terror.
Just keep going. No feeling is final.'

Rainer Maria Rilke (1875–1926)

Chapter One

Le Marché Cher, Paris

Usually, all eyes gravitated towards Lando Shillington, a blond and dashing Irishman with a tightly cut beard. But on this October morning at Le Marché Cher, it was Charles de Croix who commanded attention. The two men stood between the Corinthian columns at the entrance to the city's most exclusive department store, with a Mansard roof and an enormous glass canopy above them. De Croix turned on his heels and entered the building, with Lando in pursuit.

'Straighten your tie,' de Croix snapped at an immaculately dressed man behind the perfume counter, 'and when did these lilies arrive?'

'At five a.m. this morning, Monsieur de Croix,' he said in a trembling voice. 'They arrived from Provence as you requested.'

Change them to pink roses,' said de Croix, whose sprinkling of grey in his neatly cut brown hair was the only hint to his sixty years of age. 'The day is too cold for lilies,' he added. 'Our customers must see colour to energise their senses.'

Lando breathed in the sweet, heavy smell of lilies and wondered if they would be binned or gifted to someone worthy of a bouquet that morning. The central gallery of the ground floor looked so inviting, he was sure customers would barely have a moment to glance at any floral display. Silk headscarves, velvet hats, tortoiseshell glasses and long cashmere coats were laid out so beautifully, anyone with available funds would be unable to resist a purchase. De Croix had made temptation an art form and Lando wondered if he could replicate this talent.

'Constance Jablonski is wearing this piece in the winter edition of *Vogue*,' said a sales assistant, bravely holding up a navy girdle in front of de Croix.

'Not bad,' he said, 'though the lace is perhaps cliché.' De Croix reached for a black girdle, neatly folded on a table beside a gilded birdcage with its door open. 'This piece of lingerie symbolises obedience, and like the clever birds who flew from captivity, we encourage women to free themselves.'

'So, we remove the girdle?' The sales assistant looked confused.

'In the words of Dita Von Teese,' said de Croix, 'lingerie is not about seducing men, it's about embracing womanhood.'

'What would you suggest as an alternative?' said the assistant, whose complexion was turning increasingly puce.

'This is for your department head to decide, *non*?' said de Croix. 'Where would we be if I had all the answers in my pocket?'

Lando stood next to a rail of Coco de Mer lingerie and ran his finger around the neck of his shirt, acutely feeling the pressure of his future. He had asked his godfather, de Croix, to guide him through the most intimate running of Le Marché Cher in preparation for taking the helm of his own family department store, Shillington's, in Dublin. After all, de Croix's foresight and indomitable energy had transformed Le Marché Cher from a squalor of strip lighting and polyester to a department store so chic, queues would form each season as clothes rails were updated with the latest arrivals from the world's most elegant and exclusive ateliers. But three months under the critical eye of de Croix had resulted in Lando feeling even more unnerved about his task ahead.

The floor silenced as de Croix climbed the curved marble staircase. On the landing, with opulent chandeliers hanging from above, he clapped his hands like a cha-cha dancer and peered down at his staff. Lando noticed how each well-groomed staff member stood to attention, looking up to their boss whose puzzling combination of sternness and strength of purpose earned their respect.

'I want you to listen carefully,' he said, looking from left to right. 'We must give our customers what they want before they know what it *is* they want.' De Croix paused and drew a hand towards his right ear. '*Oui ou non*?'

The staff dressed in black trouser suits mumbled, '*Oui*, Monsieur de Croix.'

De Croix stamped his foot. 'What response is this from my ambassadors of all that is chic and *magnifique* in this world?'

'*Oui*, Monsieur de Croix,' came a resoundingly passionate response. '*Oui!*'

De Croix pressed the palms of his hands together in prayer. 'A department store of this calibre exists to feed a desire for abundance.' He breathed in so tightly his nostrils squeezed together. 'They want jewels, not only for their ears or wrists but for their houses. We must tantalise with our Forbes & Lomax light switches and tempt with technology like the computer-operated coffee system on the top floor. Maybe they want a Saint Laurent wool tuxedo jacket or a pair of cashmere Yosemite socks.' De Croix pulled up the hem of his trousers and flashed his ankle to a cheering audience, though they quickly returned to their demure composure. 'Fulfil dreams and wishes this Christmas season, and you will be rewarded not only with a bonus in your pay cheque, but a sense that you are doing the world a favour by spreading the good word of style.'

Lando couldn't imagine speaking to the staff at Shillington's in such a way. Some had worked at the store for so many years; they'd watched Lando grow up, and now their own children worked there. Others had started at Shillington's straight out of school. What would they think of Lando as their twenty-seven-year-old new boss? He didn't have his mother's authority or his late father's confidence, and though he had studied hard through university, including getting a 2:1 in business at Trinity College, followed by a first-class master's degree and a PhD over three years, it was plain to see he didn't need such qualifications to become CEO. But it had been a case of anything to give him more time before stepping into the hot seat – which was the very reason Lando had asked de Croix to take him on as an apprentice, though starting in the basement, dressed in navy overalls, and adding size cubes on top of clothes-hangers was something he hadn't bargained for.

After a mind-numbing three weeks, Lando had graduated to the restrooms, this time wearing a white coat like a lab technician, except there was no science involved as he'd passed hand towels to customers. Though Lando's proficiency in French was mediocre at best, he could easily understand when a woman had asked for his number, another had invited him into a cubical and one lady had given him twenty euros as if Lando was her grandson.

When de Croix had at last instructed Lando to dress in a suit, he expected to be at management level but instead was brought to the complaints department. His job was to deal with English-speaking customers, mostly tourists, moaning about the French sizing or the amount of tax they had to pay, and if they'd known, they 'never would have bought the item in the first place'. Finally, when deemed ready, Lando was invited to shadow de Croix, the bossiest man in Paris. And when the bells chimed for November 1st, he would fly to Dublin and accept the baton from his mother. The question was, would she really hand over Shillington's department store to Lando when the time came?

Chapter Two

The night before Lando was due to fly to Dublin, he stood
next to Celine de Croix outside her family's apartment on
rue Vaneau. A year older than Lando, and daughter to de
Croix, Celine had added unexpected complexity to the
Parisian trip. They had become close, and not only because
Lando had been invited to stay in the guest room of her little
apartment on rue Saint Dominique during his stay in Paris.
Celine had listened to Lando's turmoil about living in his
late father's shadow, and his fear of failure in taking on the
family business. They hadn't slept together, but in every
other way, Lando and Celine had become a couple. And it
wasn't as if Lando had ever had any problem persuading
a woman to sleep with him, but this was what made their
connection more interesting. She was exquisite in her French
beauty, and the sexual restraint she showed only heightened
her appeal.

'Lando,' she said, sheltering in the arched doorway from
sleeting slow, 'why must you stand with hands in your
pockets?'

He shrugged his shoulders. 'I always have.'

'And if you fall on your face?'

'I'll put out my elbows.' Lando flapped out his arms like a bird.

'Then maybe before you leave Paris, I can teach you another new habit.' Celine gently tugged Lando's sleeve from the warmth of his woollen coat pocket and held his hand. 'Let's just hope this door opens before we catch frostbite.'

'If it delays my return to Ireland, frostbite doesn't sound so bad.' Apart from Lando's nerves about his new role at Shillington's, he had hoped that three months away from Dublin would ease his guilt about what had happened the night before he'd left, but to no avail. It had been the classic cocktail error. Farewell drinks with his best friend since childhood, Immy Brooks. So intimate, they could pretty much read each other's minds. For years they had shared their own intimate world, solving each other's dilemmas and dramas, partying together, and passing out together.

When the door opened, Lando stepped back so that Celine's mother, Julie de Croix, could embrace her daughter. Julie was the epitome of Parisian elegance in a black knit dress and dark hair tied back.

'My beauty,' she said, hugging Celine. 'Lando, what do I do with this unmarried daughter?'

'Mama,' said Celine, double kissing her mother's cheeks. 'How many times have you asked Lando this question? Maybe I'll follow him to Ireland. I could even become a nun while I'm there.'

'You think they serve champagne in convents?' said Julie, winking at Lando. She must have been as confused about his relationship with Celine as he was. 'Besides, how could Le Marché Cher survive without the best Head of Buying in the whole of France, if not the world? Come on, let's open a bottle and say farewell to our handsome Irish boy.'

Julie led the way to a minimalist drawing room with a silkscreen portrait by Andy Warhol hanging above a stone mantelpiece.

'Lando, you open the champagne and I'll light a cigarette,' said Julie, sitting down on the green velvet sofa, kicking off her heels, and curling up her stockinged feet. 'And then you tell me if your godfather has taught you all you need to know?'

'I don't think it's possible,' said Lando, removing the wire around the champagne cork. 'Even with all my years of studying business and getting to know every inch of Le Marché Cher, which is the tightest ship run at the highest standards, I'm feeling more intimidated than ever.'

'You'll be fine,' said Celine, throwing a log on the fire. 'Just follow the rules, mark up the prices and sell.'

'That won't work on our customers,' said Lando, popping the cork. 'They'd all turn grey overnight if we charged more; mind you, most of our customers are over eighty.'

'Then you need to reach a new kind of customer,' said Julie. 'Out with the old.'

'That's harsh,' said Celine.

'It is,' agreed Lando, 'and no disrespect intended, Julie, but Shillington's is on its knees.' Lando poured the champagne into the delicate Baccarat coupe glasses. 'We have no marketing budget and Mum refuses to modernise.'

'Then it's just as well a new boss is coming to town,' said Celine.

'But if I can't boost sales, then I've failed everyone, including you guys,' said Lando, handing a glass to Julie. 'Your family has been incredibly kind.'

'Paris is the best place in the world to find a new perspective.' Julie took a sip of champagne and dragged deeply on her cigarette. 'It is a patient city which gives the heart time to judge.'

Lando only wished that were true. When he arrived in Paris, he messaged Immy to say he hoped she was OK and maybe the break could help them figure out what they wanted. But he received no more than a couple of lines in return, downplaying what had happened.

'I am not one to get involved in other people's business,' said Julie.

'Ha, Mama, that is what you think,' said Celine, raising her glass to Lando.

'I have a rather extreme idea,' said Julie, 'but at my age, I feel it's time to speak up for what I want.'

'What are you saying, Mama? Do you want to buy a Bugatti and drive to Monaco and rekindle a romance with an old boyfriend?'

'Nothing so exciting,' said Julie, looking like she rather liked Celine's suggestion. 'Before we reach another new year, I am wondering if there is an opportunity for my husband to take his godfatherly duties a step further and accompany you to Ireland and help boost your Christmas takings?'

'And you stay here alone?' laughed Celine. 'What would you do with your evenings, Mama?'

Julie blew out her cheeks, and with steely eyes, looked very serious. 'I would have some time to myself for the first time in years.'

'And what about Le Marché Cher?' said Celine, sounding panicked. 'The place couldn't run without Papa, not before Christmas.'

'Then you could take his place,' said Julie.

'*Non*, Mama, I would have to go with him.' Celine looked at Lando. 'Besides, I heard so much about Shillington's; I think it could be looked at as an essential research trip.'

Celine and Immy together at Shillington's? Lando's new role momentarily paled in comparison as he considered this unintentional love triangle.

'My point, Lando, is that my husband's retail experience and entrepreneurial skills are so sharp, I know he can make an impact in a matter of weeks, and then you are set to inherit a business which can thrive.'

'I don't think Papa would leave Paris, even for a week,' said Celine.

Lando couldn't work out if Celine was for or against joining him in Ireland. Maybe she wanted to travel without de Croix.

'Your father needs a challenge,' said Julie, 'even his *cinq à sept* is boring him.'

'Oh, he told you?' Celine teased as if she didn't seem bothered by her father's rendezvous between 5 p.m. and 7 p.m. with his cliché Parisian mistress.

'He doesn't need to.' Julie spoke seriously. 'The sparkle in his eyes has turned weak and I worry we are getting stale with each other.'

'Mama, that is too sad.' Celine walked over to her mother and kissed her hand.

'I don't know; maybe it's the champagne which makes me speak,' said Julie.

'Excuse our English, Lando, won't you?' said Celine. 'The movies we watch encourage us to speak with drama.'

'Both of you speak English perfectly,' said Lando.

'Then you are even sweeter than I thought.' Julie put her glass on a side table and pulled a cushion to her chest. 'You know, Lando, the pact your father and de Croix made with each other in Cambridge all those years ago still stands.'

'Don't make him sad, Mama, not on his last night,' said Celine.

'But it's true.' Julie's voice broke. 'They promised to make each other godparents to their first-born children, and to watch over them for their lifetime.'

'If my father had lived to know Celine, he would have been very proud,' said Lando, watching the flames dance in the fireplace. He felt the familiar heartache of missing a man he had never known.

'My sweet,' said Julie, 'surely your mother has told you how much you are like your father, and if you can find the courage, it could be worth opening your heart to try and give your store one more chance. If it fails, you sell the property, but maybe it can work.'

Lando felt his shoulders tighten. He had enjoyed living life on the surface these past months, knowing it was a freedom he couldn't enjoy once he returned to Ireland. The crew at Le Marché Cher, when they weren't on their best behaviour for de Croix, had taken Lando under their wing, guiding him through the best of Paris night life. From the *1988* with sequined walls, mirror balls and DJs switching between the turntables, to the velvety salons of *Moi, Moi* with cocktails named after literary characters, bookshelves, and full-size peacocks from Deyrolle. Lando had been taken on a nocturnal journey to opulence, but he knew it was time for reality to bite.

'Your father wanted to put his future on a stick and throw it over the bridge,' said Julie. Her English translations would have been amusing if the subject hadn't been serious. 'And your mother came along, urged him to face his realities and yes —' Julie paused, her eyes filling with tears ' — OK, it was a quick time for them, but they created you, Lando, your mother bravely carried on with the business and, now, it's your turn.'

Celine rested her glass on the mantelpiece. 'Mama, you are bringing us down.'

'What?' said Julie, pressing her fingers beneath her eyelids. 'Lando has this opportunity in his hand, and I know his father would want me to tell him so.'

'Then let's fix this together,' said Celine, who loved to take charge just like her father. 'Lando, it's all eyes on you – to sell up or give it a try.'

'And I want to try,' he said, 'I really do.' Lando felt so indecisive, he might have to resort to flipping a coin to make his decision.

He felt so grateful to have this talk, which would have been impossible with his own mother.

'De Croix is impressed with you, Lando; you were always on time and never complained, even when you had to put up with the odour of the ladies in Le Marché Cher, and let's face it, no matter how deluxe these women think they are, in the toilette they are no different from the farm animals.'

They burst into hoots of laughter, which felt like the best relief.

'What would your mother think of de Croix assessing the business? Then you can weigh up the realities of taking on a lead weight or a balloon that can soar high and keep your family in euros.' Julie slid her feet back to the floor and deftly put her heels on. 'Though maybe your mother would miss being in charge?'

'Mum prefers to be in her greenhouse, talking to plants,' said Lando, feeling optimistic about the suggestion. 'She can't stand the public and yet insists on wandering around the store, judging customers and scowling at staff.'

'And if Papa agrees, I'll join him in Ireland with Lando,' said Celine. 'Le Marché Cher can survive with Benoir at the helm, and it will be a chance for him to prove his abilities as deputy manager.'

'You really think so?' said de Croix, standing at the door, snowflakes sitting on his flat cap.

'Papa,' said Celine, crossing the room to hug him. 'You're home early.'

'Celine is correct,' said Julie, stretching extravagantly across the sofa to pick up her iPhone on the side table. 'What is the matter, my love? It seems you are no longer appealing to your *cinq à sept*?'

De Croix ignored his wife and crossed the room to the fireplace. 'A glass of champagne for your godfather?' he said, turning to Lando.

You could cut a knife through the tension. Julie drained her glass and held it out to Lando before he'd had a chance to pour champagne for de Croix. There was obviously some kind of marital problem going on and Lando admired Celine for her ability to sit back and quietly observe her parents.

'For you,' said Lando, topping up Julie's champagne. 'And de Croix, I'm going to fill your glass to the brim in the hope that you can return to Ireland with me.'

'And do what exactly?' said de Croix, who held the stem of his champagne coupe like an elegant David Niven. 'I've taught you all I know, Lando. You are twenty-seven, you have completed the studies; I believe you are ready.'

'It was my suggestion,' said Julie. 'I think you should complete your guidance and use your expertise in preparing Shillington's for Christmas. You know better than anyone about the income that can be generated from last-minute extravagant shoppers.'

'I can't hold his hand forever,' said de Croix, turning to Lando. 'I may be your godfather, but I am here with my wife; I can't just up and leave.'

'Don't you mean you are here with your precious Le Marché Cher, not to mention your *cinq à sept*?' said Julie.

'It sounds like you want me to leave,' said de Croix.

'What I want is for you and Celine to go to Dublin with Lando.' Julie stood up and shook out her hair. 'I'll have some peace before Christmas, and you three can sort out the future of Shillington's. The dream team, *non*?'

The dream team maybe, but how would Lando's mother handle the arrival of well-meaning but incredibly bossy de Croix's at Shillington's?

'And Lando, don't look so shocked at the mention of my husband's mistress,' said Julie, with a wry smile. 'French women don't just tolerate their husbands' affairs – we expect them!'

Chapter Three

Shillington's Department Store, Dublin

Three storeys high, Shillington's was like a fortress of a gracious age, built of exquisite red brick, with turrets and towers rising above the roof. The business began as a dry goods store in the 1850s on Kildare Street when 'Old Mrs Shillington', as she was known, became widowed and used the fortune left by her late husband to fulfil his dream of creating the most opulent department store Ireland could ever have imagined. Overlooking St Stephen's Green, Shillington's was a landmark to all, and the view across the city on a clear day was unbeatable.

Immy Brooks' twenty-seventh birthday was off to a bad start. She had accidentally fallen asleep in her disposable contact lenses the night before, having polished off a bottle of wine in front of Netflix. Then she got drenched on her way to work. Her eyes watered so much, a customer in Shillington's homeware department on the first floor asked if there had 'been a death in the family, poor love, or maybe a breakup with the boyfriend?' Immy smiled and diverted the customer's attention towards new stock, including a butter dish with the words 'Cholesterol Rules' emblazoned on the side. The Head of Buying managed to slip the occasional tacky item past Delia Shillington, insisting that 'bad taste sells', but this was not the case. Shillington's clientele was conservative, and anything vaguely humorous went over their heads like a bad shot, be it golf or shooting.

Immy was about to slope off for a hot chocolate in the staff room when she heard clicking heels approaching from the staircase. Delia Shillington, sensible from her short mousey brown hair to her court shoes, scanned the homeware department like a buzzard hunting for its dinner.

'Aren't you meant to be in beauty this afternoon?' Delia curled her hair behind her ears, checked her pearl earrings and straightened the collar of her shirt.

Immy braced herself for a lecture. Lando's mother had a way of pulling up the collar of her shirt when preparing to rant, as if the cotton rising from her neck gave her a sort of regal power.

'Janette's dentist appointment was cancelled, so there was no need for me to fill in for her.' Immy spoke as respectfully as possible as she really was not in the mood for a long interaction.

'But Janette told me she had an appointment with her optician.'

'Oh,' said Immy, picking up a milk jug and rubbing the cuff of her sleeve on the handle as if to polish it.

'Then which is it?' Delia tapped her watch impatiently. 'I don't have time to stand around deliberating as to which explanation was true or false, but I can tell you, Janette is on thin ice.'

Delia opened her crossbody purse, which she wore on her department rounds, and took out her mobile phone. 'Now where are they? The flight landed over three hours ago.'

'Sorry?' said Immy, but Delia ignored her and pressed the phone to her ear.

'Darling, where on earth are you?' she said, quickly dropping the call when a commotion could be heard on the ground floor. While Delia galloped off as fast as her court shoes could carry her, Immy looked over the balcony to find customers browsing around the beauty hall. A man in a smart navy coat and a hat stood next to an immaculate Anna Wintour look-alike, who was a beacon of style in a long red coat. Then there was a tall, model-like guy with a beard and sunglasses. Immy noticed a familiar-looking leather bag over his shoulder and the confusion lasted for only seconds until she realised who it was.

Lando took off his sunglasses and looked up at Immy, connecting his thumb and index finger into a circle. It was the same OK sign he'd been making since they were teenagers. His beard made him look even more like James Norton and his suede jacket was much trendier than anything he'd usually wear. There he was, her now ex-best friend because they'd crossed the platonic danger line. Immy's heart raced.

The last time she saw him, they had been in bed together, having had stupid and electrifying sex. She felt furious and wanted to pick up every jug and butter dish she could get her hands on and fling them over the balcony at Lando and what appeared to be his new *amour*.

'Who is that up there?' said the bob-haired beauty with a French accent, which must have made her doubly attractive to Lando.

'Just a girl in homeware.' Delia's voice echoed upwards, pinching Immy's ears as she retreated from sight.

How about that as a milestone for my twenty-seventh birthday, she thought to herself. 'I'm just a girl in homeware.' Immy desperately wanted to get back to her flat, but first she'd have to tiptoe past the French contingent downstairs.

★

Despite the perfection of Le Marché Cher, the octagonal hall of Shillington's, with a gallery on the first and second floor, never failed to make Lando's heart soar. This was the hub of the store, leading to all departments.

He had become used to the warmth shown to him by the de Croix family in Paris, clashing with his mother's expertly controlled affection.

'Darling,' said Delia, five foot four next to Lando's towering height. As she double-kissed her son Delia's voice became increasingly high-pitched. 'Your beard makes you look so much like your father.'

Like a pro, de Croix stepped in to comfort her. 'Delia, my

dear,' he said, extravagantly removing his gloves from finger to thumb before kissing her hand. 'You are overcome by your son, and why not? He is a marvellous young man.'

'Thank you, Charles,' said Delia, sounding momentarily vulnerable.

'No, Delia, you must call me de Croix, I insist on this name – there are no formalities between us,' he said. 'Even if it has been some time since we have spent time together, I feel the closeness with Gregory, who is in the Heavens.'

'You are kind,' said Delia, blinking as if to avoid tears from falling.

'Your husband was my rock when we studied together at Cambridge, and I want to be the same for Lando.'

Delia didn't look remotely happy being instructed by her late husband's friend, but even she knew his bossiness surpassed her own.

'And I present to you my daughter, Celine,' said de Croix.

'Hello,' said Celine, 'so lovely to see you again.'

'You were a tiny baby when we last met,' said Delia, 'and now look at you.'

'My godfather's funeral,' said Celine, kissing Delia's cheek. 'I think of him so much.'

'He adored you,' said Delia, 'so much so, he drank the most expensive claret he could get his hands on in Hôtel de Crillon.

'It's true.' De Croix smiled a very sad smile. 'And you were pregnant with Lando at the time.'

They were all quiet for a moment, as nobody wanted to mention how it had been the de Croix's last time with Gregory.

'And are we not lucky with our children?' said de Croix,

removing his coat and passing it to Janette, who looked rather out of breath behind a make-up counter. Lando recognised the Head of Beauty due to her famously thick eyebrows, who looked put out to be treated as a clothes horse. The last time Lando had spoken with her, before his flight to Paris, she'd sworn like a sailor about some Tinder date claiming to have forgotten his wallet on a night out. 'I've bleedin' had it with online dating,' she'd told him. 'Those lads wouldn't know a lady if she poked them with a stick.'

'Good to see you, Janette,' said Lando, diplomatically. 'You're keeping well?'

She blushed in response and seemed happy enough to carry off de Croix's coat to the cloakroom.

'What can I say?' said de Croix, gesturing to the manic layout of counters on the ground floor. 'I can't even find the words to explain.'

'What on earth do you mean by that?' said Delia.

De Croix picked up a tray of nail polish and shook his head. 'Everywhere I look, there is an overcrowding of product.'

'Papa, no,' said Celine, looking apologetically at Lando. 'It's too soon.'

'This is the first and obvious reason why your customers have fatigue,' de Croix persisted. 'And tell me why your staff members are dressed as farm hands? That girl over there seems to be wearing some kind of brown sacking.'

'De Croix, no, that's—' Lando attempted to divert de Croix's pointing finger in another direction and sent pleading eyes of forgiveness towards Immy, who rushed towards the exit next to the long jewellery counter. It was too late. Immy disappeared. He wanted to go after her but knew he had to give his mother undivided attention and further explain the purpose of de Croix and Celine's visit. Lando had told his mother the de Croix's wanted to do some market research in advance of Christmas, but he knew once de Croix explained his desire to help them save the business Delia would understand. Lando knew she'd purposely distanced herself from the de Croix family as the association with Gregory was just too painful, and yet she'd seemed quite happy for Lando to stay with them in Paris.

'Why would a department store have staff looking as if they are ready to milk the cows?' said de Croix, seemingly unaware of his insults.

Celine winced in embarrassment. 'My father's English sometimes gets a little confused – he doesn't mean to be rude.'

'The uniforms are traditional,' said Delia, clearly aghast at the bombardment of criticism. 'The collars are deliberately large; it's the sort of Princess Diana style from the eighties,' she explained. 'I always admired her.'

'And I can only ask the question,' said de Croix, 'are we still in the eighties? *Non*! And what is that sound like cats squabbling?'

'The music?' said Delia. 'It's the Shillington's soundtrack.'

'What kind of soundtrack?' said de Croix, blocking his ears for effect.

Lando and Celine looked at each other. The rockets were about to fly.

'I bought the cassette from the *Reader's Digest*,' said Delia.

'Let me guess, in the eighties?'

'As it happens, yes,' she said.

De Croix stepped back with one hand on his forehead and the other on Lando's shoulder.

'We run and hide, or we face this ear-menacing music.'

'Mum,' said Lando, 'I probably wasn't that clear on the phone last night. You see, I've asked de Croix and Celine to spend a week—'

'Or three,' de Croix, added.

'Yes,' said Lando, 'and, well, to observe, give us advice and help us to increase pre-Christmas profits. I learned so much at Le Marché Cher and I want to see if the same business structure could be applied here too.'

Lando braced himself for Delia's response but was saved by Uncle Stanley, who came rocketing down the banisters from his bedsit and landed on his feet, as he had always done. Delia pressed her fingers to her temples.

'About time,' said Uncle Stanley, reaching out a hand to Lando and pulling him into a bear hug. 'Sure, the place was about to freeze over with your mother's icy looks.'

'Stanley,' said de Croix, stepping forward to kiss him on both cheeks. It has been too many years and you are as beautifully attired as ever; the cut on that suit is exquisite.'

'Johnson Tailors of Tullow,' said Uncle Stanley, kneeling to fetch a silver hip flask from behind a headless mannequin. 'We stock only the finest hand-made tweed suits in the country. And speaking of Ireland's finest, how about a sip of Irish whiskey to get you all settled and then I'll bring you up to menswear for a gander.'

Chapter Four

The short walk along 'the golden mile' of pubs and restaurants by St Stephen's Green often helped to decompress Immy on her way home to the flat on Merrion Street. Number 30 was her bolthole in a brown-bricked four-storey Georgian house with a mustard-yellow door.

She thought of her parents and the stifling world they'd created for themselves in Marbella. Her dad played golf every day and, judging by the occasional messages, her mum rarely ventured out. When her parents had sold the family home in Ranelagh to the neighbour who'd fancied the idea of knocking through walls to create a palace for himself, they'd failed to inform Immy until the sale had gone through. It wasn't exactly out of character for her parents, as they never pretended to take any interest in Immy from the moment she'd turned eighteen. However, informing her through a vaguely apologetic email that she had a fortnight to clear her belongings from the house had been a blow.

'I think your parents have done you a favour,' Lando had said. 'You've been temping as a secretary for three years and you know it's called temping for a reason.' Immy had retaliated by pointing out that Lando still lived with his mum and 'how about that for independence?' But she knew how close he was to Delia, and how he worried about her, which must have been what gave him his drive. He'd breezed into Trinity College to study business, while Immy had scraped into Maynooth College, which she'd ventured to no more than once a fortnight and it was a miracle she had passed at all. Lando went on to do a master's degree, increasing his confidence about fulfilling the role of CEO at Shillington's, while Immy had partied and taken up being a secretarial temp as a career.

With every bone in her body, Immy had wanted to say no when Lando had asked her to take a job at Shillington's to vary her limited work experience. She'd wanted to prove she could take care of herself, but even at her most stubborn, she'd known that to carry on with the temp agency was a road to nowhere. Lando had arranged for her to stay in the company flat, which would have been sold long ago had it not been tied up in a trust connected to the store. He had even managed to persuade his mum to let the apartment to Immy for a low rate, pointing out that the flat needed a lot of work before they could rent it out properly. Until Shillington's financial conundrum was sorted out once and for all, they were all stuck.

Immy pushed her key into the front door and felt a hint of warm air from the storage heater in the hall. The tired

Anaglypta wallpaper was hardly uplifting and the same climb up the worn-out carpeted stairs to her cold flat didn't help either. In the old days, she would have lit a ciggie. Her parents didn't really care about her smoking, though she never would have dared when staying at Lando's house. She smiled to herself, as smoking was how their friendship had begun.

On a Sunday afternoon at boarding school, Immy got caught smoking, and the girls in her dorm were so disgusted they'd refused to speak to her. In the outdoor swimming pool, when Immy had swum towards one of her friends, she'd ducked her head in the water and swum away. Mooching around the school grounds, Immy had met Lando, both twelve years of age. No judgement, just a cool, lovely guy. He was much taller than Immy and managed to date girls in years above them. Lando was one of those people who fell in love quickly, constantly finding 'the one', only to be heartbroken when it turned out to be zero. As the school years progressed, Immy had listened to his heartaches, and quietly figured they were like *When Harry Met Sally* except without the ending. But she had been wrong. The ending had arrived the night before he'd left for Paris. It wasn't as if Immy had slept with many people, but she and Lando had the most extraordinary chemistry. It was like wildfire from the moment they'd crossed the line and that was the tragedy of it. A night of mind-blowing sex in exchange for fifteen years of friendship.

Immy made her way up the stairs and deduced that tonight required vodka and *Bridget Jones's Diary*, the film

Immy saved for times of utter disillusionment. She heard knocking on the front door and Lando's number flashed up on her phone. There was no way she was going to pick up. She felt so awkward and embarrassed about what had happened, and ashamed of herself, worried she had given him the wrong signals. She knew Lando's approach to women; he was never pushy, always a gentleman. And she also knew it had been something they'd both wanted, and that was the killer. They'd had their moment and now they were at a dead end. To make matters worse, while Lando had been away, Delia had quizzed Immy about her future and suggested she should 'get out of Dublin and see the world, just as your parents are doing'. Immy knew Delia disapproved of her parents and her only reason for wanting Immy to leave had nothing to do with her well-being but to get her 'out of Lando's way', as she'd once overheard Delia saying on the phone.

There was now a hammering on the front door.

'Go away, Orlando,' she yelled from the second-floor landing. She only called him Orlando when she was upset with him.

'Immy, please, we've got to talk,' came his muffled response.

Her phone rang again, which she silenced. Lando was now using the brass knocker on the door, which continued to thud as Immy reached the third floor. Then, she heard the front door rub against the coco matting and a breathless 'thank you' from Lando. Typical of him to be in the right place at the right time, scoring entry from a fellow occupant.

Immy grappled with her keys, too flustered to unlock the door to the flat before he made his way up the stairs. Within seconds, Lando had taken off his hat and got onto his knees.

There he was, spoilt, irritating and confusing. Her ex-best friend.

'Can I come in?' he said, covering his face with his hands and peeking through his fingers.

She left the door open behind her. He followed and began taking off his jacket but left it on when Immy glared at him. The flat was a mess. A far cry from the sophistication of Paris.

There was a duvet on the sofa from Immy's Netflix marathon and it didn't help that the laundry hadn't been hung up properly, so the clothes horse looked like a Tracey Emin installation. Even more annoying, she didn't want to take off her coat because of the comment the Frenchman had made about her dress. What was wrong with her? This kind of thing usually wouldn't bother her.

'That jacket looks ridiculous,' she said to Lando, feeling childish for saying it but she just felt so angry.

'It's French, Isabel Marant,' he said. 'As is this.' He took a box out of his pocket and handed it to Immy. 'Happy Birthday, and sorry.'

'Thank you,' she said, with a grumble, wishing Lando hadn't remembered her favourite perfume, Chanel Coco Mademoiselle, as it just made her feel guilty for being cross.

Immy walked into the tiny kitchen and opened a cupboard to find a box of tea bags, though she hardly ever drank tea.

Then she opened the fridge, closed it, and turned on the kettle for tea she didn't want. She opened the fridge again and wished she was small enough to climb into it.

'Immy, what's going on?' he said. 'Can you stop opening doors and look at me?'

She turned to him and stared. 'What do you want, Lando?'

'I want to know why you replied to about one per cent of my messages, and when you did, they were no more than one sentence.'

'What were you looking for exactly?' said Immy.

'I don't know, maybe you could have told me how you were feeling, you know … about what happened?'

Lando stepped out of her way as she crossed the room to stand in front of the window. She fixed her gaze on the imposing government buildings across the street and tried to pull herself together. Before, she wouldn't have cared that she hadn't so much as hung a picture on a wall or added cushions to the sofa, but this feeling of self-consciousness was dreadful.

'Look, Immy, I'm sorry,' he said.

'For what?' Immy knew she was shouting but she just couldn't help it.

'I'm not sure, that's the thing.' He sat down on the sofa and zipped up his jacket as if it were a signal that he had no intention of staying long.

'We got drunk, Lando,' she said, turning to face him with folded arms. 'It didn't mean anything.'

'Yes, but it was awkward afterwards.'

'It was a one-night stand.'

'That's what you think?' he said, looking surprised. 'You don't think it was more than that?'

'That is what I think,' she lied. 'As far as I'm concerned, it never happened.' What was she supposed to say? Lando had returned with a gorgeous French woman on his arm.

'But Immy, if it never happened, then why are you being like this?'

She couldn't help but burst into tears and, within milliseconds, Lando held her in his arms and hugged her.

'It was stupid, and all my fault, I just got carried away,' he said, releasing her from his grasp. 'The sofa was too cosy, the booze made us too relaxed and for a brief moment —'

Immy's self-confidence was in tatters. He was waltzing back in and expected everything to be back to normal.

'Lando, I don't think you realise that while you were in Paris, I was stuck at Shillington's with a boss who clearly doesn't want me there.'

'What has Mum been saying?'

She shook her head. 'It's nothing.'

'Well, it sounds like something, and it's no excuse, but I think Mum's was going through some kind of stuff.'

'What kind of stuff?'

'It's Gerhardt,' said Lando. 'Mum told me he proposed to her again.'

'Poor Gerhardt had been in and out of Delia's life like a yo-yo. Every time they got close, at least according to Lando, she'd back away. The man had the patience of a saint and how he thought he'd ever satisfy Delia, whose standards were sky-high, Immy would never know.

'Look, Im, you're my best friend, you know that.' He looked like he meant it. Of course, he meant it. They'd been each other's wingman and confidant since their teens, and it didn't matter how many romances either of them had, they'd always kept their relationship completely solid, until now.

'I'm sorry about everything.' He put his hands in his pockets and looked sincere. 'Can we get back on track?'

All Immy wanted to do was ask about the gorgeous French woman he'd returned with, but she didn't want to sound jealous.

'I went to Paris to immerse myself into the world of Le Marché Cher, and now I want to see if I can replicate it at Shillington's.'

'That sounds ambitious,' said Immy, shaking out the duvet on the sofa and folding it up.

'Yes, because I am ambitious,' he said.

Immy could feel him trying to make eye contact with her, but she continued to tidy, and began taking her laundry off the clothes horse. She hadn't realised how messy she was until now.

'The de Croix have come to Dublin for a few weeks to help us prepare the store for massive Christmas sales.'

'Good for you,' said Immy, hating herself for being sarcastic.

'Good for all of us,' he said, 'for everyone employed at Shillington's.' If he meant to sound pointed, then it worked.

'Lando, you get paid whether you turn up or not.'

'That isn't true,' he said, though it was plainly obvious that it was. 'And as for you, Immy, the store is giving you a chance to find a job you could really thrive in.'

'You're going to wave a magic wand and find a career for me, are you? What, with my less-than-mediocre arts degree, patchy temping history, and two years of being a shop girl?'

'Stranger things have happened,' said Lando, 'and if you can work at Shillington's until Christmas, by then we'll know more about the state of play at the store and all of our futures.'

Immy found it difficult to be cross with Lando, which was infuriating in itself.

'Can we go back to before?' he said.

'I'm not sure.' At least Immy was being honest. 'But I will stay at Shillington's until Christmas.'

Chapter Five

In the 1980s, Shillington's on St Stephen's Green had been a shrine to shoppers seeking the most illustrious of fashion. The windows were dressed in extravagant silks and sequins you'd expect to see only in New York or Milan, and the doormen, standing on either side of the enormous cast-iron entrance, had the gift of the gab for both Americans and locals. Gregory Shillington was twenty-seven years old when he took the helm and had only been in the job for nine months when he died. His plan had been to dispense with archaic traditions, removing the staff dress code and welcoming people from all backgrounds to create a lighter and more progressive version of the store. His wife Delia, on the other hand, was a traditionalist who held Shillington's in trust until Lando turned twenty-seven; Gregory's plans were binned. Inevitably competition arrived in Dublin, with department stores popping up with clothes, beauty and interior items at more accessible pricing.

'To hell with less expensive brands,' Delia had famously

said during her first staff meeting. 'I will not lower standards for the sake of your bottom line.'

'It's my bottom I am thinking of, Mrs Shillington,' the accountant had said, shuffling in his leather chair. 'We'll all be out on our rear ends if sales continue in this trajectory.'

Until recently, Delia's word had been gospel. 'The customer must learn it pays to buy quality in the long run.'

At the doorway to Shillington's managerial office on the second floor, de Croix stepped back and studied the piece of memorabilia from a distance.

'Delia, my dear, I've been studying the stock, from the ground floor all the way to the top, and I feel I must point out there is a lot of dust on some items.'

She looked at his dewy complexion and wondered if he wore tinted moisturiser.

'It's a large, historic building, de Croix, what do you expect?' she said, sitting on the swivel chair behind the heavy brown desk. 'The Shillingtons were never bothered by dust, and I seem to have inherited the tolerance through Gregory.'

De Croix did not look impressed and appeared to adjust his cravat as a way of conveying his dislike for the art piece.

'But how did the modern age bypass Shillington's?' said de Croix, running his fingers across the top of the box-like computer monitor. 'I have the feeling of being in a museum, or at times even a gallery.'

Delia pitied the Frenchman's poor taste as she admired the floral Laura Ashley wallpaper and matching curtains in the office. 'No need for dramatics, de Croix,' she said, gently.

'And is that truly a fax machine?' he said. 'I thought they went out with the dinosaurs.'

'Very funny,' said Delia, disguising her well-practised scowl with a smile.

De Croix sat on the mauve chair. 'Even the colour of this,' he said, shaking his head. 'I'm afraid there are some design problems at Shillington's.' Clearly reading Delia's reaction, he quickly reined himself in. 'Not that I mean to be rude.'

'Of course not,' she said, with as much condescension as she could muster.

'I began my department store experience by working in the finest perfumery in Paris.' De Croix stood up and paced up and down, his heels clicking on the hardwood floor. 'This is why I have the nose of a hound,' he said, tapping his fobble.

Delia thought how unfortunate for him, as some fragrances were beyond revolting.

'And then,' de Croix continued, 'I slowly crawled my way to senior management.'

She liked the idea of this man crawling, after such insulting comments.

'Would you like a coffee, de Croix?' Delia was ready to have a caffeine hit and then dash home to wrap up her bay tree, which never liked the frost. 'And won't you sit down?' All this pacing was making her feel uneasy.

'Thank you, but no,' he said. 'I would prefer to immediately discuss the visible problems of the store, and my worry that it might be quite difficult to turn Shillington's into a profitable business.'

'That is one point of view,' said Delia.

'It is *my* point of view, and you must know I am only honest with you.'

'Fine,' she said, 'and if we are going to exchange frank views, I might as well tell you that I did notice Celine and Lando – it seems they became close in Paris?'

'I believe so,' said de Croix. He didn't give anything away by the expression on his face.

'Celine is a marvellous girl,' said Delia. A strong and kind woman was exactly what her son needed.

'She is marvellous,' said de Croix, wagging his finger, 'and marvellously spoilt in places.'

Delia considered the potential wealth from Lando's future in-laws and felt her head nodding furiously. 'I think continuing the bond between our families would be wonderful.'

'But your boy, at twenty-seven, as sweet as he is, he lacks confidence.'

Delia buttoned up her tweed jacket. 'I agree with you, de Croix.'

'*Bon*,' he said, looking impressed by Delia's frankness, 'and he has reason to feel unconfident, as profits are sinking at every quarter.'

'Undoubtedly,' she said. 'You realise we have seventy-eight employees? That is seventy-eight families, some of whom have been working here for generations.'

'Then I see there are three choices for Shillington's.' De Croix held out his fingers.

'Go on.' Delia was ready to listen.

'One, the store gets taken over by a vulture fund, which would be too sad.'

'Agreed,' said Delia.

'Two, you sell.'

'To whom?'

'This store is positioned in the most famous area in Dublin – it will sell to the highest bidder and make you a very rich widow.'

Delia could barely afford tinned tuna at present; it didn't sound like the worst of options.

'I could put myself forward as a buyer,' said de Croix, 'as I have been considering expanding Le Marché Cher in Europe and this could be a good opportunity.'

She wasn't at all sure how to respond to this offer; as casual as it sounded, clearly de Croix had been considering Shillington's as a conquest.

'Of course, I would give you the very best of deals.'

'And three?' she said, ignoring his last comment as she didn't want to seem too keen.

'The third option is, we turn things around.'

Delia's eyes brimmed with unexpected tears. Maybe she did love the place, even though it brought her stress and aggravation almost every single day.

'Oh, my dear,' said de Croix, taking a pressed handkerchief from his pocket. 'My *grand-mère* used to say, "*des choses incroyables peuvent arriver*" … amazing things can happen.'

Delia nodded, dabbing her eyes.

'But, to make it work, I will have to reshape the crêpe, if you understand.'

'I understand,' said Delia. 'But why are you doing this, de Croix? I understand your loyalty to Gregory, but surely this generosity is going over the top?'

Widowed at twenty-six years of age, Delia had never been beholden to anyone, and she wasn't about to start now with de Croix. She needed to know what was in it for him.

'Christmas is the opportunity you have to boost the sales,' he said, 'and if you can't make it add up this season, I can categorically tell you, Delia, it will never happen.'

'But why are you really here, de Croix?'

She knew he didn't like her persistence, but if he was going to review the company books and make suggestions, all cards needed to be on the table.

'My wife,' he said.

'What about Julie?'

'She tells me I am stuck in, what you say in English, in a rut?'

Delia longed to be in such a place. To her, a rut meant security and repetition, which was something she'd never had. Every day, there was another problem to solve, a member of staff kicking up or bowing out.

'Are you talking about your business or your marriage?'

'I think I've become boring, to tell you the truth.'

'I long to be boring,' said Delia. 'I long to sit with a crossword in my conservatory, drinking tea.'

'No, it isn't enough for Julie,' he said, scratching the side of his face. 'We've been married for twenty-nine years.'

'I remember your wedding, and what a stunning bride she was, married in Les Invalides, the bells, the grandeur —'

'And the morning sickness,' said de Croix. 'Julie was three months pregnant, though you would never have known.'

'And you've been together all this time?'

'Yes, and I didn't think she was bothered by my mistresses.'

'Excuse me?'

'Oh, come on, Delia, you know what we Parisians are like.'

'And Julie, does she have a man?'

His face filled with dread. 'I don't know,' he said. 'All I know is she practically told me to leave, to honour Gregory and guard Lando's future inheritance.'

'So, Shillington's is your pre-Christmas escape route,' she said, feeling guilty for finding some kind of relief that their marriage wasn't perfect. She often wondered if she and Gregory would still be together now if he had lived.

'I am taking three weeks to escape from my life,' he said, tapping the face of his Cartier watch, 'and I may as well help you at the same time.'

'And you truly think sales this Christmas is the last chance we have?'

'I fear so,' said de Croix, looking genuinely sorry, 'and

we are already late. Your competitors surely opened her Christmas shops in September – Halloween barely makes a dent in profits, it's Christmas that sells.'

'Oh Lord,' said Delia, longing to get home to prune her geraniums.

'But let us put our worries into action,' he said, getting to his feet. 'May I accompany you around the store and I can explain my concerns?'

'I will listen,' said Delia, rising from her chair and feeling grateful to have worn her sensible lace-up leather shoes, 'but you must know, all decisions rest with me.'

'Yes,' he said, opening the door for her.

'And I never, ever take the lift,' she said.

'Not even to the top floor?'

'Not even to the top floor. We are blessed with legs, and I intend to use them.'

Prints of polo, foxhunting and horse racing by Snaffles lined the walls as Delia and de Croix made their way up the dark wooden stairs to the third floor. Delia felt like she was part of a scene in Agatha Christie's *Poirot*.

'I note there is a woefully small amount of signage here,' said de Croix, wobbling the banister. 'How can customers find their way around without direction?' Relief came when they walked into the women's department, painted in Delia's favourite colour of Summer Pudding.

De Croix paused by a rail of Leslie velvet waistcoats and moleskin trousers.

'If a woman is on her way to the lingerie department, we

want to tempt her with incredible luggage perfect for her husband's Christmas present.'

'Right,' said Delia, understanding de Croix's approach.

'And for those dropping by for lipstick or eye shadow, we first salivate their palates with a display of handbags and sunglasses.'

'I see,' said Delia, 'and so we want these items to be centre stage in the beauty department on the ground floor.'

'Precisely.' De Croix reached his hands out in front of him as if having an epiphany. 'There must be temptation at every turn, leading customers to areas they had no intention of visiting, including the VIP lounge.'

'VIPs? I'm not sure we have any these days,' said Delia, 'and if we did, we certainly don't have a lounge for them.'

'There are always VIPs,' said de Croix. 'Indeed, one of my talents is scouting for those who like to spend money. These customers can make up to thirty per cent of annual sales; they cannot be forgotten.'

'I suppose I've become used to our regular customers,' said Delia, 'some of whom are big spenders.' She immediately thought of Gerhardt and felt pangs of guilt. A dozen red roses had arrived last week, and she still hadn't called to thank him because she was so confused about how she wanted her future to play out.

'Then I suggest you reacquaint yourself with three pretty letters, V-I-P, and the more luxurious and elaborate the lounge, the longer we can woo these big spenders of yours and keep them shopping.'

A fact de Croix overlooked was that there was no money for renovation, but Delia felt too proud to tell him.

'At Le Marché Cher our lounge is decorated with extravagant clocks, large-screen TVs and Baccarat chandeliers,' he said, polishing his fingernails on the lapel of his jacket. 'And all items are for sale, I might add. It is a place where clients can relax, get their head into shopping, and build up energy to swipe their bank cards.'

'I'm afraid the sentimentality I have for Shillington's will prevent any immediate changes,' said Delia.

'No matter,' he said kindly. 'We will add the festive touches we can afford and sprinkle in some *je ne sais quoi*.'

'And the VIP lounge?' said Delia.

'We'll make it unique, and if you can find some old photographs of Shillington family members through the years, we can frame and display them.'

'I'll look in the house. Gregory was such a hoarder and in twenty-six years, I haven't thrown out a thing.'

'One more thing comes to my mind,' said de Croix, adjusting his glasses.

'Go on,' she said.

'Uncle Stanley. What are we to do?'

'An age-old question,' she said, openly sighing. 'He is Gregory's paternal uncle, and they were very close.'

'And how does he get in and out of the store when it's closed?' said de Croix. 'Surely there are security alarms to protect the building and stock. He can't be responsible for turning everything on or off when he leaves.'

'There is a side door he can get out of, so he doesn't have

to roll up shutters or unlock the main doors,' said Delia, wondering what on earth would happen if they had to sell Shillington's. Uncle Stanley had lived at the store for as long as Delia had been married, and his entire diet consisted of the menu in the tea rooms. He was a household name at Shillington's and both customers and staff adored him, though his eccentric stories and witty banter with customers didn't exactly fit with her vision of an upmarket department store.

'I take it he has shares in the business, or an income at least?' said de Croix.

This question was rather too nosy for Delia's liking. 'I've never been entirely clear,' she said, thinking about Uncle Stanley's recent request to set up some kind of welcoming station inside the arched doorway to Shillington's. He had always been a creative thinker, sprinkling artistic licence into his tales of Irish mythology for customers from overseas. But what if he was a liability? What if he said or did something truly outrageous and got Shillington's well and truly cancelled?

'Then I suggest you clarify,' said de Croix, tapping his nose, 'for clarity is one of life's greatest assets.'

Chapter Six

The windows in Shillington's beauty department towered eight feet high and when the sun shone through the stained-glass feature, created by Harry Clarke in the 1920s, there was no place like it. Stanley was always on the hunt for ways to promote Shillington's and he'd recently discovered *Golden Moments Off Grid*, a Dublin news site for tourists. He sent an email to the editor, claiming 'if one sees one's own reflection in the Shillington stained-glass window, it brings not only prosperity but stonking good looks too'.

'Sure, why not?' he'd told Immy that same morning and it had at least brought a smile to the poor girl's face. Stanley had been setting up his kiosk in the hall, charging a 'tenner a pop' for a photo by the 'Window of Prosperity', when Immy's pretty face had peered through the huge glass doors. She'd arrived far too early for work, claiming she had to restock the winter crockery in homeware, but as far as Stanley could tell, she'd do anything to distract herself from her misery. He understood Lando was oblivious to the fact that bringing home the French girl, as charming as she was, had done no favours to his long-term prospects. Stanley believed his grand-nephew and the discreet Dublin beauty were meant for each other, but how he'd bring them together was a matter he'd have to leave for later.

Shillington's opened every day, except Sundays, at 9 a.m. The store had only been open for moments when a group of Americans arrived to test out Stanley's rumour. From homeware on the second floor, Immy leaned over the balcony watching two ladies posing by the window while their husbands held up their iPhones.

'Honey, make sure you get my best side,' said one of the women. 'Can you see my reflection clearly? I really want this to work before my birthday.'

'It'll save you a fortune on cosmetic surgery,' said the other man, sounding like he meant it.

Immy was fighting off a hangover. She'd stupidly stayed up far too late watching an eerie sci-fi series and managed to drink an entire bottle of red wine. In the good old days, she would have split a bottle of wine with Lando. Though she had given herself an order not to think about him, she wasn't doing very well. Immy was used to his flings and surely his interest in Celine would be no different. All she wanted was to get through the rest of November, and then the store hype leading up to Christmas would keep her occupied. Last year she'd worked fifteen-hour days from December 15th to Christmas Eve. She and Lando had been so exhausted, they'd fell asleep in the tea rooms until security had woken them up and sent them home.

At least her parents had invited her to Spain from Christmas Eve to St Stephen's Day, and hopefully it would go well. Then she planned to take the new year by the horns. Try and try again, that was her mantra.

★

In homeware, de Croix stood behind a kitchen dresser with handmade crockery and exquisite table mats. He observed several tourists circulating a table laid with silverware, Waterford Crystal and delicate pudding bowls. Immy connected with the large group, making firm eye contact, and asked them about their travels and what their favourite experience of Dublin had been so far. She was impressive and appeared to have a talent for putting people at ease so they could relax and almost fall into shopping without thinking too hard about it.

'Who is Head of Personal Shopping?' de Croix asked Delia in a text message.

'Head of?' Delia responded. 'There is no personal shopping service.'

De Croix felt his eyebrows rise as his mind began to conjure up a solution.

Department by department, de Croix assessed Shillington's from the ground floor upwards. He asked Lando to lead the way, with Celine following behind. They appeared to whisper and laugh a lot. Perhaps they were even the picture of love.

In the soft furnishings and bedding department, on the fifth floor, there was no one to be seen. Wooden beams ran across the ceiling, blending beautifully with tartan throws and handmade Irish rugs lying across armchairs and beds. The space was rather mesmerising.

De Croix stood still and raised his hand for silence. 'Wait, what is that sound?' he whispered.

'What sound?' said Celine, speaking softly in response.

They walked slowly towards a double bed, raised on a platform in the centre of the department. The duvet rose and slowly fell.

'Is it alive?' said de Croix, feeling genuine concern. He'd once found a nest of baby rats beneath the blankets of his bed as a little boy. But concerned his parents would harm the rodents, he'd told no one and had slept on the floor for several weeks until the family had vacated. His wife was the only person he had told, for who would believe such a thing? Even his mistress had laughed when, one evening, he'd felt sentimental and had an urge to share a tale from his childhood of poverty, and a degree of neglect. Julie had always taken him seriously, and being away from her made him pang for his wife for the first time in months.

The grunting and grinding sound from the bed continued. De Croix stepped back and watched as Lando grabbed a curtain pole and poked the duvet.

'Jaysus,' yelled a man with a double chin of stubble, shooting bolt upright. 'What in hell's name?'

Celine squealed.

'Martin,' said Lando, 'what's going on?'

Flinging back the duvet, the man jumped out of bed and began smoothing out his jacket and tie. 'I had no idea you'd be doing the rounds,' he said to de Croix. 'I'm mean, I'd heard of folks coming over from Paris, but I didn't expect you to—'

'Inspect?' said de Croix.

'Well, yes,' he said, reaching out his hand. 'I'm Martin.'

'And you actually work here?' said de Croix.

'I'm the Head of the Soft Furnishings and Bedding Department.'

'I have to say I'm surprised,' said de Croix, revolted by Martin's wrinkled clothes and wishing to place him directly onto an ironing board.

'My missus is going through menopause and she's snoring something awful.'

De Croix was not in the mood to take pity. Julie didn't as much as sniff during her menopause.

'And the rents in Dublin are so pricey, my son's in the spare room, you see?' said Martin, now shaking out the pillow and pulling up the duvet like a chambermaid. 'I've got no option but to put up with the missus and, to be quite honest, I'm knackered.'

★

Like archaeologists on a research trip, Lando descended the stairwell with de Croix and Celine. His mum had taken the day off, which was a relief. He loved the place, like a second home, but there were ghosts, particularly of his father. From an early age, Lando got the sense that even before his father had died, Shillington's had eaten into their private life, though he had only officially been CEO for nine months.

Celine's smile shook Lando out of his daydream. She looked gorgeous, and the chocolate-brown polo neck hugged her torso like a perfect day.

'Lando?' said de Croix, looking irritated. 'Are you going to introduce us?'

'Yes, of course,' he said, not realising they were on the first floor already. Lando was relieved to find six or seven customers browsing through glassware. 'This is obviously the home appliance area in homeware,' said Lando.

Shirley Gandon, wearing an apron with 'Tender to the touch' blazoned across the front, waved a spatula in the air, signalling for them to join her at her kitchen island.

'Follow me,' said Lando to Celine and de Croix, hoping that Shirley would keep her zany comments to a minimum.

'Shirley,' Lando said, 'I'm very happy to introduce you to Charles and Celine de Croix, who have generously come from Paris to help rustle up ideas for Shillington's this Christmas.'

She laid down a spoon covered in green slime, wiped her hands on her apron and reached out to greet de Croix with gusto.

'It's lovely to meet you,' said Shirley. 'I've just been whipping up a spinach smoothie.'

De Croix raised up both his hands. 'I wouldn't want to contaminate the juicer.'

Shirley broke into cackles of laughter. 'That's funny,' she said, 'sure wouldn't sweaty palms only add to the flavour of the smoothie.'

Lando eyeballed Shirley, suggesting she got on with the display.

'Grand,' she said, holding up a cucumber, snapping it in two and dropping it into the large jug. 'Today I'm demonstrating the Doily 360, the one-stop shop for blending.' Shirley dropped in a pack of blueberries and picked up a cardboard pack of juice. 'I love a kiwi or two,' she said, 'and I'm partial to mango, which makes me feel like I'm on my holliers.'

'What kind of juice are you pouring into the smoothie?' asked Celine, as if she was trying to get her father interested.

'I'm not totally sure,' said Shirley, pulling glasses from her messy bun and reading the packaging. 'It's called Made from Concentrate so it can't be all bad, can it?' Further cackles came from her. 'Now for the magic.' She pressed the button, forgetting to place the lid on, and the juicy concoction went flying out of the jug and onto her head.

Lando covered his eyes for several seconds, to avoid the inevitable look of dismay from de Croix.

'Not to worry,' said Shirley, wearing a tea towel around her smoothie-covered hair. 'Maybe come back around teatime, and I'll have had a bit more practice in by then.'

'By teatime, I'll be drinking Irish whiskey,' said de Croix, just loud enough for Lando to hear him.

Chapter Seven

The next morning, de Croix was ready to break bad habits at Shillington's like a spoon cracking through crème brûlée.

Frank the doorman was discussing the racing from the day before with his co-doorman, Bob, who had a copy of the *Racing Post* in his pocket.

'Sure, the ground didn't suit him,' said Frank.

'Not a bit,' said Bob. 'I needed a nip of whiskey after that race, what?'

De Croix watched as the duo gazed out over St Stephen's Green. 'Aren't we the luckiest men to have this as our view? Sure, Fifth Avenue couldn't even beat it.'

'The door, gentlemen, please,' said de Croix, who had been waiting for an unacceptable amount of time. 'Keep the horse observations to the racetrack or you'll find your work will involve opening doors to stables rather than this establishment.'

'Right you are, boss,' said Bob.

'Race track it is,' said Frank.

★

The new rota, devised by Delia to cover staff shortages, had Immy working in a different department every day. She hadn't spent much time in the women's department and relished the opportunity to check out the winter stock, not that her wage would enable her to buy anything, even with the ten per cent staff discount. She stood by a long mirror outside the fitting rooms while a woman swished from side to side in a red cocktail dress with mid-length sleeves.

'I want to love it,' said the woman. 'Can I try a higher pair of heels, just in case that makes a difference?'

Immy went to the storeroom and returned with a nude pair of six-inch heels. The woman slipped on the shoes, and she would have toppled over if it hadn't been for Immy leaning her shoulder forward in the nick of time.

'What do you think?' said the woman, staring at her reflection. 'It's too red, isn't it?'

'It is a very red dress,' said Immy, 'there's no denying it.'

'But is it too red?' said the woman. 'I mean, too obvious for an office party.'

Immy didn't hesitate in her response. 'It depends on who it's for.'

De Croix stood a professional distance away from the women's fitting room but close enough to observe and hear. He was surprised to hear the sales assistant ask who the dress was for. This personal question was close to crossing the professional line.

'My boss,' said the woman. 'But he's divorced,' she quickly countered.

'And have you been out together?'

'Not unless you count company bowling night.' The woman blushed. 'God, I'm ridiculous. I'm acting totally desperate, aren't I?'

Immy paused for a moment. 'How about I bring you an alternative?'

'Please,' said the woman, who disappeared behind the changing-room curtain.

Immy returned with a black cocktail dress. Simple, elegant and with a high neckline. She passed the dress through to the woman, who within moments was standing by Immy's side in front of the full-length mirror.

'I'm actually speechless,' said the woman.

'This dress says *confidence*,' Immy replied.

'I never thought this kind of neckline could look sexy,' said the woman.

'I guess it's all about the mystery of what lies beneath.' Immy stood back to allow space for the customer to pose in front of the mirror.

'This is the one, isn't it?' asked the woman.

'I think you've answered your own question,' said Immy. 'And you know what, if he's right for you, he'll come your way.'

'I really hope so,' said the woman, 'not that I'm, you know, desperate.'

De Croix observed the women laughing together, both content with the outcome.

He stepped forward as Immy sent the satisfied customer towards the pay desk.

'Might I trouble you for a moment?'

The girl was still dressed in that dreadful shapeless brown uniform, but tomorrow was another day.

'I want to ask you about the lady you just served.'

'Yes?' said Immy.

'The red dress she tried on, that was by Bishope Altertate, was it not?'

'Yes,' she said, looking immediately guilty. 'Was I not supposed to have—'

'You may not know,' said de Croix, cutting in. 'You see, Altertate is very expensive, in fact his dresses must be amongst the most designer Shillington's carry.'

Immy nodded in agreement.

'Well, I have to tell you—'

'You're not going to give me the sack, are you?'

De Croix chuckled. 'No, I am not; instead I give you praise and a new job title that will give you not only a pay rise but your very own office.'

The girl shook her head in disbelief.

'Tell me your name.'

'Immy Brooks,' she said.

'Then, Immy Brooks, I want you to be Head of Personal Shopping for Shillington's.' He would battle it out with Delia later. Decisive action was required if they were going to make a sales impact by Christmas. The clock was ticking.

'Personal shopping?'

'Your honesty is everything,' said de Croix. 'You weren't thinking of the price tag when you were with that lady.'

Immy continued to shake her head.

'You thought of the situation she was in, and what was appropriate.'

'That's true,' said Immy. 'I didn't want her boss to think she was desperate. She deserves more than that.'

'And I couldn't agree more,' said de Croix, feeling a rush of the retail business. A feeling that had become so foreign to him the further up the ladder he'd climbed. 'When our clients go home, they must feel satisfied with their purchase. It is not our job to soothe the ears and tell them what they want to hear, but for the clients to feel the love from the clothing and from all they buy at Shillington's.'

'Do you really mean it?' said Immy. 'I'm going to be the Head of Personal Shopping?'

'As of this moment I anoint you.' De Croix took a Montblanc pen from his pocket and tapped it on either side of Immy's shoulder. She curtsied and smiled. 'I will see to it that the rota is re-worked. I see no shortage of staff members here. In fact, if anything, the Shillington's have too many people given the number of customers they deal with.'

'But do you think anyone will actually come to see a personal shopper?' said Immy, which was a fair enough question.

'With the right marketing, I believe the answer is yes.'

'Thank you, Mr de Croix.'

'No need,' he said. 'Business is business, and I always do what needs to be done.'

★

In the beauty hall, Celine walked next to her father, who was in critical form as he stopped by each counter, made of walnut, and heaped with products and perfume, and make-up display cabinets. The walls were beautifully frescoed, and the shelving was low for easy access. The floor was divided into two departments. The windows on three of the four sides and high ceilings made it possible to see the jewellery department from the beauty department and vice versa.

Celine spied Janette, Head of Beauty and Well-being, behind the lipstick counter, chewing gum and scrolling on her phone. Sensing her father was about to pounce, Celine stepped ahead of him.

'I love this lip gloss,' Celine said, hoping Janette would have the sense to put down her phone. 'You wouldn't believe how many lipsticks I possess, and yet I seem to wear the same gloss every day.'

'It's amazing, really, to have all this kit for women, when we have just one mouth,' said Janette.

'It's true,' said Celine, waving her father away.

'Mind you, yesterday a woman came in looking for a cream to make her lips less pouty.' Janette didn't crack a smile.

'She was serious?' said Celine, quite fascinated.

'I told her I thought her mouth looked more than fine,' said Janette, 'but she genuinely seemed to want the opposite of what women request at the Botox clinics.'

'So, what did you do?'

'I felt sorry for her, so I grabbed a load of samples and told her to take it day by day.'

'I like that,' said Celine. 'At Le Marché Cher, I don't think they'd be so kind.'

'Sure, she was harmless,' said Janette, opening a brand-new mascara and adding to her already thick lashes. 'You've got to be tough to work in retail.'

'I agree,' said Celine, though she wished Janette would ease up on the mascara and was about to advise when her father stopped abruptly by the counter.

'Janette,' he said, looking down at the range of lipsticks.

'Yes, Mr de Croix?'

'I have appointed Immy Brooks as Head of Personal Shopping.'

'Very fancy,' said Janette.

'Can you take bookings from VIP clients?'

'Can I offer them a makeover while I'm at it? I do very high-end eyes,' she said. 'Brown and gold, soft smoky, deep blue or a simple day look, it's all possible at Janette's make-up counter.'

'Just take the bookings,' said de Croix. 'And this has no business being here.' He pointed to a raspberry lipstick. 'You think Victoria Beckham would wear this? Celine, go through the stock and remove any item that is insulting to the senses.'

Celine looked apologetically at Janette, who didn't seem remotely bothered.

★

'You realise this wallpaper dates back to the 1830s?' Delia told de Croix in the tea rooms. 'Each bird of paradise, every feather exquisitely painted by hand. I adore the blues and greens and purples. Don't you? So vibrant.' She reached out her hand and lightly touched the wall.

De Croix squeezed his eyes together. 'I'm the sort of person who tends to look forward rather than back and so I suppose historical items don't impress me as much as they should. You know, this place could be converted into six or seven hundred apartments.'

She had to catch her breath before she could speak. 'I think your way of thinking is very sad,' she said. 'Gregory was so proud of his family history and took pride in pointing out details of the building to customers, from gold leaf cornicing to the intricately carved clock embedded in the first balcony above the hall. He believed Shillington's was part of the social fabric that made up Dublin city, and he viewed the store as a historic art piece.'

'Surely this room should be a museum rather than a place for women to eat cake, for which their hips will hate them forever.'

'And surely you are the most blatant misogynist I have ever come across.'

Delia turned without comment and made for the side door. What had Lando done, bringing this hideous business version of de Croix into their lives?

★

De Croix sat opposite his daughter in the tearoom and felt unnerved by Delia's attitude, not just about the wallpaper but about the business in general. She was hot and cold, like a woman who couldn't decide if she would join him in bed. He knew he'd been impetuous in taking on the project, and he also knew why. He and Julie needed a break, that was obvious, as did his mistress. He'd rarely had problems in pleasing women, be it business or romance, but right now he felt like he was riding a runaway reindeer. Christmas may be the most wonderful year for the public, but for retailers it was the most stressful time. He was in two minds as to whether Shillington's should continue in the family's hands. The boy was lacking in leadership skills, and if it wasn't for his obvious attraction to Celine, de Croix was doubtful if Lando would come into work at all. Delia, meanwhile, was running on stress and coffee. On the plus side, Celine was surprising him more by the day with her decisive thinking and high energy for business. The same could not be said for the tea rooms, with sloth-level displays of movement by the waitress.

'Is this a saltshaker?' said de Croix, picking up an almost empty glass jar. 'Where are the real flakes of sea salt? It is no wonder it fails.'

'Papa, keep your voice down,' Celine whispered.

'Here she comes,' said de Croix, 'now for answers.'

The waitress arrived at the table. Where was the notepad, and why was there a J-Cloth in her hand?

'Would you mind if I moved you, love?' asked the waitress.

Why were they being asked to move rather than which kind of morning cake they'd like? De Croix didn't say a word but instead glared at the woman.

'It's the plug socket,' the waitress explained, as if it should be obvious. 'We like to take our breaks at this table and plug in the phone, you know how it is.'

'Do I?' said de Croix.

'Papa,' said Céline, smiling up at the waitress, attempting to detonate a bomb that was already exploding.

'How about I ask you a question.'

'About the plug socket?' she said.

'No. Why do people leave their carrot cake behind?'

The waitress looked genuinely interested and didn't seem to be picking up on his point. 'It might be a little dry?' she said. 'Ross does his best, and he has the odd off day, but it has to be said, he does like a good plain cake.'

De Croix felt his eyeballs popping. 'Where is the influencer Instagramming their tarte au citron?' he said.

'Tarte au what?' said the waitress.

Céline was about to wave a white flag but backed away when de Croix gave one of his steely looks. He glanced around. The tablecloth pattern had faded, the staff seemed disillusioned, and the place was cold.

'And so, you wouldn't mind moving?' the waitress said again, before slowly retreating with her J-Cloth.

De Croix looked at his daughter. 'I want you to take pictures of problem areas, from displays on the counters to walkways and lights, then place luminous red stickers on the relevant counter so we see what needs to be corrected.'

'Of course, Papa.'

'And remember, it is the little things that matter a lot, and though we don't have the budget to bring in decorators as we do at Le Marché Cher, we can do some DIY to bring in the VIPs. Offline can be our gold mine,' he said. 'Let the other stores go fishing for customers online, but I know it is impossible to replicate the feeling of entering a Shillington's for real.'

'You think so?' said Celine.

'There has never been a better time to offer customers the personal experience, the kind of service that was quite normal when shopkeepers cared for those visiting their stores. Taking pride in a business may seem like gold dust these days, but with a little attention, it is possible for Shillington's to regain its popularity.'

Chapter Eight

Bring me lobster on a clean plate, thought Stanley, leaning against the door to his flat in Shillington's. Gone was the day when he'd order his lunch from housekeeping, where a choice fillet was always at the ready. George Bernard Shaw was bang on the money when he said, 'Reminiscences make one feel so deliciously aged and sad.' Stanley patted his tummy and wondered if a visit to the tearoom could be worth it. Friday's quiche wasn't always bad, and he had bothered to wear his blue velvet three-piece, the same suit Gregory used to say signalled the weekend. He may have been his nephew, but Gregory had always felt like a son to Stanley, and their bond was no doubt the reason Stanley lived in reasonable comfort in his Shillington's rooms. But he was no fool and knew Delia was becoming tighter by the minute and any day now she might turf him out. They had known each other for twenty-eight years and yet he'd never managed to break through that hard exterior. But he wasn't one for overthinking and felt compassion for Delia more than any other emotion. For her to have lost her life partner after only nine months of marriage, she deserved to be given all the space she needed to be her own boss. However, the time was coming for Stanley to think seriously about his next steps.

'Morning, Uncle Stanley,' said Immy, carrying an armful of dresses.

Such a jolly lass and pleasant, he thought, though God knows she had a hard time.

'Looking so smart as always,' Immy added.

'Let me help you with that lot.' Stanley stepped forward and managed to lift over half of the dresses. Being a lightweight, he knew his limits.

'Do watch your back, won't you?' said Immy.

'I do, particularly when Delia's around.'

Immy giggled, though she was always loyal to her best friend's mother and tried her best not to complain.

'Where are we off to?' asked Uncle Stanley, flinging a green cocktail dress over his shoulder.

'To my new department,' Immy said, with added zing in her voice. She was the prettiest girl at Shillington's and though she wore little make-up, she could outclass any Rose of Tralee. 'You're looking at Shillington's first ever personal shopper,' said Immy, opening a door to a generous-sized room overlooking the green, which was full of winter's morning sun.

'We'll have to arrange a big desk for you, like J.R. Ewing,' said Stanley.

'I think I'll try channelling my inner Fallon Carrington,'

she said, having just watched the re-make of *Dynasty* on Netflix. 'And you know de Croix has instructed me to stop wearing the brown tent and instead wear a different dress every day from Shillington's stock.' Immy ran her fingers along the brass rail of dresses.

'Then let the personal shopping begin!' said Stanley, reaching for Immy's hand, and twirling her. Funny how life can lay on incredibly joyous moments when least expected.

★

In her suite at the Merrion Hotel, Celine opened one eye and then the other without moving from her nest of feathered pillows. The vaulted ceiling reminded her of long summer holidays at her grandmother's chateau in Normandy, where she used to curl up with her spaniel, Truffe, and wish for siblings.

Being an only child, Celine got a lot of attention from her parents, but they worried about her just the right amount and gave her enough freedom in Paris, so life wasn't too suffocating. Her role at Le Marché Cher hadn't just been handed to her on a plate, no matter what people might have thought. She had worked her way through the ranks, sourcing and introducing products, along with travelling to showrooms and manufacturers to meet the extravagant palates of their customers. She was confident in her decision-making and was always two seasons ahead, thinking of winter in the summer and spring in the autumn. If only she could be more decisive when it came to Lando. He was a darling young man, so handsome and funny, and yet something wasn't clicking. When they kissed, she didn't feel the sparks, though she felt so good walking around with him, arm in arm, hugging and goofing around. Her father had a mistress and how he continued to have his wife's loyalty was beyond comprehension. Celine didn't think she could ever handle that sort of life. What is the value of tradition if it is disrespectful? It troubled Celine, just enough to feel a small percentage of guilt for staying in one of Dublin's most beautiful hotels. But then her mother's enthusiasm for Celine to join the trip to Dublin, especially so close to Christmas, was quite out of character. Change was coming, she could feel it.

At midday, wrapped in a yellow coat with an alpaca hat covering her hair, Celine moved through the lobby. She walked past marble columns in the hallway and smiled at the top-hatted doorman who held the door open to the middle of Georgian Dublin. This was a decadent hour to appear and even more so to go straight to lunch with Lando Shillington. Today, she was going to go wild and order a pint of Guinness, not the sort of thing a Parisian girl should do. Too often, her life of privilege felt nothing of the sort. It had been a good time to leave. Celine had complicated things with too many people, ghosting lovers and teasing those she fancied without following through. Her phone had become an explosive device, streaming notifications from too many dating apps. She couldn't recall a single romantic walk, let alone philosophical talk, that had come from an online liaison. Sex was always fine but these days she wanted more.

★

The café in the National Gallery was alive with hungry art lovers and shoppers carrying early Christmas presents. Lando and Celine stood at the counter gazing at the ready-made lunch options.

'What are you thinking?' said Lando, deciding between roast beef and tomato, or humous and roast vegetables.

'Not a sandwich, that's for sure,' said Celine.

'Why is that?'

'They make you fat.'

'I was born with lean genes,' said Lando, blowing her a kiss for fun. 'All the photos of my dad, he was very slim, even though Mum says he cut butter so thickly, it looked like he was spreading cheddar cheese on his toast.'

'Maybe your father would have been overweight in his forties, or a big fat man by the time he was sixty,' said Celine. But she must have read the expression on his face, as she had tears in her eyes. 'Oh my god, I'm so sorry, Lando.' She hugged him tightly. 'I thought I was being funny, please forgive me.'

'Always,' he said, kissing her cheek. 'It's so weird, you know I'd never thought of what sort of shape he'd be in later in life. After all this time, it's incredible that I still have new questions that just cannot be answered. It's no more than supposition.'

'Then, one thing we can be sure of is that you'd better have the low-fat sandwich,' said Celine, with a beautiful smile, 'and I'll have vegetable soup.'

'No bread?'

'I had planned on drinking a large glass of Guinness,' she said, picking up two bottles of water and placing them on their sides on the tray, 'and I guess it's just as well they don't serve it here.'

'I'll take you for a proper pint of Guinness this weekend,' he told her.

'I'd like that, and maybe you can bring Immy?'

'Sorry?'

'Immy.'

'Have you met?'

'I've tried to find her, but she seems to be with customers anytime I see her.'

No surprises there. He knew Immy was still feeling very sore about everything.

'I think better just the two of us.'

Celine looked at him closely. 'You know, I think I've got to know you well over the past months, Lando Shillington, and if I were a gambler, I'd say you have got some business with that pretty girl.'

'No,' he said, feeling himself blush. Besides, why was Celine even asking this? She didn't seem even vaguely jealous. In fact, she treated him more like a cousin than a boyfriend, if that's what he was. But then he didn't really know what they were.

'You know what I was thinking when I woke up this morning?' said Celine, pulling out a chair and sitting down.

'Tell me.' Lando lifted the bowl of soup from the tray and placed it in front of Celine.

'We are both in similar positions,' she said.

'In what way?'

'We are both only children and the heirs to our family businesses.'

'A curse or a blessing,' he said, looking at the humous sandwich and not feeling even vaguely hungry.

'But I can't imagine what it has been like for you,' she said, dipping her soup spoon into the bowl. 'My father has been guiding me all along, but you and your mother are strong together, and I admire that.' She took a mouthful of soup. 'Life is what we make it.'

She was more than adorable, but she wasn't Immy, and maybe it was the guilt he felt for hurting her, but he couldn't get Immy out of his mind.

Chapter Nine

The fluorescent lighting throughout Shillington's had been called to Delia's attention by de Croix, who implored her to make an adjustment. At this point, it would make little difference financially to the hole they were in, and Delia gave the go-ahead to replace the bulbs with soft glow versions in a bid to turn Shillington's into a place of Christmas elegance.

'Remind me of your name,' said de Croix, standing in Immy's new personal shopping headquarters.

'Immy,' she said.

'As in Imogen?' De Croix sniffed in the kind of way that a handkerchief wasn't required. 'Do you notice a delicate, slightly citrus scent running through the air filters? It is a little magic trick of mine to intoxicate the senses.'

Immy sniffed. 'I actually can,' she said. 'A hint of orange?'

'Correct,' he said, looking satisfied with her reaction, 'orange to stimulate appetite, and a little lavender to calm the senses and encourage customers to feel at ease.' De Croix appeared to survey the room, pressing his hand flat on the tartan sofas facing each other with a coffee table in between.

Uncle Stanley had bequeathed a beautiful collection of Dublin pubs by the acclaimed photographer Patrick Donald. Each frame looked so elegant and interesting on the walls, telling the story of each establishment.

'If you don't mind, Imogen, we will use your full name to accompany your job title, as I feel it more appropriate.'

'OK by me.' Immy kept waiting for de Croix to burst out laughing, as he seemed to be taking this personal shopping business very seriously.

'Sadly, there are presently no resources to train you as a personal shopping executive to my usual standards, but we must work with what we have, and you are what we have.'

This was a relief. The thought of having to spend any longer than expected with de Croix made going to the dentist seem preferable.

'I'll do my best,' said Immy.

'In essence, Imogen, you are to represent Shillington's as our highly skilled gift-curating expert. You have an unrivalled knowledge of every item in-store—'

'I do?'

De Croix nodded. 'You do, and I want you to focus on your extraordinary ability to find the perfect gift, the right clothes, shoes and accessories.' He looked at Immy so deeply, she may as well have been on stage with Keith Barry for hypnosis. 'You will solve all of your clients' dilemmas.'

Immy admired de Croix's imagination, not to mention his optimism, and it was an improvement on re-arranging butter dishes in homeware.

'I'm flattered you think I'm up to the task,' she said.

'Failure is not an option,' he said. 'But remember, the best thing about your job is that you are, without question, making people happy. You will transform the faces of customers from flustered to fabulous as they find relief through your guidance.' De Croix kissed the tips of his fingers. 'Some clients may actually kiss you when they leave, I've seen it happen with my own eyes.'

'You're really sure you wouldn't prefer me to be more behind the scenes?' Immy wanted to double-check but de Croix ignored the suggestion.

'The main condition is for you to achieve client satisfaction and sales targets, no matter what, and get Shillington's back in the game.'

'I'll do my best.' Immy would have to borrow some fashion magazines from the staff loos, and at least it was Thursday, so she could swot up on the latest winter trends in *The Gloss* magazine.

'I want more than your best,' said de Croix, walking to the door. 'We must make the profits if Shillington's is to survive.'

★

'Can you pass me a fresh tea towel, please, Lando,' said Delia, wiping the cookery books with a damp cloth and carefully stacking each one into a cardboard box.

The main kitchen in number 58 Fitzwilliam Square looked more like a stocktake at Shillington's, with piles of plates and dishes, napkins and photo frames taken from cupboards to be dusted and labelled.

'I'm not sure you're going to fit all of this downstairs,' said Lando, feeling increasingly stressed about the prospect of his mother moving into the basement.

'Nonsense,' she said, 'and once it's stored correctly, it will fit.'

Lando put a couple of slices of bread into the toaster. 'And when do the tenants move in?'

'In four days,' said Delia, finding a Christmas card squashed between pages of *Simply Delicious* by Darina Allen.

'You OK, Mum?'

Delia looked up and smiled the kind of smile she used to hide her sadness. It was a smile Lando knew all too well. 'Of course,' she said.

'Who was it from?'

'Sorry, darling?'

'The card.'

'Oh, it's nothing.' Delia slipped the card back into the book.

In the past, they had been reasonably open with each other, or at least as open as an old-school person like Delia could be. But lately, she wasn't sharing her thoughts with him and he could sense there were things beyond the uncertainty of Shillington's on her mind.

'Fine,' he said. 'And it's a twelve-month contract for the tenants upstairs.'

'Yes, which will be heaven to my bank account.'

Lando understood the need for his mum to downsize, but did it have to be into his own flat?

'I'm determined to be prepared for every eventuality,' said Delia, 'and if we can hold on to Shillington's, then we're going to have to continue tightening our belts until the place takes off again.'

Lando didn't want to say it, but he just couldn't help himself. 'And if we sell?'

'If we sell?' Delia said. 'If.'

'Yes, *if* we sell the store, you can keep this place—'

'And then you'll be free to do as you wish, if that's what you mean.' Delia said it in a voice that made Lando feel like a dreadful son.

The grandfather clock in the hall struck six o'clock.

'Thirty minutes to go until a glass of wine,' said Delia. 'De Croix brought me a lovely bottle earlier in the week.'

'He's good with wine,' said Lando.

'And with parenting; Celine is the first decent girlfriend you've had.'

'Steady on, we're not exactly serious.'

'I know what I see,' said Delia, 'and my chemistry radar is on full alert.'

'Then maybe dial it down a little.'

Apart from Celine's obvious beauty and charisma, she and Lando still hadn't slept together. He was interested in her, not in a notch-in-the-belt kind of way, but more because their pace was unusual. When Lando liked a girl, he'd have her on his arm before you could say Tinder, though no dating app had ever been necessary. Maybe because he was easy-going, plus he didn't take much interest in his appearance, though he knew he looked OK.

He looked at the photo stuck to the fridge of his dad kidding around, sitting back to front on the saddle of a bay hunter named Wishful. The photo had been in the kitchen for as long as Lando could remember and, as he grew older, his father became younger. It was one of life's paradoxes that he found hard to get his head around.

The toast popped up, but Lando had lost his appetite.

'It isn't like you and I will be housemates forever,' said Delia, passing a jar of Marmite to him. 'If things go well, you and your future *you know who* can move upstairs.'

'And you'd be living in the basement?'

'Where else would I go?' she said, opening the cutlery drawer and taking a knife out for Lando. 'I've lived in this house all my married life.'

'Mum, you were married for nine months.'

Delia slammed the drawer closed in response.

'Mum, I didn't mean—'

She looked devastated. Her eyes brimmed with tears, and she bit her bottom lip as if to stop herself from yelling at him.

'I made a promise to your father,' said Delia, lowering her head as she pressed her hands against the island. 'For better or for worse, and I got the worse.'

Lando walked over to his mum and put his arms around her, holding her as tightly as he could.

'I didn't mean it like that, Mum, I'm so sorry.'

'I know,' she said, burying her face in his shoulder, 'and I shouldn't blub in front of you.'

'Blubbing is good for you,' he said, smiling down at her. 'You need to blub, it's important, Mum; you're not a robot.'

Delia began to smile and then even laughed a little. 'Thank you,' she said, and reached for the paper towel and tore off a square.

'And you know what, Mum? In terms of our house-sharing, or not sharing, I don't think there's any chance of me bringing home "the one" anytime soon.' He thought of Immy. She loved to laugh about 'the one', and whenever Lando had a new girl on the scene it was always the first thing she'd ask - 'is this *the one*?' - knowing full well it wasn't. 'I'm doing something I'm sure Dad would have approved of, and that's called—'

'Yes, I know it, playing the field, which he never got to do, did he? He chose me, without looking at anyone else, never gave himself the chance to look around.'

'Mum, come on.'

'And then you arrived. You were your father's real true love, even though he only met you once, but to have seen him holding you in his arms—'

'Don't upset yourself again, Mum, it's OK.'

'I'm fine,' she said, and turned to pick up a spoon and stir the pot of soup on the Aga. 'It's just not fair, is it?' she continued. 'I know you've heard me say this repeatedly, Lando. He was your father, and it was your right to have him.'

'No matter how many times we go over it, Mum, losing Dad will never make sense.'

Delia put down the spoon and turned to hug him tightly. 'If we have to sell the paintings, you know which one I want to keep, don't you?'

'The one Dad put his elbow through,' said Lando.

'Yes,' she said, looking up at him. 'The restorers did such a good job, but it really wouldn't be worth anything to anyone but us. Captain Hook, on his twenty-sixth birthday,' she said, picking up the spoon again. 'And the older I get, the less I can believe I had the courage to dress as Tinkerbell.' Delia attempted to laugh. 'I'd be an old woman to him now.'

'No, Mum, you're gorgeous.' Lando never knew her to be so unconfident.

'You know, I never understood when people talked about becoming invisible in their sixties. I never thought I would.'

'I see you, Mum.'

'You are a good boy, Lando,' she said. 'Your father would be so proud of you.'

Chapter Ten

There was a knock on the door of the personal shopping suite, and Janette, wearing sparkling green eye shadow, appeared with a young man next to her.

'Good morning,' she said, in a funny formal accent. 'May I present Mr Bill O'Brien.'

'Lovely to meet you,' said Immy, reaching to shake hands with Bill, who took off his green flat cap and blushed. His corduroy jacket was buttoned up to his neck.

'Wishing you a lovely consultation,' said Janette, reversing out of the room. She must have been briefed by de Croix with a sales script and how to articulate her words.

Immy walked to the centre of the room and wondered how on earth this was going to work, though her new wardrobe had given her a lift. De Croix arranged for a fortnight's worth of dresses and trouser suits, chosen by Celine, to be delivered to her office. Today, she chose a wrap dress made from green jersey fabric. The tie at the waist made her feel more feminine than she had ever felt in her life. It was amazing what a piece of fabric could do to lift the spirits, and hopefully she could create the same feeling for her future clients hunting for new clothes.

'Would you like to sit down?' she said, gesturing to the sofa. She sat across from him and poured a glass of water from a crystal carafe she'd chosen from the bridal department. A start at least.

'What can I help you with today? Are you looking for anything in particular?' said Immy, thinking it wasn't a great question.

'No clue,' said Bill, who looked like he was about to collapse with nerves.

She'd have to try a different tack. 'And tell me, where are you from?'

'County Monaghan,' he said, clasping his hands together.

'OK, and what do you do there?' He seemed very shy.

'Dairy farming,' he said.

'I hear that cattle prices are up in Monaghan.'In the newsagent's this morning, she'd bizarrely noticed and remembered a headline in the *Farmers Journal*. Lando always told Immy she had a photographic memory.

Bill's eyes appeared to light up. 'Didn't I hear the very same?' he said, almost animated. 'Charolais bulls are selling well at the minute,' he added, 'and Aberdeen Angus-cross heifers sold well above.'

The perfect icebreaker.

'That sounds positive, doesn't it?' said Immy, wondering what she could follow with.

'Not too bad,' he said.

'And to get the ball rolling, what sort of things are you

looking for today?' Some kind of direction would be helpful. She hoped he'd say something to do with his house because crockery, candlesticks and cushions were a cinch for her. Immy could choose salad bowls or egg cups in her sleep.

Bill rubbed the back of his head. 'My sister saw on social media that you have a service to help people shop, and I can tell you, I've never been a good shopper in cities.' He eyed the water and Immy poured him a glass. 'In the mart, sure I could spend a million no problem, I'd know exactly what I'm looking for, but when it comes to clothes I wouldn't know where to look beyond a pair of overalls for the yard.'

'Your sister sounds very thoughtful.'

'I wouldn't say that now,' he said, bunching his flap cap between his hands. 'She's over in America and sends back instructions like she's the boss.' He took off his Leslie coloured jumper to reveal a white and blue checked shirt. 'It's warm in here,' he said.

Immy got up to open a window and looked out at the sky, dark with snow clouds.

'What sort of instructions does your sister send to you?' said Immy. She was intrigued, mostly because she didn't have any siblings, but more so because his sister sounded a little like Immy's mother. Barking instructions from a distance.

'She's got some award ceremony in America and her boyfriend's away, so I'm to get something called a lounge suit.' Bill was now on a roll. 'And says I to her, the only lounge I'll be getting into is my local, to watch the hurling.' He picked up the glass and drank almost all the water.

Never in Immy's life had she shopped for men's clothes, let alone a lounge suit.

'Do you live alone?' said Immy, to find out a little more about him, which may bring further clues as to what kind of suit he'd like.

'I do, but I'm only ten minutes from Castleblaney,' he said, 'the same place my sister took the bus to America.'

'When was that?' said Immy, topping up his water glass.

'I'm twenty-nine, and I would have been eleven when she left.'

'Eighteen years ago?' said Immy.

'That's it,' he said. 'And I've been working on the farm ever since.'

'Did you want to get on the bus with her?'

'I did,' he said. 'How did you know?'

'Just a guess.'

'Mammy and Daddy would have sent me away if I hadn't been needed for the farm.'

It might have been a joke if he hadn't looked so serious.

'Did you ever think of following her out there?' said Immy. 'When you were older?'

'Daddy died the next Tuesday; God rest his soul.'

'And you were next in line?' Immy had not expected this kind of conversation.

'I was, and there was no question but for me to take on the farm.'

'How did your sister end up in America?'

'Ah, she was always going to go. She was singing in the

church choir and listening to records. Once she hit eighteen, she couldn't wait to get away.'

'And she's doing well?'

'Ah sure, she's singing and doing what she loves in New York, and I'm back at the farm.'

It could have been so different if his father hadn't died, and he'd joined his sister when he turned eighteen. Sliding-door alternatives started racing through Immy's mind until she realised Bill was staring at her.

'Sorry, I got distracted.' Immy picked up her brown leather notebook and pen, which de Croix had given to her. 'I'm just taking a few notes, and then I'll ask one of the sales assistants in menswear to take some size measurements.'

'No need,' he said, putting up his feet on the coffee table as Immy stood up. 'You should find my details in an email by now.'

'Really?'

'The boss, AKA my sister, sent a car for me,' he said, with a chuckle. 'She likes me travelling in style, so she does, and didn't the driver measure me up?'

'Your driver took your measurements?' said Immy, excusing herself so she could check her laptop on her desk by the window. She quickly looked out over St Stephen's Green. It was going to be a frosty night; she could tell by the sky. Maybe she'd curl up in front of *The Holiday*. The film was like a comfort blanket to her. Lando used to say that in another life he could have played Jude Law's part as Graham, and then Immy would call him vain, and they'd cackle, tease each other and pretend not to imagine life in the idyllic cottage. The simple life, Lando called it.

'My sister leaves no stone unturned,' said Bill, looking very relaxed on the sofa. 'She worries about me without reason and sends all kinds of crazy treats my way.'

'She sounds like some lady,' said Immy, closing her notebook and feeling intrigued by Bill. 'And she sent a driver to bring you here?'

'Wasn't it a nice change from bumping around in my Zetor.'

'Zetor?'

'My tractor,' he said.

Brilliant, thought Immy. She felt like she was starring in some kind of mini-series about *Unlikely Encounters*. 'I'll be back in ten minutes,' she said, 'and then we'll pull out a few options for you to try on.'

Immy closed her office door and wondered how she was going to choose a suit for a man who rarely dressed up and whose micromanaging sister was going to be hard to impress. She took a moment to check her iPhone for messages, of which there were none, but an email had arrived from Bill's sister's PA, to say 'money is no object'.

'Uncle Stanley,' Immy called out, seeing him outside the door to his bedsit.

'There you are,' he said. 'Aren't you the one looking smart now?'

'You like it?'

'You look like a stylish woman on a stylish mission.'

'A mission to the unknown, more like,' she said. 'I'm supposed to be choosing a knockout suit for a man who's more comfortable in trousers held up by baler twine.

Uncle Stanley straightened his tie and pulled down the ends of his waistcoat. 'If you'd like a little steerage, I'll be happy to escort you to menswear?'

'Would you really? Yes, please, you're a lifesaver.'

Uncle Stanley put out his arm, Immy took hold, and together they descended the staircase to the fourth floor to find few customers, and no salesperson to in sight.

They stood on a 1950s yellow rug in the centre of the department. 'What colour are we thinking?' said Uncle Stanley. 'How about a lovely bright mustard?'

'I'm not sure,' said Immy. 'I have a feeling he'll want something discreet. He doesn't strike me as the kind of man who wants to stand out.'

At that moment, Celine strode through the door with Lando in tow.

'Fabulous timing,' said Celine, 'marvellous to see you both.' She was wearing thigh-high black boots, a cream jumper dress, and a fitted jacket. 'Oh my God, Immy, you look incredible! Lando, look at her.'

Lando had his head stuck in *The Week*. He looked up and smiled at Immy.

'Looks nice,' he said.

'Nice?' said Celine. 'Uncle Stanley, wouldn't you agree this dress was literally made for Immy? The neckline is beautiful, and the green brings out her eyes.'

Immy felt herself blushing, which was ridiculous as Lando had seen her in everything from fancy dress as Queen Elizabeth to her most faded pyjamas.

'She always looks fabulous in my eyes,' said Uncle Stanley.

Immy smiled gratefully at him. Anything to avoid having to look at Lando.

'And what am I thinking?' said Celine. 'Immy, I am sorry, we haven't formally met, but I've seen you many times from afar and so I feel like I know you.' She stepped forward and lightly touched Immy's shoulders before kissing her on both cheeks.

Immy had no intention of liking Lando's new liaison, or fling. She wasn't sure how to describe it. Usually, Lando didn't put Immy through such torture, most likely because he didn't want to receive one of Immy's eye rolls as if to say, How long with this *one* last?

'Are you happy with the rail of outfits we sent up to your office?' Celine seemed genuinely interested. It was such a massive change to be in a position at work where people sought Immy's approval.

'The clothes are gorgeous,' she said, trying not to be so formal in front of Celine, but knowing she was de Croix's daughter, she couldn't quite help it. 'I'm actually in the middle of choosing suit options for my first client,' she said, trying to deflect attention away from herself.

'I've suggested mustard—'

'And it's so kind of you, Uncle Stanley,' said Immy, jumping in, 'but for my client—'

'Let me guess,' said Celine, 'he wants something he can throw on and look great in, something seasonless.'

Wow, she was good. 'Sounds about right,' said Immy. 'It's for an awards ceremony.'

'You're a mind reader,' said Lando, looking at Celine.

Immy couldn't help feeling annoyed by his enthusiasm.

Celine walked over to a rail next to Lando. 'You have the size?' she said, turning to Immy.

'Forty in the suit and a thirty-four waist,' said Immy, reading from her iPhone.

'Thanks,' said Celine, passing the cream suit to Immy. 'Fashion is all about attitude and feeling good in what you're wearing. The cut in this suit is flattering, I'm sure of it.'

'What about the fellah in the pink tuxedo in Paddington?' said Uncle Stanley. 'Now that's what I call a suit.'

Immy wasn't sure where her impulse came from, but she gravitated towards a rail of navy suits and searched for the size tags. 'I kind of think navy would be better for my client; much easier to keep clean.'

'If you want,' said Celine, 'but I think you should bring him the choice, no?'

Immy wanted to turn to Lando and ask him to keep his girlfriend's views to herself, but instead she found herself saying, 'Good idea,' and passed the navy suit to Uncle Stanley, to carry while she retrieved the cream suit from Celine.

'Good choice,' said Celine, waving them off. '*À bientôt*.'

Chapter Eleven

In Delia's office, de Croix was on the visitors' side of the desk with an espresso and slice of carrot cake, which the tearoom chef was working hard to improve upon. Delia attempted to appear as if she didn't mind de Croix eating. If there was one thing she couldn't stand it was crumbs on her papers.

'I'm pleased to say this carrot cake has improved greatly,' said de Croix, tapping the pudding fork on the side of the plate. 'This is a good sign, for it signals that staff are listening to my advice.'

Alternatively, Ross, the tearoom chef, may have been lucky with his cake mixture this morning. Delia had had lengthy discussions with Ross over the years, who'd been at Shillington's for almost as long as Uncle Stanley. Sentimentality really did put a spanner in the works when it came to being ruthless. Delia was sure if she hadn't loved Gregory so much, she would have thrown many staff members out on their ear, including Martin upstairs, whom she heard had passed out in bed as de Croix was doing the rounds.

As a young widow, Delia had made hard decisions including land sales and dismissing well-meaning relatives' advice. One of Gregory's close single friends discretely offered to marry her, and though she was fond of him and wanted a male role model for Lando, she suspected Shillington's department store was where his interests lay and so she declined.

'I have been thinking about pricing,' said de Croix, drinking the espresso in one mouthful.

'Go on,' said Delia, thinking she may send an order to the tea rooms for a decaff cappuccino. She had been sleeping badly since Lando's return and there was no way she'd risk caffeine so late in the afternoon.

'To use this cake as an example,' said de Croix. 'You are selling a slice for two euro seventy-five.'

'Our customers wouldn't pay a cent more,' she said.

'Then we add some trinkets.' De Croix moved his hands as if he were a magician conjuring up a trick. 'A puff of cream, a spray of golden glitter, we add theatre to the plate and fifty cents more to the charge.'

'And you think this is going to save Shillington's?'

'No, it is merely the beginning,' he said, tapping his index finger against his temple. 'We must remember the golden rule of retail: four times the cost price and add on the VAT.'

'Hike the prices and we'll lose the customers we already have.' Delia felt utterly deflated. The man made no sense.

'We simply find new customers.'

'How exactly? Are you going to wave that invisible magic

wand of yours?' Delia had never been one for sarcasm but there was a time and a place for everything.

'The facts are that Shillington's footfall is down by more than half, and now we have four weeks until Christmas Eve to make a serious amount of money.'

'And do you think we can do it?' she said. 'What exactly are you trying to tell me, de Croix? Just spit it out.'

'Can we do it? Who knows?' he said. 'Because despite what you may think, I am not God.'

Delia wasn't suggesting for a moment that he was.

'At Le Marché Cher,' said de Croix, pressing on with his mini lecture, 'I hire the very best because we earn a lot of money. But for Shillington's, we are down to the bone.'

'I don't follow,' said Delia.

'We have little meat, but we must boil the bones, make the stock and attempt to salvage what is left of money-making opportunity for this Christmas.'

'Are you comparing Shillington's to a carcass, de Croix?'

'Of course,' he said, brashly. 'As one of my icons, Graydon Carter, says, "Life is about a succession of minor failures; the key is to keep them minor", and though I realise there may be no option but to sell Shillington's, let's see if we can do this the old-fashioned way.'

'And what is the old-fashioned way?' said Delia, so close to losing her cool.

'We call in the favours … isn't that a favourite of the Irish? But most immediately, we require staff. I want you to employ the best person you can find to run the social media accounts for Shillington's.' De Croix brushed the crumbs from the desk onto his hand, which was a relief to Delia. Had he let the crumbs hit the floor, she might have thrown the jar of paper clips at him. 'We need,' de Croix continued, 'at least one young blood to invigorate this ageing dinosaur.'

'And are you expecting this young blood to put up the Christmas decorations?'

'No, I am delegating this task to my daughter; the budget is so small it wouldn't even cover what she spends on shoes in a month.'

Chapter Twelve

In her PS Headquarters, as it had become known, Immy sat at her desk and read over her notes about Bill O'Brien. She wondered about his sister, clearly bossy but she must care a huge amount for him if she was getting involved in what he was going to wear to an awards ceremony. She was still smiling about the *Farmers Journal* and wondered if she should do some research about each client before they met. Her midday meeting was with David Clock.

The now familiar door knock came, along with Janette sporting glittery eyes and introducing 'Mr Clock' in her well-practised and increasingly eloquent voice.

With David Clock there was no hesitancy. He shook hands with Immy, sat down and said, 'I'm short on time, sorry.'

'That's OK,' she said, trying not to think of the fact that his name was Clock and how ironic that time is practically one of the first words to come out of his mouth. 'Tell me how I can be of help.'

'Well, if you were a therapist I'd sit back and ask you

to tell me what the hell I need to do with my life.' He laughed unconvincingly. 'But I'm here to feed my habit of procrastination.'

'Which is?' Immy sat down on the opposite sofa and opened her notebook.

'I'd like some new clothes.'

'OK,' she said, relieved at the simplicity of his request. For a moment she wasn't quite sure what he was going to say.

'It sounds ridiculous, and you wouldn't think I'm the MD of a software company, but we have our office Christmas party coming up and I need something to wear. You know, something to shake things up.'

'Formal or casual?' said Immy.

'I'm told there will be karaoke, God help us all with my voice,' he said. 'At least that's what my PA tells me, but I trust her completely. She has very good taste actually.' He examined the palms of his hands as if he were trying to read his own fortune. 'Not that we've spent time together out of the office, but I have a feeling she chooses well in all kinds of areas.'

Immy didn't have to say a word for him to realise the question she wanted to ask.

'We aren't together, no, not at all,' he said, shaking his head defensively. 'I'm in the middle of getting divorced.'

'I'm sorry,' said Immy.

'No need, better all around,' he said, looking down at his shoes. 'I think we both stopped trying; not sure why, just one of those things.

Immy thought he was going to cry. 'Would you like a glass of water?' she asked.

'Please.'

She took the lid from the carafe and filled a glass for him.

'Though, there have been times when I've wondered if she might like something more,' he said.

'Sorry,' said Immy, 'I don't follow.'

'My PA' he said. 'I feel like there's something between us, and it has nothing to do with the collapse of my marriage.' He clearly felt the need to defend himself. 'The whole thing had disintegrated by the time Elaine came to work for us.'

'Elaine is your PA?'

'Yes,' he said, 'but it's hard to tell.'

'What do you mean?'

He looked awkward and didn't answer.

'It's OK,' she said. 'Nothing you say will go any further, and I know we've just met, but just so you know it's between these four walls.'

'There's something in the way she laughs at my jokes, and I'm really not very good at jokes.'

Immy chuckled, and said, 'If you say so.'

'And she asks me how I am in a way that I feel she really means it.'

'She sounds nice,' said Immy.

'She really is, and she tells me about finding tickets to a play, but she didn't want to go alone and that it's a real pain ordering takeaway for one person, and hardly worth it to pay for the delivery service.'

'She's single too?' said Immy, figuring that his PA is almost definitely interested in out-of-office activities.

'She is.'

Immy had to get a grip; she was here to sell things for Shillington's, not turn into an agony aunt. 'So, David, let's talk about the kind of clothes you're seeking.'

'Yes, I'll get on to the clothes,' he said, 'and I'm surprising the hell out of myself by even saying this, but I'd dearly love someone to tell me how the hell I can tell.'

'Sorry?'

'If she likes me,' he said, 'romantically, that is.'

All at once he seemed embarrassed and eager to tell all.

'And I wonder, if I do ask her out, would she want to go clubbing and that kind of thing? Because, you know, when it comes down to it, I want to snuggle up on the couch, watch movies, walk along Sandymount Strand, and just talk, you know? I sound like an old fart, and I'm not even that old, but at fifty-one I don't think I could handle Copper Face Jacks.'

'If you're short on time, how about you give me your measurements and I'll put some outfits together for you to try on next week?'

'Would you really? That's so good of you; I mean, it would be a load off my mind.'

Immy noted down David's measurements and when he left, she jotted down his references to long walks, movies, and cosy evenings along with questions about body language. This was a subject that interested her, as she had noticed how Lando seemed to have his arms folded every time she had seen him since his return from Paris. Did it mean something?

★

Five interviews later, Delia was aghast at the youngsters she was meeting. To say they were demanding put it lightly; she almost expected them to request payment for the time they spent preparing for their meeting with her. One more candidate to go, and then she would go home to write Christmas cards. She'd just received a delivery of the most exquisite stationery from Plunkett Press. Handwritten correspondence was more important to her than any social media account could ever be.

'Next,' she hollered, and slower than she liked, a young man arrived at her doorway and hovered.

'Do come in,' she said, curtly. Dressed in cream trousers and a zip-up cardigan, he appeared to have excellent deportment. He sat down, lightly touched his hair, which was so curly it looked like it had been sprayed in salt, and lay his iPhone on the desk.

'Is it necessary to have a device present?' said Delia, wondering if he had set the iPhone to record mode.

'It's my right to have my device with me for support.'

'Fine,' said Delia. 'It's Christian, isn't it?'

'Yes,' he said.

'Let's get started, shall we?'

'First,' he said, 'it's important for me to know where your

clothes are coming from. When I choose brands, I want to know that the clothes are in style but that the brands are in line with my own values.'

'Such as?' Delia was put out that he'd dived in, in front of her, as if to lead the interview. Much too headstrong; there was little chance of her choosing this young man, if first impressions were anything to go by.

'Sustainable, for starters.'

'All right,' she said, 'we can discuss such detail *if* I decide to hire you.'

'Fair enough,' said Christian.

'Let me brief you as to your potential role here at Shillington's —'

'It's important to me that my needs are met,' he said. 'This is my second job, and I want to be recognised for the value I'll be bringing to this company.'

'And what is your first job?'

'I handle social media campaigns for property,' he said, 'mostly rentals. Often people attempt to bribe me with cash to get them to the front of the queue, and I have to say, whoah, I've got morals, which are more important to me than the zeros.'

'Well, that's good to know, and fits very nicely, as it happens,' said Delia. 'We'd like you to promote Shillington's throughout the Christmas season.'

'Did I mention that salary is definitely a priority of mine?' said Christian.

'I thought you said that you don't put cash before a job.'

'In terms of bribery,' he said. 'I could never accept cash for bribery but in terms of my being paid for my worth, I'm very fixed on that.'

'I see,' said Delia, feeling rather overwhelmed by his rhetoric. 'Tell me about your strengths, and weaknesses too, if you wish?'

'I'm all about equity and if I think another gender is being paid more than me, I'll call it out.'

'I can't see how that is a strength, or a weakness; surely it's more of an opinion?' said Delia. 'But to answer your question, I think you'll find everyone at your level will be paid the same.'

'Six hundred and fifty euro per week and I'll do your socials: FB, Insta, Twitter, you name it. I'll get new energy for this old place online.'

'Isn't that a little steep for part-time?'

'If you don't get your socials in order, you may as well shut up shop because you'll be going nowhere.'

Delia knew he was right.

'And just to point out, I'm not greedy,' said Christian. 'I like to cover my costs and my hair doesn't pay for itself.' He took the end of the curl between his fingers and made it spring.

'You perm your hair?'

'We're not in the eighties, Mrs Shillington. These days it's called "new wave and much less rigid".'

'Well, it's very natural looking,' said Delia, 'and I do like the gentle wisp at the front.'

'My hair was literally poker straight,' he said, 'and I was

looking for something simple to style, so the salon came up with this.'

'Maybe I'll consider a new wave for my own poker-straight hair,' she said. 'I could definitely do with something to pep me up.'

'So do I have the gig?'

Another interview would surely tip Delia over the edge. He seemed like a competent young man, and most youngsters these days knew about social media.

'Then yes,' she said, feeling relieved. 'Let's go for a two-month trial, and if you do really well, I'll give you some vouchers for the tea rooms.' She waved him out of the office before he could think of any conditions.

Chapter Thirteen

The music in the menswear department had changed to jazz with a hint of South America, notably improving the atmosphere. Immy looked around for a staff member, but could only see Celine, re-arranging jumpers on a trestle table.

'It's all about the layout,' said Celine, giving Immy a warm smile. 'Papa taught me from a very young age. I even arranged my Barbie clothes in a particular way.'

'Sweet,' said Immy. 'My bedroom was like a jumble sale; I couldn't find my Cindy dolls let alone their clothes.'

'And what about Lando? Was he more Ken or Action Man?' said Celine.

'Definitely neither,' said Immy, as she began to help folding jumpers. 'I think he spent a huge amount of time here, especially in the days when it was so busy. When he was little, Lando thought the lady who headed up the haberdashery department was his actual grandmother as he spent so much time there. When she left, Lando said he was devastated. I guess she had been like his unofficial nanny while Delia was working here.'

Celine began stacking the folded jumpers on top of each other.

'He's so sweet, isn't he? And such a dreamer. My mother adores Lando.'

'That's nice,' said Immy, thinking of her own mother who had made no effort to get to know her friends, particularly Lando. Immy had spent practically every summer and most half terms with Lando, running up and down the flights of stairs in Shillington's, playing tricks on Uncle Stanley and hiding in the basement in Fitzwilliam Square.

'How long have you known him?' said Celine.

'Since we were twelve. It was a boarding school in the south of Ireland.'

'Lando tells me you're such a good friend to him,' said Celine. 'I'm so glad.'

Immy smiled that smile of hers which she saved for times when she didn't know what else to say, which she had been doing a lot of lately. Celine seemed to be a cool girl, and on top of that, she had model looks.

They both looked to the doorway, hearing sounds coming from the creaking stairs, and there was Lando, with a woolly hat pulled over his ears and dressed in a huge Canada Goose parka.

'Have you come from the North Pole?' said Celine, striding across the floor to hug him and kissing both his cheeks. Immy stayed where she was, and she noticed how Lando barely made eye contact with her.

'I've just been waiting in a building that definitely hasn't been updated since about 1810,' he said, rubbing his hands together. 'This place feels like the Bahamas in comparison.'

'What were you doing?' said Celine. 'Buying my Christmas present?'

'Uncle Stanley asked me to collect some legal papers from him but next time I'm going to bring an electric blanket and plug it in to the first socket I find in the waiting room.'

'You are so good to your uncle,' said Celine, 'or should I say grand-uncle?'

It was as if she knew his entire family background, but then Immy considered that maybe she did. Lando could have given her his entire history over pillow talk.

'So now you are lucky to have two girls to warm you up?' said Celine, full of humour. 'I think we are a good team, don't you think, Immy?'

'As in, you and Lando?' said Immy. 'Very good, obviously, you're a very good team.' Why did she always have to say *obviously* when things just weren't obvious?

'Lando, what do you think?' said Celine.

'Sure,' he said, though he looked as uncertain as Immy felt.

They all looked up when a man with dark curly hair, smartly dressed in a suit and overcoat, coughed awkwardly for their attention.

'Sorry to interrupt,' he said, in a slightly hoarse voice. 'I was looking for a pair of jeans.'

'Of course,' said Celine, striding towards him. 'Anything you want, I'm sure we can help you find the perfect fit.'

The man cranked his neck in Immy's direction. 'Hello,' he said, smiling.

She smiled back shyly and could feel everyone looking at her.

'You two know each other?' said Celine.

'Not as such,' said the man. 'I'm Flynn Rooney, TD North Dublin.'

Immy began shuffling hangers from left to right.

'Very nice to meet you,' said Celine, smiling at Flynn and then at Immy. 'Let's take a look at some fabulous jeans, shall we?'

'Who's that, Im?' said Lando, gently elbowing her when Celine and Flynn were out of sight.

'You heard what he said – Flynn Rooney, TD North Dublin.'

To keep herself busy, Immy continued where Celine left off by piling up the folded jumpers.

'He seemed to know you, that's all.'

'He's a regular customer, Lando, but we haven't met formally.'

'OK,' he said, 'no need to be so coy.'

'Coy? Sorry, Lando, but what's it to you how I might know him or what our relationship is?'

What was he thinking, giving her the fifth degree? He was the one who chose not to pursue their relationship further after he went to Paris, he was the one openly flirting with Celine and intimating there was something between them. Why should he have any say in who Immy knows or what she does?

'Christ, Immy, there's no need to be so defensive.'

'I'm not defensive,' she said, fetching jumpers to stack when Celine came running through the archway.

'Immy,' she said, 'I've just been chatting with Flynn about the beach.'

'The beach?' said Immy. 'But you've only been with him for a split second.'

'I asked him where he was from, and he said he lives next to a beach in somewhere that sounds like Dollymount, or something like it, and I thought, why don't we go there in the morning!'

Lando gave Immy the look as if to say, 'She really is fabulous, isn't she?'

'We can't just go to the beach,' said Immy, purposely scowling at Lando. 'Apart from anything else, it's freezing outside.'

'The air will be good for our skin,' said Celine, on high energy.

'In minus one degree Celsius, I'm not sure,' said Lando. 'And what about your new friend?'

Immy couldn't believe how jealous Lando had become; it sounded like he really minded Celine even meeting the guy.

'He's fine,' said Celine, looking through a shelf full of jeans. She turned to Immy. 'So, like I say, I think it's time Papa rewards us for our hard work, don't you?'

Immy would swap the beach for a day in bed, any day.

'I'm going back to Flynn, but I'll pick you up at eight a.m. And Lando, will you give Immy my mobile number?'

Lando looked at Immy.

'Celine, it's time for hibernation,' said Immy.

'No,' she said, twirling as she made her way towards the arch, 'it's a time for us to get to know each other!'

Chapter Fourteen

A freezing wind blew through the passenger window while Celine dangled her arm out of the black Range Rover. Immy couldn't work her out. In one way she was a sort of precious, manicured urban beauty, but then there were flashes of an untamed tiger.

'Today, we can do as we wish,' said Celine, 'and I wish to dip my toes in the Irish Sea.'

'Even though it's minus one outside?' Immy wore leggings beneath her jeans, double socks and had wrapped a long red scarf several times around her neck. She wasn't a morning person, but even she had to admit the sight of the sea on a silvery winter morning felt good.

Celine's driver didn't say a word as he drove up the narrow road to Dollymount Strand, passing well-wrapped-up dog walkers, diligently picking up their dogs' 'parcels', as Immy's mum would have called them. She never could bring herself to mention the word 'poo', which is most likely part of the reason they moved to a gated community in

Spain, which had a strictly no-pets policy. Immy suggested this might stretch to a no-grandchildren policy, and her mother didn't disagree.

The driver parked at the summit of narrow cement steps, and, following Celine out of the Range Rover, Immy zipped her fleece up to her neck. She watched as Celine ran down the steps, seemingly oblivious that she could slip on ice and go flying. Immy reached the pebble beach stretching out to spectacular views of the Dublin Mountains and an elegant row of Victorian houses. There was no sign of Celine, except for a pile of clothes on the shoreline. For a split second, Immy felt panic, especially as there was nobody else on the beach. But then Celine launched out of the sea like a superhuman with a grin on her face, despite the white horses on the water. Raising her hand, the driver seemed to appear out of nowhere with a long fluffy navy Dryrobe and boots. Celine hadn't mentioned she was wearing a wetsuit beneath her clothes.

'This is the way to live,' said Celine.

'Whatever about the temperature of the water giving you a heart attack, you nearly gave me one; for a split second I thought you'd disappeared.'

'I'm used to the freezing sea,' said Celine, drying her hair with the hooded towel. 'My mother and I go to Båstad in Sweden every spring and sit in a wooden sauna on stilts over the Baltic Sea. We plunge into the water, back to the sauna, and over and over. It feels incredible and I'm sure that's why I'm in such good shape.' Celine spoke without a hint of irony.

The sky was brightening and Immy began to look at Celine differently. This girl had guts and kick-ass confidence.

'I can just about take a cold shower,' said Immy, 'and even then, it's probably more on the lukewarm side.'

'Then push yourself,' said Celine, now striding along the beach. 'I'm sure that's what Lando would want.'

'What do you mean?' And since when did Celine know what Lando would want?

'He told me about you,' said Celine.

Immy wasn't sure what to say to that, but she felt defensive. 'I don't think Lando's in a position to talk about people pushing themselves.'

'Oh, he is,' said Celine.

'How?'

'He was very focused at Le Marché Cher. He was always on time, he didn't complain, even when he had to hand towels in the lady's toilette.' Celine slapped her thigh as she laughed. 'Papa said he has some good ideas and a good work ethic, but really it's confidence and people believing in him that he needs more now than anything.' Celine must have read Immy's expression, which was one of surprise. 'I think he's really something, Immy.'

It was as if Celine knew a completely different Lando.

'Oh my,' said Celine, as they came across a man stretched out on the sand in all his glory. 'Even in this weather you have nudes. It's normal in France, but at this time of year, that is crazy.'

Immy averted her eyes but noticed the man was reading

Ulysses. She wondered if his watch had stopped like Bloom's had.

'We've totally earned this,' said Celine as she and Immy stretched out in the spa at the Merrion Hotel, enjoying a lifting massage and LED light therapy. Immy was surprised to find herself drifting into a blissful trance-like state and was woken by a hand mirror being held in front of her.

'Oh crikey, what's happened to me?' Immy was the least vain person she knew, but her face was so red.

'Don't worry,' said Celine, reclining on her bed. 'The micro-needling makes the skin a little flushed; it will settle down in a few hours.'

'I'm so lazy about this sort of thing,' said Immy. 'I rarely have any kinds of treatments.'

'I have a facial every four weeks.'

That explains Celine's dewy glow.

'My last lover had a puppy who loved to lick my face in the morning; he must have liked the taste of my night cream.'

'The only kind of night cream I'm familiar with is ice cream,' said Immy, who was serious. She and Celine had a genuine, proper giggle. Maybe she wasn't so bad.

'And what about Flynn?' said Celine.

'Flynn?'

'The handsome man looking for jeans yesterday.'

'He comes to Shillington's every couple of weeks and seems to find something to buy in every department,' said Immy. 'I hadn't spoken to him before, but I've seen him around.'

'I think he likes you,' said Celine.

'No,' said Immy, 'not like that.'

'Yes, like that.' Celine sat up and tightened her white spa bathrobe. 'But you agree he's handsome?'

'Yes, obviously.' Immy smiled and threw a towel at Celine, which she caught and threw back. 'Good catch!'

'You're a good catch, Immy,' she said. 'I think it's time for you to improve your self-esteem.'

'Honestly, my self-esteem is fine. It's my direction in life that's the problem; I literally have no idea what I'm doing.'

'My mother taught me that life just takes practice, and so I practised shopping, and the more I shopped, the more I absorbed about fashion.' Celine lay back down on her bed, mimicking a patient in a therapy session. 'At Le Marché Cher I worked in the perfume boutique and then I worked in trend forecasting, and before I knew it I became Head of Buying and I love it.'

Celine was turning out be much less threatening than Immy had originally thought.

'My mother doesn't care about my career,' said Celine. 'All she wants is for me to marry and give her grandchildren – I come from a noble family and that's just how they think.'

'The opposite of my mum, who doesn't seem to have any interest in children of any kind,' said Immy, also lying back down on her bed.

'We are caught at either end of the spider web,' said Celine. 'But what about your love life? Who is your perfect man?'

'Ha, good question,' said Immy, who was looking forward to asking Celine the same thing. 'I've had some disasters, mainly because I was so embarrassingly naive. I remember meeting a guy at a wedding a few years ago, but he only gave me his work number and when I called his office they said he was on holiday for a fortnight. I never questioned it.'

'And?'

'I called back two weeks later, and they told me he was away indefinitely. I hadn't realised the holiday was just an excuse, and that he was there the whole time, but didn't want to speak to me.'

'Then he was missing out,' said Celine. 'And so, you do flirt?'

'I guess, but I'm pretty rubbish at that sort of thing.'

'French people love to flirt, it's in our genes, even when we know there is no hope of it leading anywhere. I think it's good for you; it's an innocent game. I do think flirting is good for health.'

'Wow, you could be a spokesperson for flirting,' said Immy. 'And what about Lando?' There, she'd said it.

'Lando? What about Lando?' Celine smiled so broadly when she said his name.

'Are you guys, you know, dating?'

'Ah, the very question my father asked me yesterday because Delia asked him the same question.'

'And what did you say?'

'I said I think Lando is *wonderful*.'

'You guys are a couple?' said Immy, who really wanted to know so that she could kick Lando out of her mind.

'I haven't really thought about it,' she said, and she didn't look remotely bothered about it. 'While we wait for the manicurists to pretty our nails, why don't you ask me more questions, Immy? I love to share.'

Immy figured she might as well learn what she could from Celine, as she appeared to have a straightforward, uncomplicated take on life.

'OK, Celine, so how does flirting work in France? How would someone know they are being flirted with?' Immy asked this with her recent client, David Clock, in mind, who was unsure if his secretary was flirting with him.

'Good question! So, when a French girl is flirting, she'll smile a lot, play with her hair, laugh out loud at your jokes and she may even make the first move.'

'Really? French women sound brave.'

'Yes,' agreed Celine, 'and as for French men, well, they are men so they are usually happy to oblige in a night of fun, but you may never hear from them again.'

'I think that's universal,' sighed Immy.

'I think the game is often more important to the men, with their egos. My father has a mistress, and honestly, my mother doesn't seem to care. She gets to have dinner and doesn't have to bother with sex.'

'Wow.' Immy wasn't sure what to say, being shy on the subject.

'At least, my mother never used to care but lately I've been wondering,' said Celine. 'But it wouldn't work for me if my lover had another lover,' said Celine. 'I couldn't do without sex.' She must have noticed Immy blushing. 'Sorry, Immy, we French women are very direct?'

Chapter Fifteen

A large bottle of Anaïs Anaïs sat in front of Celine in the beauty hall, her mother's favourite scent. It was so reminiscent of her childhood: blackcurrant, and honeysuckle. Celine took off the lid, spritzed her neck and felt like she was back in her mother's arms. She loved this aspect of retail, enabling the senses to travel through textures and smells.

'I'd say there won't be much on your list for Santy this year,' said Janette, dropping her fake leather handbag on the make-up chair. 'Your bathroom must be bursting with freebie products.'

'You startled me.' Celine put the lid back on the perfume and stood up. Janette was a force of nature, seemingly unaware of her loud voice.

'With my face, I even startle myself when I look in the mirror,' said Janette. 'I'm just back from having my nails done, but no need to tell the boss.'

'You're quite unique, aren't you?' Celine was endeared by the self-deprecation that poured out of this boisterous woman.

'That's one word for it.'

Janette flipped open a compact mirror and added a layer of mascara to her lashes. 'I appreciate life all right, especially at six p.m. on a Friday when I've got a vodka and lime in my hands.'

'You don't like it here?'

'It's fine but what I really want is to start my own make-up line with proper, lip-smacking colours.'

Janette picked up a colour palette of eyeshadow, balancing it on the palm of one hand like an artist, with a brush in the other.

'Women, men, all sorts come to me and ask for the same old boring products, beige and brown shadows, nude lipsticks and waterproof mascara.' This was the first time Celine had seen Janette excited by her work. 'But with these babies, I can create multidimensional looks. Dark orange, cranberry, teal, sea greens – they're all here and given the chance, I can brighten people's eyes and make them feel alive. The power of make-up is incredible, it really is.'

Celine picked up Janette's handbag, put it on the floor and sat on the make-up stool.

'Then maybe start with me?' said Celine, checking her phone. 'I've got twenty minutes before I'm meeting with Papa to prepare for the arrival of Christmas decorations, so let's go crazy, any colour you want on my eyes, I'm all yours.'

'Crikey,' said Janette, 'you're on!'

★

Immy's morning client was a woman this time, and the most timid person so far.

'I'm Leslie McAdoo,' she said, with hands trembling as she took off her waterproof jacket to reveal a ribbed polo neck and black polyester trousers full of static. 'I wasn't sure what to wear, so I thought I'd go practical.'

'Of course,' said Immy. 'Don't worry, we're pretty relaxed here at Shillington's.' Which was not at all true, thinking of the Delia and de Croix combination.

Immy took Leslie's jacket and guided her to the sofa.

'And thank you for your email,' said Immy.

'Well, I thought no harm to give you an idea of why I'm here.' Leslie sat back on the sofa, her dark hair pulled back into a tight bun. She wore no make-up but quite a few gold necklaces, and stud earrings.

'Aren't your toes chilly?' said Immy.

Leslie smiled. 'I haven't been up in Dublin for years and I wasn't sure what the right thing was, so I thought these laces would do the job.'

'I'm hopeless with shoes,' said Immy, trying to find common ground. 'I'd wear runners every day of the week if I could, and the only reason I'm wearing these heels is that I'm meant to be a beacon of fashion as a personal shopper.'

They both laughed and Leslie visibly relaxed.

'Tell me how I can help,' said Immy, reaching for her notebook.

'It sounds silly, but I'd like something special for Christmas Day. It will only be my sister's family and it isn't as if there's anyone to dress up for.' Leslie sat forward, as if ready to confide. 'You see, my great-aunt left me a bit of money, most of which I've put into my investments, but I'm thinking I may as well treat myself with the bit I have left over.'

'Quite right,' said Immy. 'And do you live alone?'

'I do,' she said. 'I thought about a cat, but then, knowing my luck, I'd end up being known as the Cat Lady, and all the same, I don't want to be tied down.'

'I don't mean to be rude, Leslie—' Immy was taking the plunge here '—but surely you aren't much older than I am.'

'Thirty-two,' she said quietly as if she were in a confession box, 'thirty-three on Stephen's Day.'

Immy tried to imagine what sort of dress Leslie could wear. She had quite a good figure, and taking her hair down would make her look and feel so much more glamorous.

'And do you have a career?'

'I used to run our local post office in Duleek before it closed down, so it was a blow to me when I had to leave,' she said, rearranging the buttons of her cardigan. 'Well, I suppose it was a blow to the whole community really.'

'I'm sorry,' said Immy. 'And the building is empty?'

'No, I live above the shop still and volunteer in the Family Resource Centre.'

'Then you're a busy lady. And any time for romance?' Immy knew she was being cheeky, but she thought, why not?

'Sure, who'd want me? I can't even pick out a dress.'

'Then, Leslie, you have come to the right place,' said Immy. Why should this wonderful woman feel unwanted?

'And when we find the right dress for you, I'm going to give you some tips on making it clear to someone you like that you actually like them.'

'Who would I like? I never see anybody outside the village.'

'You never know,' said Immy. 'Life can be full of surprises.' She wasn't sure what had got into her, but Immy was feeling optimistic and gutsy, like she wanted to stand up for those who thought they weren't worthy of finding love. Immy wanted to show them how.

'It's all about making eye contact with the other person,' said Immy, trying to drop in some advice without being pushy.

'Oh, I'm not sure I could do that,' said Leslie.

'It would be the most natural thing, literally holding someone's gaze for a tiny second longer than you'd usually look at someone.'

'If he were to look at me in return?'

'Then I'd say it's all looking good,' said Immy. 'Remember *Fifty Shades of Grey* and how he looked at her?'

'How did he look at her?'

'Like he really, really wanted her.' Immy could hardly believe the conversation, but it was fun.

Leslie began fanning her face. 'Could I have a glass of Prosecco? I'm feeling slightly overwhelmed,' she said. 'But in a good way.'

Immy was confident that a call to Celine could help Leslie's wardrobe tremendously. It was time to dial the Paris helpline.

Chapter Sixteen

The hot chocolate in the Shillington's tea rooms had risen to high standards since de Croix had flown Benoir, his head barista, over from Le Marché Cher for a day's training.

'Wouldn't get better in the Kardashian household,' said the waitress, arriving to a corner table with a cup and saucer, a small teapot, and a side plate of homemade marshmallow fluff for Immy. 'When you're ready,' she said, 'I'm going to pour hot chocolate over this lovely-looking chocolate ball inside the mug.' A perfectly white linen napkin had replaced the J-Cloth on the arm of the waitress, and orders were carried on circular gold trays.

'Fire away,' said Immy, smiling up at the waitress, who seemed thrilled by the theatrics as the gold-dusted ball melted in the cup.

'And now for the marshmallow,' said the waitress, taking a tiny pair of tongs from her apron to place the fluff on top of the hot chocolate. '*Bon appétit.*' She readjusted her dangling reindeer earrings, which de Croix had presented to staff along with neck scarves sporting miniature snowmen. Benoir the barista carried them as hand luggage, when de Croix remembered stock left over following a Christmas promotion at Le Marché Cher several years ago.

'I'm working on my French, thanks to Benoir,' said the waitress. 'He was as dishy as this new drink,' and she walked away with such flourish it seemed that she may be enjoying all her Christmases at once.

Immy took a sip from the cup, and it tasted like French gold. She surveyed the room, noticing salt cellars had been replaced with sea salt and ground pepper, and tiny lights trailing around the windows. Plastic tablecloths had been replaced with red and holly green linen, and the tables had a miniature gold Christmas tree at their centre. Even Immy, who was not sentimental when it came to the festive season, felt a twinkle of Christmas magic.

However, the flip side of all the good the de Croix were doing for Shillington's was the gasket blowing off her friendship with Lando. She was mourning a friendship, which they'd both thrown under a bus the moment the sofa had got too comfortable. They were equally to blame, getting caught up in a moment, catching each other's glance, lingering too long while instrumental movie music played on the screen in her sitting room three months ago. He'd gently pushed a tendril of hair behind her ear, rubbed his fingers along her jawline and rested the tip of his finger on her lips. Like a stable door opening to a horse desperate for the summer grass, they'd kissed so intensely, as if every single moment of their lives had culminated in where they were. As they'd kissed, he'd held her face with such passion there was no turning back.

They'd melted into each other, removing layer by layer until their bodies had magnetically joined and it had been the most indescribable pleasure Immy had ever experienced. This was what made it so bad. She had never felt so physically, so deeply, and it had been with her best friend.

She was furious with both Lando and herself for being so utterly disloyal to the friendship they had spent their lives shielding from venturing off track. But off track they went, and this was the price they paid for that one, gilded night.

Immy opened her notebook and took another sip of hot chocolate, the deliciousness easing her angst as she sat back to review information on her next client. Tanya Mortell, the 2002 Rose of Turpinstown, who worked for a phone company. Her email requested a 'complete makeover in body and soul'. Well, Immy was no exorcist, but with Celine and Janette on standby, she could talk through the client's wants and then delegate accordingly. With only four weeks to go until Christmas, Immy may as well delay quitting. Maybe when she arrived in Spain she'd experience a divine inspiration and never return to Ireland. At this point, she felt so distant from Lando that she was beyond caring. Though she knew that wasn't true, she'd run with that line for now.

Tanya crossed her legs of sherry tights on the sofa, with long tousles of blonde hair extensions and all the confidence of a woman once crowned Rose of Tralee. She wore a top that showed a lot of cleavage.

'My flatmate's got a new boyfriend,' Tanya told Immy.

'They met in a pub, and he asked her out for a drink the next night.' She took a vape from her handbag.

'Sorry, would you mind not vaping?' asked Immy.

'Grand,' said Tanya, swapping the vape for a pack of chewing gum. 'And now they're like Ben and JLo, totally mad about each other.'

'And this is a bad thing?' said Immy.

'It's incredible,' said Tanya, 'except that they've bonked themselves silly in the flat and I've moved back into my mum's while they get it all out of their system.' She winked at Immy and put three pieces of gum into her mouth at once.

Tanya reached into her bag for a nail file. She couldn't seem to keep still for as much as a minute.

'Men just stare at me,' she said. 'I used to get so paranoid about my bum, worrying it was too big, but then thanks to the Kardashians, big bums are in.'

'And, sorry, Tanya,' said Immy, trying to work out the path they were on, 'in what way would you like me to help?'

'I think I need a new look,' she said, 'and before you ask, I don't have a huge amount of money to spend.'

'It's definitely important you feel comfortable in what you're wearing, and if you feel men are ogling you, then maybe a wardrobe refresh is the answer.'

Tanya said, 'The other night, I was on a date in a restaurant with a guy who was sweating his head off and barely made any eye contact. It felt like a real waste of time.'

A light bulb in Immy's head switched on, and instinctively she opened the notebook to her research pages on body language.

'I wonder were his arms at ease?' said Immy. She looked up at Tanya. 'It's just I've been doing some research on dating and apparently if your date folds their arms, it isn't a great sign.' Immy quickly wondered if this might sound utterly loopy.

Tanya folded her arms in response. 'I'm just fed up being single,' she said. 'What else does your research say?'

'If he reaches out to make contact with you, then this is good,' said Immy.

'Go on.'

'And even better if their legs are crossed in your direction.' Immy was relieved Tanya didn't think it was odd a personal shopper had dating advice on tap. 'Did he sit next to you in the restaurant or across from you?'

'Next to me,' said Tanya.

'Did he lean forward?' Immy checked her notes as she spoke.

'I think so.'

'Then this is a good sign,' said Immy, looking up and smiling at her.

'You think so?'

'I do.'

'Sometimes I worry my looks take over.' She was serious, and Immy hadn't thought of this point of view. 'I know I'm good-looking, but there's a kind of pressure for me to look good *all* the time and it's just exhausting, and if I don't have a boyfriend—'

'You feel like a failure?' said Immy. 'Sorry for cutting across you, but I think I can see where you're coming from.'

'Exactly,' said Tanya. 'I'm beginning to think my looks are a curse.'

This was deep-end stuff, and in a way, Immy wished Leslie could have been there to hear this woman complaining of the downside to being gorgeous.

'Before we begin devising your new wardrobe,' said Immy, following her instinct, 'how about we talk through your concerns about the date?'

'Sure,' said Tanya, 'like an artist meeting their subject before painting.'

Immy smiled. 'Something like that.'

'He was quite attentive,' said Tanya. 'He sounded quite enthusiastic when we were chatting and he definitely made me laugh; in fact, he was hilarious.'

'This is sounding very good so far,' said Immy. 'It seems like he was flirting with you, and the fact he's making you laugh feels so good, doesn't it?' The last time Immy had a proper laugh was with Lando. They'd been watching a Swedish thriller, which wasn't meant to be a comedy but Lando's commentary on the characters had made it hilarious.

'Maybe it wasn't as disastrous as I thought it was,' said Tanya.

Immy turned the page of her notebook. 'How about clothes?'

'He was in a hoodie,' said Tanya, 'and he looked pretty gorgeous, sort of like Jay-Z, and I love Jay-Z.'

'How about his hair? Apparently, when men touch their hair, they're drawing attention to their eyes, which means they like you.'

'Really? Well, he was checking his reflection in the window when we were reading the menu outside the restaurant.'

'There you go,' said Immy, 'and his feet – did you notice if they were pointing towards you?'

'Not really, but one thing which was a turn-off was the way he ate the garlic bread with his mouth open; it was totally gross.'

Maybe this guy wasn't her knight in shining armour after all.

'But none of us are perfect, are we?' said Tanya. 'And what does it mean if he was fiddling with his glass? I remember reading somewhere that if guys peel the label off a beer bottle while they're speaking to you, it means they fancy you.'

Immy read down the checklist of pointers she'd made. 'OK, great, so yes, you are right, this apparently means he wants to have physical contact with you.'

'It sounds like some kind of spy language,' said Tanya.

'Well, if you still like your James Bond, the advice here is to mirror his body language.'

'I would,' said Tanya, 'but he hasn't called.'

'Since when?'

'Saturday, and it's Thursday. He should have called by now.'

'Maybe he's had a busy week,' said Immy, but she didn't want to give him a free pass. 'However, your time is precious, Tanya, and being the fabulous girl that you are, your diary is now booked up for the weekend.'

'Um, no, it isn't.'

'This is where we get creative. When he calls to arrange your next date—'

'If he calls.' Tanya rearranged her mane over the shoulders.

'*When* he calls,' Immy persisted, 'tell him you're busy and you don't have to say how or what, just that you're busy.'

'But he'll think I don't like him,' said Tanya.

'No, you can still sound like you're interested, but it's important to get this right. He needs to know if he wants to spend time with you, he's got to up his game with his communications.'

'Girl power!' said Tanya, stamping her feet.

'That's it. We all need to channel a little Spice Girl, otherwise we'll get walked over.'

'Did that happen to you?'

'In a way—' she could only think of Lando '—which is why I really want you to get this right.'

Immy turned the page of her notebook, and as she thought, there was the point she'd meant to say from the beginning. 'All in all,' said Immy, 'men are slower on the uptake. It takes them three times as long to realise someone is gazing at them.'

'We have to stare?' said Tanya. 'Because sometimes I get really dry eyes in clubs.'

'Not exactly, but I guess it takes longer for men to get the message.'

'I want someone who'll curl in front of Netflix with me, go out for dinner with me, and hold my hand,' said Tanya. 'I think I'm looking in the wrong places. I need an older man, don't I?'

Chapter Seventeen

'Welcome to November twenty-first,' said de Croix, standing on a chair behind a display of Shillington candles. He relished motivational talks and, looking up at the galleries peppered with employees, it felt satisfying to have so many paying attention to him.

'This is the scent you want for your home,' he said, holding up a glass vessel filled with golden wax. 'This candle exudes luxury, and will elevate not only a room, but your mood.'

Celine took the candle from her father and, in exchange, passed a bottle of perfume to him.

'This bottle of fragrance,' he said, 'is a scent of family and of Christmas gifts.' He passed the bottle back to Celine. 'I urge you all to intoxicate your senses with this perfume, and I promise, this will make you feel festive to your fingertips.'

'Just as well,' whispered Janette, standing next to Celine. 'I'm having diamanté added to my Christmas Eve manicure.'

'Pass the bottle around,' said de Croix, peering down at his daughter. 'Don't be shy.'

Martin immediately spritzed the scent across his chest

and gave Janette a wink, who did nothing more than roll her eyes dismissively.

'This evening,' de Croix continued, 'when you go home to your warm beds, a select number of employees will coordinate a Christmas makeover of this store.' There was a lovely sound of bodies shuffling in reaction to the Christmas makeover idea. 'This year, under my guidance, we transform Shillington's to a place of stylish celebration and luxury.'

'Hip, hip,' said Martin. 'Does that mean I can wear my Christmas jumper tomorrow?'

De Croix turned to Martin with a neutral expression. 'No, Martin, you will wear the very fine blazer Shillington's have provided you with, and let it be known that this Christmas sales period will define the future for Shillington's and for you all.'

'Meaning?' said Janette.

De Croix was skilled at delivering lines of drama. 'It is up to the gods of retail,' he said as if treading the boards with Shakespeare, 'whether Shillington's survives.'

'Keep it positive, Papa,' said Celine, tugging his sleeve, 'Delia would lose her head if she knew you were saying this. Tell them more about the decorating.'

'From tomorrow, Shillington's will be transformed into a Christmas ball of sparkle, and this will warm us up.'

The sound of heels clipped in the distance, and all heads turned to Delia, and Lando. What was that young man doing, hands in his pockets? Had he learned nothing in Paris?

'Madame Shillington, and Lando, fabulous you are here.' De Croix knew his voice was lacking in enthusiasm.

'All right, de Croix, no need to cause a fuss.'

He really wished she'd lighten up a little; she carried a tension that was most unattractive in a woman. Perhaps it was romance she needed. De Croix thought about Gregory and felt sentimental for a moment before getting back to business.

'Now, I implore you all to remember that the words we use are crucial to bringing confidence to our customers.' He took a handkerchief from his pocket and dabbed his forehead. 'The word "selling" is a no-no for we are—' he put his hand to his ear, but no response '—yes, for we are *providing*, and always avoid the word "problem" and instead say "challenge".'

Shirley from the home appliances department popped up her hand. 'Sorry, sir, but when somebody returns a faulty product, that is a problem.'

'First, you smile,' said de Croix. 'Then you could say, "Madam (or Sir), it seems this product has been a challenge for you, and I do apologise for this inconvenience".'

'We were told never to apologise,' said Janette, flatly.

'Who told you this?' De Croix could not bear these modern-day mannerisms.

'I did a make-up course, and they said if you apologised, you're stuffed and they'll sue the pants off you,' Janette said in all seriousness.

'I can assure you the pantaloons are safe once you show respect to the customer,' said de Croix, looking to his daughter. 'After all—'

'The customer is always right,' said Celine. 'And I add

to my father by saying the phrase "no problem" is one to rule out. 'When a customer thanks you, simply say, "You are welcome" or "Thank you too".'

'Correct, Celine,' said de Croix, feeling proud of his daughter. 'Recognise what your customers are looking for and give them what they want, and I want interaction, social media and influencers.' He raised a bottle of scent and began spritzing the air. 'I want hashtag Shillington's at Christmas to be on the tips of your tongues.'

'How about securing a brand ambassador?' said Christian, slightly out of breath as he slipped in behind Janette.

'That is a smart question,' said de Croix, glaring at Christian, 'as is punctuality. But as I know from my store Le Marché Cher in Paris, we prefer to have genuine endorsements from celebrities, and may I say, if a celebrity visits Shillington's you are —' he raised his hand for extra clarity '— not allowed to let them know you know who they are.'

'And if Taylor Swift arrives with her entourage, you're telling me I have to pretend I don't know who she is?' said Janette.

'That is precisely what I am saying,' said de Croix.

'Matt Damon's always hanging out in Dalkey. Sure, he might pop in one day,' said Shirley. 'Can I not give him one of my demo smoothies on the house?'

'The same applies to actors,' said de Croix. 'You must treat them like everyone else; that is what they want, and at Shillington's we give people what they want.'

'Does that include a pay rise?' said Martin, clapping his hands with a big smile on his face.

'And absolutely no selfies,' said de Croix, ignoring Martin. 'And all departments must place gift cards near the tills for impulse purchases.'

The staff nodded their heads like they understood.

'The socks, Papa.' Celine passed a pair of socks to de Croix.

'I almost forgot,' he said, dangling a pair of long, red socks out in front of him. 'These are no ordinary socks, but cashmere, and they deserve their reputation of luxury.' He wondered if this gesture would be lost on the employees of Shillington's, but then this was surplus stock from Le Marché Cher, so why not? 'You know, it can take an entire year for a goat to produce cashmere for only a scarf, and so these socks are precious and to be respected.' De Croix loved the feeling of deluxe fabric in his hands.' Tonight, I urge you to pull off your common cotton synthetic socks, clean your feet and treat your tootsies to the beauty of cashmere.'

'Is there a pair for everyone in the audience?' hollered Janette.

'I suppose there is!' And de Croix's ears were delighted with a cheer. Who would have thought socks could win him such a popularity ticket? He surveyed the desperate-looking staff in front of him and deduced he had never seen so many people in need of makeovers in a single space.

Chapter Eighteen

Frank and Bob stood either side of the arched doors to Shillington's and, perfectly in sync, they held both doors open for Immy.

'You're looking nice and warm in that coat,' said Bob. 'It was minus two last night in Drimnagh and took three saucepans of water to defrost the car.'

'Well, I saw a woman going flying in her high heels on Baggot Street the other day and so runners are my mode of transport,' said Immy, doing a curtsey.

'The environment will thank you for that,' said Frank, 'and now on you go before we let out any more of the hot air in the building.'

'And sure, there's no shortage of hot air, is there?' said Bob. 'Your man, the French fella, was telling us yesterday that he's going to turn Shillington's into Europe's most famous department store.'

'Next to his own gaff, that is,' said Frank, with a wink.

'Miracles do happen,' said Immy, walking through the

doors and wondering where she'd be this time next year, or even next month. The light shining into the beauty hall was breath-taking, and even though there were only a few customers browsing the counters, Immy noticed that not a single staff member was on their phone. The 'de Croix' effect, as it had become known, must be kicking in.

★

De Croix decided to start the day in the beauty hall. The young lady, Janette, showed promise and would benefit from a touch of wisdom.

'Good morning, Janette,' he said, 'how are we today?'

'Could be worse,' she said. 'Better if we got a pay rise.'

'Ah, yes, indeed; it's all about the money, isn't it?'

'I wouldn't say all,' said Janette, contemplating his statement. 'But it's definitely relevant.'

De Croix moved behind the counter next to her. 'You see that lady and gentleman over there?'

'The man in the baseball cap?'

'Exactly, and that is not just any baseball cap, but a Loro Piana baseball cap – like the one Kendall Roy wore in *Succession*.'

'God, I loved that show,' said Janette, re-applying lip gloss.

'It is what we call quiet luxury,' said de Croix, speaking just above a whisper and looking in the opposite direction to the couple. 'Such a display of wealth is only noticeable to those who know what they are looking for.'

'What you're saying is, just because some guy is wearing ripped jeans, don't think he isn't going to be a big spender.'

'Yes,' said de Croix, impressed that Janette was catching on. 'We must give all customers the opportunity to be exposed to our most luxurious brands. People don't want to show off these days, and so they will be discreet—' he removed his Montblanc from his pocket to scribble a note to self on his business card '—but they will spend, you can be sure of it.

'We want to attract what social media likes to call "the freshly minted"; they are chic but anonymous. Take Brunello Cucinelli as an example. He creates uniforms for the wealthy, but there are no labels, no showing off, and you can be sure each item he produces is made of only the finest materials. Items of quality do not have to be showy or scream to the world, "I'm insanely rich".' De Croix pulled his shirt cuff over his Rolex and continued with his soliloquy. 'And you know that posting wealth on Instagram is a no-no for those in the know,' he said, holding up his iPhone. 'Not bragging about the finery around you gives you power, though one must stay connected to those who know the next big thing, where to go and what to buy.'

'Papa, there you are,' said Celine, holding an iPad to her chest, 'and Janette, how are you?'

'Intrigued,' she said. 'Your dad is giving me the lowdown on how not to be flashy.'

'I was just saying that Gaucherie is no longer acceptable,' said de Croix.

'Papa, who uses that word anymore? Why be so old-fashioned.'

'Then let's use the word *discretion*,' said de Croix. 'It is the true key ingredient to style, and on that deluxe note, Celine, I want to order dress sneakers from Berluti.'

'With pleasure,' said Celine. 'You know these shoes, Janette?'

'Are these the runners that will set you back at least a thousand smackers?'

De Croix enjoyed Janette's expression. 'Even more than *one thousand smackers*, as you say, though you wouldn't know unless you knew.'

'It's like the Harmony bangle from Hemmerle,' said Celine, 'people will spend a fortune even though the bangle looks nothing more than a bangle.'

'Low-key baubles,' said de Croix, 'they are all the range.'

'And how do you keep up with the trends?' Janette reached for a copy of *The Gloss* magazine. 'This is my go-to for fashion and beauty.'

'Yes, and like you, we do our research,' said de Croix, tapping his phone. 'Our team at Le Marché Cher have their fingers on the buzzer, ready to order the next big thing before they can say *"Oui,* Jean Pierre" on *Qui veut gagner des millions?'*

'Sorry, I'm lost,' said Janette.

'It's an old TV programme in France,' said Celine. 'Who Wants to Be a Millionaire?'

'I do,' said Janette, 'and as soon as I am, I'm going to buy a pair of those Berluti runners.'

★

In PS Headquarters, Celine arrived with two rails of dresses, tops, and trousers for Immy's second appointment with Leslie, while Janette laid out her make-up brushes.

'Even though Christmas is just over three weeks away, it feels like it's here,' said Celine. 'I get so excited for makeovers.'

'So do I,' said Janette. 'And you, Leslie, are you a fan?'

'Of Christmas? I try to be,' she said, 'but most years I wind up feeling disappointed.'

'Generally, or for a particular reason?' Immy sensed Leslie was nervous to be there.

'It's silly really,' said Leslie, holding a mug of tea in both hands. 'Every new year I say to myself, "this year, I'm going to meet someone", you know, my *other half*, but then it's me and my family, and I'm Ms Single, the old maiden aunt.'

'This year will be different,' said Celine, with a confidence that was infectious. 'We are going to find dresses that make you feel like you are whole, and let me tell you, I believe we depend on ourselves for happiness.' She picked up a dress and held it up in front of Leslie.

'I've never really thought of myself in that way,' said Leslie. 'I don't have a full-length mirror in my house, and I wear about a quarter of my clothes in my wardrobe.'

'My wardrobe is the same,' said Immy, moving behind her desk, as Leslie was clearly in safe hands.

'Then it's time for both of you to empty your wardrobes,'

said Celine, 'and give the clothes you no longer wear to charity.'

'The French lady has spoken,' said Janette.

'I'll do that,' said Leslie, blushing. 'I'm not really used to this much attention, but I'm very grateful for all your help.'

'The wardrobe is the window to your soul; have you heard that, Leslie?' said Celine. 'You can wake up in the morning and get excited about the clothes you're going to wear. It's fabulous.'

Immy and Leslie smiled at each other.

'And it isn't that we want to be obsessed by our appearance either,' said Celine, 'but it does make you feel good.'

Immy felt like she wanted an instant makeover.

When Immy led Leslie to the full-length mirror outside the dressing room in PS Headquarters, her reaction made them all feel like this was more than just a game of dress-up. They were bolstering a woman who had forgotten her importance in the world. Janette had applied very natural make-up, with a light lip gloss and mascara, and with her hair down around her shoulders, it lengthened Leslie's face.

'I'm speechless,' she said, gazing at her reflection. 'The dress feels so soft, and these heels feel so easy to wear.'

'The V-neck shape looks incredible,' said Celine, 'and the trumpet sleeves are so flattering.'

'Red really is your colour,' said Immy.

'Thank you all so very much,' said Leslie.

'Here to serve,' said Janette, with a wink.

'You wouldn't believe how much time Immy has spent listening to me, banging on and on.'

'Not at all,' said Immy, 'that's all part of the service.'

'Well, I'll definitely buy this dress, and shoes,' said Leslie, swishing in front of the mirror. 'And the make-up. So at least Shillington's will make something out of me.'

Immy was about to suggest Leslie try on another dress when there was a knock on the door.

'I'm sorry, Leslie, we're not meant to be disturbed but honestly, that dress looks incredible,' said Immy, pushing the clothes rail out of the way.

'And with your hair down, it's magic,' said Celine. 'Maybe we try some boosting underwear.'

'The French are very good with underwear, aren't they?' said Leslie, staring at her reflection.

Immy opened the door and, without a second to stop him, Bill O'Brien arrived into the room.

'Oh lord Jesus, I'm sorry for disturbing you,' he said, taking off his cap. 'Have I got the time wrong?'

'You're actually three hours early, Bill,' said Immy, 'but don't worry, no harm done.'

But Bill didn't say a word, and just looked at Leslie, who smiled at him.

'Hello,' she said.

'Aye,' he said.

They stared at each other.

'Is that you, Leslie?'

'Hello, Bill,' she said softly.

'You two know each other?' said Immy.

'We went to primary school together,' said Bill.

'Twenty-five years ago,' said Leslie.

'That's right,' he said, almost breathless.

Janette discreetly left with her make-up case, and Immy excused herself with Celine.

'What just happened?' Immy said to Celine in the corridor.

'I think Cupid's arrow has just shot across your room.'

Immy walked home through St Stephen's Green. There was frost still visible around the garden edges, where the sun hadn't reached. It was a novelty to leave work in daylight, and de Croix certainly improved his popularity status by giving everyone cashmere socks and, even better, the afternoon off so they could blitz Shillington's with Christmas decorations by the next morning and avoid disrupting key shopping hours. She thought about Gwyneth Paltrow in *Sliding Doors*; what were the chances of Bill and Leslie meeting at Shillington's after twenty-five years.

She felt so happy when Bill and Leslie looked at each other. She could not help thinking about Lando and wondered about the way he looked at Celine. It appeared to be going well, and it was so annoying that Immy could never say out loud that Celine seemed like a genuinely lovely person. She was so sweet to Leslie, and to Bill, and the navy suit Immy had chosen for him looked so smart. Celine didn't even care that Immy had overridden her suggestion of a cream suit.

Historically Immy had detested Lando's choice in women, but this time his choice could not be more perfect.

She thought about David Clock, who had an appointment tomorrow to try outfits Celine had found for his Christmas party. Immy wanted to get some insights about body language.

If Immy could bring Bill and Leslie together, maybe she could help with David too?

Chapter Nineteen

In her cashmere socks, Immy lay beneath the duvet and a multitude of blankets on her double bed and stretched out her arms. She had landed in bed much later than planned. When she'd seen her wardrobe earlier that evening, she hadn't been able to resist taking Celine's advice and hurling out things she literally never wore. Two hours later she had colour-coded her wardrobe, much of which was looking forlorn and in need of a dry clean, along with three bags of clothes for charity. She'd have to save up and be her own personal shopper. And now sleep or the iPad? David Clock was due to arrive at Shillington's at 10.30 a.m. tomorrow morning and something was telling her that a little research could only be helpful.

Her mind was buzzing, and so she reached for her iPad and with David Clock and his PA in mind, she asked Google, 'How do I know if there's chemistry between us?' She was led to snowflakesinlove.com, where romance expert Lucinda Amour proclaimed dilating pupils to be a sign that the game is on. *'The greater the size of the pupil, the sexier they think you are.'*

Immy had never studied someone's eyeballs in that way, so she may gloss over this piece of advice.

★

The pale-blue drawing room in the Shillingtons' home on Fitzwilliam Square stretched the full width of the foundations, and the place was not unlike a museum displaying extraordinary plasterwork, along with peeling paint. In advance of the tenants' arrival, Delia had asked Lando to empty the drawers in the walnut desk and to do a last tour of the rooms to make sure she hadn't left any 'personal items', as she put it, behind.

The top drawers were mainly full of old, dry envelopes, stuck together and ready for recycling. There were endless pens, brass drawing pins, a pack of cards and US dollars, which must have been from his father's time as he didn't think his mum had ever travelled to the States. He removed the contents of each drawer into a box and placed a cardboard file on top. Without thinking, he flipped the file cover open and found his parents' marriage certificate. Jane Delia Harrison and Gregory Harold Shillington. 5th January 1997. He noticed his father's signature, which angled upwards. A good sign, Lando supposed, of optimism and maybe ambition too. Next came Lando's birth certificate, and there were his parents' signatures, his father's still curling upwards. He should have closed the file and wished he had when he saw a thin A4 page and felt a shiver down his spine. 'Official Report from the Coroner's Office.'

The doormen were long gone by the time Lando arrived at Shillington's that evening. Unlocking the front door always gave him a thrill, maybe because he used to play invisible hopscotch with Frank and Bob, pushing and pulling doors open for customers. For his eighth birthday, the doormen had given Lando his own Pershing hat with the Shillington's crest engraving. The hat still hung on the back of his bedroom door. When Lando told the doormen he wanted to be like them when he grew up, Frank and Bob would crack up and tell Lando that as he'd be paying their wages, he'd better be the boss. Now that day was coming ever closer and Lando Shillington, fourth generation of a department store, had just days to prove himself to the world.

It came as a surprise that Celine and de Croix were taking a physical lead in dressing Shillington's for Christmas. At best, Lando had expected a list of directions and suppliers, along with criticisms about how behind the times Shillington's was, but he couldn't have been more wrong. Celine had mapped out areas for gigantic golden balls of sequins to hang on every floor. Meanwhile, de Croix had delegated hundreds of gift cards to be stacked and shuffled into silver holders and placed at every till and counter.

'The lights,' shrilled de Croix. 'Don't tell me they've sent multicoloured?'

'Papa, calm,' said Celine, heaving a box out from behind the men's razor section. 'Why must you always think the worst?'

'Because then at least I have the joy of being pleasantly surprised when I'm wrong, though it is rare that I am wrong,' said de Croix. 'And here he is, the man of the house.'

'Ho, ho, ho,' said Lando, feeling flat.

Celine looked like she was about to ask if he was OK, but instead picked up a box of lights and handed them to him. 'These are all yours to decorate,' she said.

'What are these for?' said Lando.

Celine led the way as Lando carried the box around the back of the candle counter, through women's hair accessories and up one flight of stairs, where three gold Christmas trees had been lined up like toy soldiers.

'You still don't notice?' said Celine.

'Notice what?'

She pointed out over the gallery.

'Now that is a tree,' said Lando, admiring the delicate roses made of coloured paper, silver ornaments and hundreds upon hundreds of tiny lights. 'Is it real?'

'Of course,' she said. 'Twenty feet of splendour, from Rathcon Christmas Trees in County Wicklow.'

'I don't think we have ever had a tree that size in the hallway before,' he said.

'I know,' shouted Delia, who looked up at them from the hall. The acoustics in the gallery must have been very effective if she could hear their conversation. 'But your father always insisted on tall Christmas trees at home before he took over, and this one he would have loved.' His mother sounded almost emotional, which was rare for her. 'Such a fine fillet of a tree at the top.'

Celine leaned over the gallery. 'A good tree brings good luck, so my *grand-mère* told me when I was a little girl.'

'Then that leads nicely to something I'd like to show you,' said Delia. 'Can you both come downstairs?'

Chapter Twenty

'Beautifully packaged products set the tone,' said de Croix, wiping his brow. 'I want bright colours to lift the spirits of staff and customers.' He began scanning the shelves in Shillington's newly located Food Hall, already winning hearts and taste buds. The footfall in the basement had been minimal and the time it took to move stock to the empty space next to the tea rooms was worth it. Wood panelling made the dry foods look wholesome and the room felt alive as winter light poured in through the tall sash windows.

'Who doesn't love a biscuit?' said de Croix, 'and the packaging, it could be a hat box! It is exquisite, this pink, it is electric; how can a box be so beautiful?'

'The Lismore Food Company know their biscuits,' said Shirley.

'Let's place the Orange with Dark Chocolate variety on the central table and put the Salted Smoked Almonds next to the stocking fillers.'

'And how about I give you a quick demonstration of my five-minute Christmas pudding recipe?' said Shirley, tightening her apron.

'No, thank you,' said de Croix, rolling his eyes, 'and to be honest, unless you are going to turn the puddings into gold, I have little interest.'

'I can add edible gold glitter?' she said, but de Croix had already galloped off with a box of All Butter Irish Shortbread under his arm.

De Croix arrived in the hallway to find Delia, Celine and Lando around a huge paper sketch spread out across the parquet floor.

'Papa,' said Celine, 'we want to show you our idea for the main window display.'

'Very well,' he said, 'but first I want to discuss my proposed extravagance to swathe Shillington's entrance in gold foil.'

'We can't possibly afford such a thing,' said Delia, looking horrified, 'and don't you think foil sounds rather gaudy?'

'It will be both tasteful and possible,' said de Croix, 'as I shall cover the cost.' A gold display would draw public attention and complaints from the county council, all helpful for PR. 'This years Shillington's Christmas window must be so beautiful that customers are lost for words by the sheer magnificence of what they see.'

'Then may I present my vision?' said Celine.

'Of course,' said Delia, with a large box resting at her feet. De Croix suspected she had some ghastly cloth or Christmas ornaments in there.

'I want us to take a natural approach,' said Celine, 'something to contrast with your gold foil, Papa.'

De Croix looked at Lando, who didn't appear to be taking much interest in what his daughter was saying.

'We are creating a Christmas window of biodiversity,' said Celine, holding up luminous pods of dried lunaria. 'These come from Amelia's Garden Flowers, and all of their flora is entirely organic and grown from seed.'

'We are not a garden centre,' said de Croix, thinking that he must have a hot shave in the morning. The self-care he was so used to in Paris had been overtaken by too many full Irish breakfasts too. Julie would not applaud him if he returned home with an expanded waist.

'Papa, this window will tell the story of time, dried flowers through the season,' said Celine. 'This lunaria is the most natural alternative to gold, and when you see the flowers shimmering in the winter light, you will be amazed.'

'If you say so,' said de Croix. 'Lando, what are your thoughts, if you are even awake?'

'Yes,' he said, 'very much so, I agree.'

'And Delia?'

'Well, I have something I think might add to Celine's window design.' Delia knelt beside her cardboard box and removed the lid.

De Croix had collected trains as a boy and this one he recognised instantly. It was a Carette.

'This is immaculate,' he said, kneeling next to Delia and lightly touching the train carriage. 'Georges Carette, probably one of their best locomotives.' He looked up to see what Lando thought, but he had gone.

★

De Croix wasn't the only person put out by Lando's exit. Celine was furious and couldn't understand why he was so hesitant in stepping forward. He rarely voiced his opinion about the store and seemed to be operating on automatic pilot.

She walked across the ground floor, through the beauty hall and into the jewellery department, gently lit by tiny floor lights.

'Lando? Is that you?'

She saw the outline of a man hunched on the floor, in the corner of the room.

'It's lucky for you the alarms haven't been turned on yet,' she said, but then changed her tone as she moved towards him and sensed that something was very wrong.

'Lando, what is it?' She knelt by his side, instinctively taking his hand in hers. He had been crying and tried to shield his face from hers. 'It's something to do with the train?'

'It was my father's,' he said.

She felt so sorry for him, thoughts of his father bubbling beneath him all this time.

'Had you seen the train before?' she said.

'Yes,' he nodded, 'but this afternoon I found my father's coroner's report.'

Celine wrapped her arms around him.

'Most of the time I'm OK, but sometimes I wonder what would have happened if I hadn't been born.' She could feel his shoulders trembling, and she held him tighter. 'Mum would never have been alone, working her guts out to keep this place going and all I've done is educate myself to avoid having to step into my father's shoes.'

'That's not true,' she said. 'Everyone moves at their own pace; there is no rule to say what time is the right time to make a transition.'

'But it's so obvious that Mum wants to get out; she is totally worn down and it's all because I'm so bloody well terrified of failing.'

They sat together in silence, Celine knowing there was nothing she could say to ease his mind. Lando was the only person who could decide on his future. It was all up to him; she knew it and she knew he did too.

★

A lively office party spilt onto the footpath from a club on St Stephen's Green. Despite the freezing weather, women were without coats or fear of slipping on ice, lit cigarettes in hand and speaking loudly into their iPhones.

Lando felt the opposite of their high spirits. He'd managed to exit Shillington's without seeing his mother or de Croix, both of whom must be unaware of his breakdown unless

Celine had told them, and now he was at a loss for where to go. Merrion Row was awash with pub-goers, some in Santa Claus hats, vaping, and flirting.

He couldn't stop thinking about the train set, which he hadn't seen since he was five or maybe six years old. His childhood was blurry at best, but the memory of finding the set beneath his mother's bed and Delia's hysterical reaction, screaming at him that he had no right to touch what wasn't his, was imprinted in his memory.

Seeing the coroner's report, his father's 'presumed instant' death, had caught him off guard. If he hadn't been born, Gregory wouldn't have been at the hospital; he wouldn't have been standing at the traffic lights when the lorry had lost control and driven straight into him. Lando desperately needed to say these thoughts out loud.

Celine had been so sweet when she'd found him, saying little and holding him tightly, which was just what he'd needed at that moment. He wondered what his father had been like; would he have been strict? Fun? Would his parents have stayed married? Would they still have Shillington's? Lando felt entirely overwhelmed and found himself walking towards number 30, Merrion Street.

Chapter Twenty-One

Lando managed to leave the house without seeing his mum, though, knowing her, she wouldn't have mentioned anything about him disappearing from the window display the night before. She was a master when it came to selective memory. Unable to sleep, Lando had googled department stores around the world, once household names and now retail history. Hecht's and Kaufmann's across America, Harding, Howell & Co. in London, and Switzers in Dublin, famous for the see-through umbrella. Once upon a time, these businesses had been a dream come true for the owners, followed by long, lingering disappointment. But what if Shillington's didn't have to join the trail of has-beens? Seeing the coroner's report was of course unsettling, but it reminded Lando that he only had one shot at representing the next generation, and maybe if he could put his catastrophising to one side, he could take on the job and relieve his mum once and for all.

★

On the third floor, next to the women's department, a room of exquisitely hand-carved oak walls was the jewel in Shillington's crown that de Croix had hoped for.

'Why this room has been ignored, I will never understand,' said de Croix, stepping over dusty curtains on the floor. 'These murals of operatic figures painted by the great Salina Semley are the icing on this cake.'

'What about old Mrs Shillington's printing press over there,' said Uncle Stanley, dressed in a navy corduroy suit. For a man in his eighties, his figure was admirable. 'Now she was a woman who liked to surround herself in style while she printed.'

Lando looked at Uncle Stanley resting on his cane and then at Celine, divine in a cream jersey one-piece. She had barely let him out of her sight all day though she was incredibly discreet, with no mention of finding him in the jewellery department last night.

'Do you remember your grandmother?' said Celine, turning to him.

'Sadly not,' he said.

'She died only a few years after Lando's father,' said Uncle Stanley. 'You were only a tot, weren't you, Lando?'

Lando smiled at his only uncle, who symbolised all the easy life. He almost always had a smile on his face, a witty line and knew when a pat on the back was needed, helping Lando to feel robust throughout his childhood and teenage years.

There was rarely judgement if Lando turned up to work with a hangover, or dodged afternoons to see a girlfriend or to catch a lift to a country dinner party. He was like a second father, or maybe even Lando's first father.

'Mrs Shillington was a fine woman,' said Uncle Stanley. 'No hesitation in using the hand-cranked press herself, creating the most beautiful letterhead and invitations.' He tugged a cotton sheet off the printer. 'It looks small, doesn't it? But I can tell you it's mighty. When I think of the smart Dublin ladies coming in with lists of their drinks and dinner parties, hunt balls and christenings, the quality of the card the invitations were printed on was close to being stiff as a board.'

'I see,' said de Croix. It was hard to know what his levels of interest were when it came to history and sentimentality. 'It's certainly old and I think makes for a very good start in making our VIP lounge unique.' He ran his hand over the printer's wooden handles. 'I suggest we do the opposite of lounges in Japan, Paris and New York by filling this room with items that are not for sale.'

'A little museum?' suggested Lando.

'Something like it,' said de Croix. 'We create a historic world of Shillington's and customers can learn the story of where they are.'

'It sounds like a gamble,' said Uncle Stanley, resting his elbow on the printing press. 'But I've never been shy about putting a few quid on the horses, so why not? And that Christian fella can add to the Shillington's promotions on social media.'

'Oh no,' said de Croix, 'the VIP lounge is not something we promote.'

'Then how will people know it's here?' said Uncle Stanley.

De Croix moved closer to Uncle Stanley and almost whispered in his ear, but loud enough for Lando to hear.

'You see, Stanley, one must be *invited* to the VIP room.'

'I see,' said Uncle Stanley, 'then it's a shame Old Mrs Shillington isn't here to print the invitations.'

'It is indeed,' said de Croix, turning to a grandfather clock. 'Oh, how I lament modernisation at times, and yet, at Le Marché Cher our VIP lounge is more deluxe than Sarah Jessica Parker's wardrobe. Shopping is a commitment of time, and these lounges can turn an outing to the department store to a day *event*. Stores like these were once the people's palace; they would dress up to dine in the tea rooms, and clothing was brought out for customers to try on rather than displayed on rails on the shop floor.'

Lando felt like he was back in history class but in a good way. De Croix knew his stuff.

★

A Louis IX high-backed sofa arrived in the VIP lounge with Martin at one end and Christian at the other.

'I obviously don't have to reiterate that moving furniture is not part of my contract,' said Christian to Delia, following him up the stairs to the fourth floor.

'True,' she said, 'and literally just a couple of more items and you can return to your whizzing about online.'

He didn't look overly put out, Delia decided, and it was good to get him out of the broom cupboard office. Not that she understood half of what Christian was achieving online, but it did seem that word of Shillington's Christmas promotions was circulating. The personal shopping service was popular, so much so that Immy was rarely seen around the store and each morning headed diligently to her headquarters. Maybe, at last, Immy had found something she was good at.

'Here is a pink Chinese rug with a very pretty floral design,' said Delia. 'Do roll it out, Martin, so we can admire.'

'I'll be tempted to lie on it and go to sleep,' he said. 'The wife's snoring something terrible at the moment.'

'And this is a framed set of 1918 signed invoices,' said Delia, ignoring Martin. She was sorely tempted to give him the sack, but a snoring watch had arrived in the tech department, which she may direct him to.

'And what do we have here?' said de Croix, picking up a shoe box.

'Costume jewellery,' said Delia. 'We're going to display it.'

'It looks almost real,' said de Croix, picking up a diamond choker. 'And this emerald ring?'

'Fun, isn't it?' said Delia. 'I think it's what's known as *bling* these days.'

'Yes,' laughed de Croix. 'Julie loves her statement jewellery, but only a single piece at a time. It's the Parisian way, less is more.'

Delia ran her fingers around her pearl necklace. It was the only necklace she wore, given to her by Gregory on their wedding day. Could she ever wear another necklace? Such a huge part of her longed for change, but her fear of venturing into the unknown froze her every time she considered anything new.

'Here's the curio cabinet for you, Delia,' said Martin. 'Not a bad-looking piece of furniture.'

'Perfect, thank you,' she said. 'The jewellery can go on display.'

'And what about these bank notes?' said de Croix, holding up a large glass frame. 'Very clever to frame these, Delia, and just look at all those characters.'

'I'm not sure what James Joyce would have thought about being on a ten-pound note, but he did like being in print,' said Delia, as Martin carried in a big heavy cash register. 'And this is a very old till made of red brass.'

'We'll polish it up,' said de Croix, 'and I think it will be fascinating for people to view, and think about spending lots of money, like the good old days, yes?'

'And what about the dogs?' said Martin. 'Can they come here while waiting for their appointment with Doggie Hairdos?'

'Everything is possible for VIPs,' said de Croix. 'If they want to bring a goat, then the goat will be welcome. VIP has no limits and André at Doggie Hairdos will facilitate.'

Chapter Twenty-Two

The next day, commuters habitually rushing by Shillington's began to slow up and press their noses against the Christmas window display. Lavish garlands of dried helipterum in pink, fluffy miscanthus and creamy white pampas grass hung over a large easel, with show-stopping globes of dried hydrangea faded to antique pink interspersed with bluish pops of echinops suspended from the ceiling. Uncle Stanley added an old cash register, which he'd been keeping in his room upstairs, along with a *Shillington's at Christmas* sign from the 1960s. A mobile of feathered angels and invisible twine flew above a wooden chest of drawers and centre stage, a life-size polar bear and wooden train, both once belonging to Gregory. Shillington's shone like a thousand stars. The enormous Christmas windows, with gold foil around the portico, shone brilliantly thanks to floodlights beaming up from the basement. No building in Dublin, or

Ireland, was comparable, especially in the moonlight, with windowpanes of snowy whiteness.

For Immy, PS Headquarters had become a welcome distraction. She'd woken up to three missed calls from Lando the night before, but he hadn't left a voicemail, which made her feel more awkward than ever about their non-relationship. Sitting in at her desk, Immy's mind drifted back to their night together, remembering how he'd looked when he'd held her face in his hands, but that was nothing but playing about with Hollywood dreams.

'Hello there,' came a voice from outside Personal Shopping HQ and Flynn, the TD, popped his head around the door. 'I hope I'm not disturbing you?'

'Oh, hi,' said Immy, who couldn't think of anything better to say. She stood up from her desk.

'I thought I'd do a little Christmas shopping,' he said, 'just to get ahead.'

Immy nodded and prayed he wasn't going to ask her out. She had noticed his lingering stare when they met in menswear and it wasn't as if she didn't find him attractive, but the thought of a date made her squirm.

'I didn't see you in homeware, then they told me you'd moved up here.' He smiled. 'Very smart.'

'Oh, thanks, I'm quite enjoying my new role.'

'No more gravy boats then?'

Immy didn't get the joke and then laughed. 'Oh yes, the good old gravy boat.'

'My mum still uses one,' said Flynn, 'she's a great cook.'

'Where does she live?'

'Leitrim, actually,' he said, unravelling his scarf. 'Lovely Leitrim.'

'Yes,' said Immy, checking her phone and feeling relieved to have an honest excuse. 'I'm really sorry, but I have a client about to arrive.'

'Sugar,' he said, glancing at the door. 'It's just, I have some tickets for a thing.'

'What kind of thing?' Immy was quite taken by his shyness.

'It's for the Snow Ball, and well, it's a sort of dinner thing and there'll be music and food, quite good apparently.'

'And snow?'

'Well, I'd say they'll do their best and the forecast is giving for it to be very cold over the next week all right.'

'I love snow,' said Immy, meaning it.

'Then would you like to join me?' He pressed his chin to his chest and looked up at her. 'It's December twentieth in the Mansion House.' He put his hand into his pocket and pulled out a business card. 'I know it's old-fashioned, but I've always liked to have a way of giving my contact details that doesn't involve a phone.' He handed a card to her.

'Thank you.' Immy studied the card. 'Can I let you know?'

'You bet,' he said, awkwardly stepping back, and then

bolting for the door before popping his head back around with a wave. 'Bye then,' he said, finally.

'Bye,' said Immy, feeling slightly shocked and excited all at once.

Immy sat on the sofa opposite David Clock, who checked his watch again and folded his arms. Not a good sign, according to Immy's body language research.

'Celine is usually very prompt,' she said, apologetically, and thankfully she saw his mouth curl into a smile.

'I seem to attract things to do with time,' he said. 'As a child, I used to get very confused when I heard in school that the clocks were moving back, and I'd run into the house and ask my mum where we were moving back to.'

'Sweet,' said Immy. 'If it had been my mum, she would have said she was moving, and I was staying put.' She tried to laugh, but then realised it wasn't a joke at all.

'Tough childhood?'

'It's hard to say, isn't it?' said Immy. 'I hear all kinds of horror stories and my own experience is so insignificant.'

'It depends,' said David, unfolding his arms. 'It was your childhood and if someone made you feel unwanted, and I'm not trying to insult your mother, but if she made you feel insecure, then that was your reality and yours alone.'

'I guess that makes sense,' said Immy, 'but we're not here to dissect my life, but to instead show you some fabulous clothes.' She was there to sell, after all. 'I'm sure Celine will be here any moment.'

'Then, if you don't mind my asking, I've been wondering ever since our conversation about Elaine.'

'Elaine? Oh yes, sorry, your PA.'

'I've been paying more attention to the way we've been interacting.'

Immy reached for her notebook. 'I'm actually so glad you mentioned this, because the same conversation prompted me to do a little research.'

'Go on,' he said.

'OK,' said Immy, 'so, when, for example, you speak with Elaine, is her voice quite upbeat?'

'I'd say so, yes,' he said.

'Good,' said Immy, folding over a page. 'From what I've read, if we sort of copy the way people are with us, and in your case, Elaine, it's meant to speed up the attraction process.'

'Sounds like work,' he said.

'I know, and I could word it better, but this is my understanding and I think it won't feel like work once you find the right person.'

'But that's just it – since I last saw you, there are a couple of things that are bugging me about Elaine.'

'Oh,' said Immy, thinking, trouble in paradise before it even began. 'What happened?'

'She says she's vegetarian.'

'And?'

'Well, I saw her on Instagram eating a Big Mac.'

'Perhaps a McPlant burger?'

'Good point, but my ex lied a lot,' he said, scratching his nose.

Immy thought it better not to comment.

'She had an affair with my then brother-in-law,' he said, 'as in, her sister's husband.'

'Holy cow.'

'I used stronger language than that when I heard,' he said, scrunching up his face.

'OK, so how about another idea?' she said. 'Are you familiar with the Law of Attraction?'

'No,' said David, 'but I'm at the stage where I'm open to anything. I mean, what have I got to lose?' He looked down at his arms and legs. 'Look at me, probably half the reason my marriage didn't work out.'

'There are a few tricks that can help to encourage love into your life.'

'I'm all ears,' he said.

David was so matter of fact they could have been discussing a sales spreadsheet in a boardroom. His eyes weren't brightening around Immy, that's for sure; she felt like she was boring him. But then again, he was here for an outfit, not for relationship advice. What was she doing? And yet, she couldn't stop it.

'If you can empty half your wardrobe,' said Immy, reading from her notebook, 'this makes a signal to your brain that you're ready to share your life with someone.'

'But what would I do with my clothes?'

'Good point, do you have a guest room or another hanging space?'

'I suppose I could even bag some up for charity. I've got far too much stuff as it is.'

Immy went on to suggest David parked his car outside his house as if making room for a second car. And that he slept on one side of the bed.

'But I've only just trained myself to sleep eagle-winged,' he said. 'Mind you, my ex-wife literally hogged the entire bed, and I wouldn't be keen to go back to sleeping as if I were on a park bench.'

'I totally get it,' said Immy, though she hadn't shared a double bed with anyone. Apart from Lando, she had slept with two other men in her life, both of whom had lasted less than the time it takes for a kettle to boil, and not even a full kettle.

'The same goes for your dressing table,' said Immy, 'and your sock drawer and bedside tables – literally making room for another person to come into your life can trigger your brain, and body, to radiate vibes that you are available.'

David looked quite interested. 'So, you're saying it's an almost scientific approach?' he said.

'Yes, with a dash of good will from the universe. The best of both, I like to think.' And Immy was a positive thinker, but also surprising herself as a risk-taker. She checked her watch and wondered what was taking Celine so long.

'It's me,' said Celine, 'and I have the pieces I was searching for; sorry it took longer than expected.'

'Thanks, Celine,' said Immy, making eyes at her. 'Is that all?'

'No,' she said, 'you actually seem to have double-booked a personal shopping client.' Celine ushered Tanya forward, dressed in a mini wool skirt, polo neck and long brown boots.

Immy looked at David and saw his eyes widen at the sight of Tanya. Perhaps his PA wasn't 'the one' after all. And then her mind wandered to Flynn and his invitation to the Snow Ball.

Chapter Twenty-Three

For Stanley, the fuss about Christmas decorating was over the top. It was not the decor that needed dealing with but the camaraderie. Delia had little idea as to the amount of energy he'd put in over the years to make visitors feel welcome. Bob and Frank did a fine job on the door with the *céad míle fáilte*, but it was Stanley who doled out the tailored compliments to men and women on their clothes, all to encourage a splurge on Shillington's overpriced products.

He knew all too well the eye-watering markup that went on handbags, the hefty margins on mattresses, and the over-priced cosmetics, much of which contained oil and wax. He couldn't believe they could get away with charging such premium prices. It was all for a good cause though; at least that was what he told himself to sleep comfortably on his pillow at night. The store was a loyal employer and some of the staff had been there decades, with family members taking over when elders retired. Shillington's was a way of life for many, but he knew D-Day was coming. Stanley did his best to twirl his walking stick and fan out the compliments, but his arthritis was playing up and he needed to know his position was secure.

The electric kettle in his kitchenette came to a boil. He added a splash of boiling water to the silver teapot and poured it down the sink a minute later. The thought of using a tea bag made him shiver, and he could still hear old Mrs Shillington saying, 'Tea bags were made of the sweepings from around tea chests.' There were also words she wouldn't tolerate. 'Polyester' had to be whispered by the soft furnishings and bedding department, and it was the same with 'bath foam'; she literally couldn't stand the words. She also refused to eat a sandwich with points and had the tea rooms prepare circular-shaped sandwiches with no trace of a crust.

Stanley added a couple of generous spoonfuls of Darjeeling to the pot and was about to add the water when he heard a knock at the door. There was only one person who knocked on the pineapple brass door knocker with such impatience. Lando had been doing that since he was tall enough to reach.

'I want to change my name,' said Lando.

Uncle Stanley didn't respond. He sat quietly, legs crossed, arms folded.

'Aren't you going to say anything?'

'What would I say?' said Uncle Stanley.

'Bad idea, good idea, I don't know.'

'And what if I had no opinion.'

'Do you?'

Stanley took the hip flask from his pocket and twisted open the lid. He paused before taking a sip. 'What your father would have to say about it is a different matter.'

'Why?'

'He was proud of his name. The place was started by his father's father, remember. That's three generations, and you are to be the fourth. Even if you give up on this place, it doesn't mean you can't still be a Shillington.'

Lando felt overwhelmed. Tears rushed to his eyes and, in a bid to stop them, he began coughing and sniffing.

'I feel like I'm failing Dad,' he said. 'I'm meant to take the reins, but I can't. This business has always felt foreign to me.'

Uncle Stanley reached out and pressed his hand on Lando's shoulder. 'You're no different to thousands before you; what do any of us know what we're doing. If we thought about things that much, we'd never do anything.'

Lando felt a release.

'Look at me, I've been in this place for sixty-two years. Shillington's is my life. You think I could survive anywhere else?'

'I'm not sure.'

'And I'm even less sure. To tell you the truth, I'm scared out of my life to leave this place. I've been on that top floor since I was sixteen years of age. And it was your grandfather who let me. He saw I was lost but he never once made me feel like he was doing it for any other reason than I was worth employing and up to the task.'

Lando thought of Immy. Was that what she meant when she said she felt like a charity case? He'd never meant it to be that way. She was like family to him, or much more than that, which confused him. They were so close, it didn't fit into a category, and the more he tried to work out what they had, the more damage he caused to their relationship.

'I'm not sure that French girl is for you.'

'Why do you say that?'

'She's a fine girl, it's not about that, and I shouldn't even be giving my opinion when you haven't asked for it, but in case you were wondering, I'm just not sure.'

For as long as Lando could remember, his life had been assessed. If Delia wasn't watching closely, then Uncle Stanley was, or members of staff. There was always someone to comment on his latest move. Perhaps this was the lot of an only child, but surely more intense when all eyes were on Lando as next in line.

'This company would have folded in twenty-nine if it wasn't for your ancestors' perseverance,' said Uncle Stanley, shuffling the knot of his tie from side to side. 'Their spirits may have evaporated during the war, and yet they bounced back with positivity.'

'And I guess you're thinking that's where my happy-go-lucky attitude comes from?' said Lando. 'The only reason I push my positivity is because I'm afraid if I stop, I'll collapse.'

'And what about Immy?'

'What about her? She seems obsessed with her personal shopping.'

'That girl has continuously supported you, Lando, despite your mother turning up her nose at every opportunity.'

Lando shrugged his shoulders.

'You think I haven't noticed?' said Stanley. 'And now you turn up with a rich Parisian beauty to solve all your problems.'

'And what is that supposed to mean?' Lando was becoming impatient.

'It means exactly what you think it means. Christmas makes people do funny things, so keep a hold of yourself, that's my advice.'

Chapter Twenty-Four

Strong odours of onion and garlic swirled in the air of Lando's basement kitchen. He could just about make out Bing Crosby's voice beneath the sound of the ear-crunching extractor fan.

'Hey, Mum?'

'Hi, darling,' said Delia, standing over the oven and looking like a mad scientist with goggles on her head.

'Do those things really work?' he said, opening the fridge and taking a chicken leg from last night's supper.

'You know how sensitive my eyes are to onions, and if wearing goggles makes me look ridiculous, then so be it.' An orange Le Creuset pot began to boil over and Delia quickly turned down the gas. 'I've never been great at cooking on anything other than an Aga,' she said, 'but darling, you are so sweet to have me living down here with you.'

'How about the tenants?' Lando opened a jar of mayonnaise and was about to dip in the chicken leg.

'Don't you dare,' said Delia.

'Hah, I was just testing,' he said, picking up a knife and dipping it into the jar.

'Just as well,' she said, pouring him a glass of wine. 'And to answer the question about the tenants, I met the mother the other day when I was parking, and she said they're planning a huge family Christmas, though they're not sure if it will be here or with their in-laws.'

Lando thought of their own family Christmas. Last year Uncle Stanley got 'lucky on the horses' and brought them to Patrick Guilbaud's where they ate the most incredible pheasant and got drunk on Chateau Margaux. The staff loved Uncle Stanley so much that they presented him with a bottle of port on the house.

'Mum, what's that smell?'

'What's that, darling?' she said, seemingly oblivious to the stench and taking another sip of wine.

Lando kneeled in front of the oven and could see something that looked like chicken roasting.

'I'm going to take a look,' he said and, reaching for the oven gloves, he opened the door and the most hideous stinking steam gushed out. 'Oh my god, Mum!' He closed the door immediately. 'What the hell is that?'

Delia clasped her hands across her mouth. 'I didn't, did I?' she said.

'Didn't what?'

'Oh Lando, I forgot to take the entrails out of the duck!'

He ran to open the front door, followed by both the sitting room windows. 'There's no way we can stay here, Mum, it's hideous.'

'But de Croix's coming over for dinner.'

'Sorry?' said Lando, doing a double take. 'You and de Croix are having dinner? What about Gerhardt?'

'What about Gerhardt?'

'I thought you two were, you know, seeing each other?'

'Lando, I've made it perfectly clear that he is most welcome to spend his fortune at Shillington's, but I cannot be bought.'

'Fair enough.' He had never pegged his mother as even vaguely feminist, but, clearly, Shillington's wasn't the only thing that was changing around here.

'I merely want to thank de Croix for all he's doing for us, and as I can't afford to take him out to dinner, I thought I'd cook.' It was hard to take his mother seriously when she had onion goggles resting on her forehead.

★

An early-evening pint of Guinness in the Cellar Bar was tempting as Lando strolled by, especially as he could still taste the odour of roasted duck entrails. But he was determined to get things back on track with Immy. They had barely spent any time together since he'd returned from Paris and when he did manage to see her at Shillington's, she was distracted and even enthused by her new role as personal shopper. He had never seen Immy properly interested in any job, ever, and what was more ironic was that she had never been into shopping, let alone fashion.

He stood in front of the yellow door on Merrion Street, which had a Christmas wreath hanging around the large brass door knocker. Three floors up. In the old days, he would have thrown a piece of gravel at her window, but he figured he'd better be on his best behaviour and pressed the buzzer.

'Come on up,' said Immy.

The catch on the front door released and Lando climbed the wide, shallow-stepped staircase. The door to Immy's flat was slightly open but again, he knocked on the door just to be on the safe side. In the small landing between the kitchen and sitting room, he was surprised to find a rail of clothes and, even more so, Immy dressed in a corduroy jumpsuit with brown Chelsea boots. Her hair was tied up in a top knot and she wore eyeliner.

'Hey,' he said, studying his old friend to see if he could spot any other tweaks in her appearance.

She looked up at him from the table, where she was painting her nails. 'Afraid I don't have too long,' she said.

'Let me guess, you're going on a date,' he said.

'Yes,' she said, looking happy.

He was joking, Immy literally didn't date. She might have snogged someone at the odd party, but on a formal date? She just didn't go for that sort of thing.

'You look good,' he said, meaning it. 'Different, but good.'

'It's all down to Celine persuading me to try new clothes and make more of an effort. Life's too short, she keeps telling me, and that I should be living it up.'

Lando sat on the sofa, taking in the smell of nail varnish, which was an improvement on the odour of duck entrails.

'So how are you, Lando?' she said, almost as if they had

met at a party and they didn't know each other that well. 'And how is your romance?' she added.

'There's something off about Mum,' he said, ignoring the Celine question. 'She's sort of flighty and more on edge than usual.'

'That could only be a good thing, surely,' said Immy, blowing on her fingernails. 'I mean, a more relaxed version of your mum would be an improvement.'

'You're always so diplomatic, Im,' he said, noticing how a tiny amount of make-up enhanced her eyes.

'But go on, tell me about Celine.' She seemed to want to know.

'Well, it's a sort of slow process.'

'OK,' she said, putting the lid back on the nail polish. 'In what way?'

'She is quite formal, in terms of ... well you know.'

Immy nodded her head as if she understood what he was referring to but he wanted her to give him the third degree. He wanted her to say, 'You haven't slept with Celine? Are you serious? Lando, you're losing your touch.'

How bizarre to have found himself in a position of wanting to spend time with both, and in different ways. Celine liked deep, philosophical talks, walking around galleries, and eating out. In Paris, he did not see her make anything beyond coffee in her *pied-à-terre*. Whereas Immy loved to curl up with home-cooked pasta and laugh in front of movies. She had always made him feel like he had nothing to prove, until now.

'Your mum seems to be happy about her,' said Immy, getting to her feet.

'Understatement,' he said.

'You've found your dreamboat,' she said, pulling on a camel overcoat and grabbing her phone from the table. 'I'm happy for you. Now I'm sorry but I've got to go.' Immy checked her phone as she left the flat, asked Lando to close the door after him, and went ahead of him down the stairs. He just stood there, wishing he had said more, wishing he had explained his genuine, heartfelt dilemma.

★

Heading down Kildare Street, Immy knew she'd made it sound like she was meeting a guy, but she had to do something to make it clear she didn't mind about Celine. She obviously did mind that Lando had found a beautiful Parisian girl, but she couldn't bear the feeling of jealousy and was determined to overcome it. She knew they hadn't even slept together. He didn't say it explicitly, but she could tell. In the old days, Immy would have straight out asked him if he'd slept with her, just as Lando would have asked who Immy was seeing. Things were different and terribly awkward, even if neither of them wanted to admit it. Maybe this was the right time for Immy to accept Flynn's invitation and venture into a new relationship.

Café Insane was a favourite hangout of the staff at Shillington's, just off South Anne Street. They served happy hour cocktails on Wednesdays and Thursdays, and as many pretzels as you could eat. Janette and Celine had already arrived, both dressed in black.

'Is this a wake?' said Immy, hugging both girls, 'or Janette, maybe you're adopting Celine's Parisian chic?'

'I wish,' said Janette. 'I haven't even been to Paris.'

'You should come,' said Celine, 'and you too, Immy.'

'If we survive Christmas,' said Janette. 'I don't know what it is about this year, but customers are more needy. They want more samples, they want everything to be wrapped, they seem harder to satisfy.'

Celine drained her margarita and nodded frantically. 'Why do you think I've just downed my drink in two mouthfuls? My father passes on all the stories to me, and I must sit in the office and listen.'

'Tell me about it,' said Janette, who had just ordered a round of holly jollys for the three of them. 'I was standing in for one of the girls this morning in the home appliances department, and a woman dressed up to the nines asked me to help her choose a hairdryer, and I said, "Of course, madame."' Janette did a little curtsy. Immy hadn't realised she had such a good sense of humour. 'So, I hand a hairdryer to the woman, and she reads the side of the box and tells me she wants one that won't electrocute her if she accidentally drops it in water.'

Celine and Immy sipped their drinks as Janette told her story. 'Then I say, you can't drop anything that is electric into water, and she said there was no way that was right, even though I showed her the warning label of every hairdryer I could get my hands on. Then off she walked, just like that.'

'To the customer,' said Celine, raising her drink, and the three girls clinked their glasses. Immy didn't usually gravitate towards a group of girls, but Celine and Janette made for uplifting company. She hadn't realised how much time she'd spent with Lando, and as a result she'd stopped trying to make new friends. Maybe this was the silver lining to their bump in the road.

'Can I ask your advice?' said Immy, taking another sip of Dutch courage.

'Of course,' said Celine.

'You know the TD guy?' said Immy, swirling the remains of the cocktail in her glass.

'The dishy one?' said Janette.

'He's invited me to the Snow Ball.'

Celine and Janette immediately clinked their glasses and whooped merrily.

'You have said yes, haven't you?' Celine looked so excited.

'Not yet —'

'I'm ordering another round,' said Janette, 'and can I do your make-up?'

'And leave the dress to me,' said Celine. 'I've got the perfect dress for you.'

'But I haven't even said yes —'

Celine picked up Immy's phone on the bar and handed it to her. 'Now is the time.'

Immy felt so buoyed up by Janette and Celine's company that she couldn't not follow through and quickly found herself text a straight-up 'yes' to Flynn's invitation. Within seconds, he responded to her message with a star emoji.

At last, Immy felt a sense of optimism that she'd been missing for too long.

Chapter Twenty-Five

In Shillington's staff canteen, Lando polished off the spice bag and popcorn chicken he'd bought at Hilda's Hotdog Stand outside the main gates to St Stephen's Green. He'd been so hungry, he would have eaten a deep-fried shoe, but luckily for him, Hilda had a fresh batch of chips ready to bag up.

'Lando,' said Uncle Stanley, standing at the door and taking a sip from his hip flask, 'would you not even have the decency to try one of Ross's lasagnes? It's half decent and wouldn't you be supporting the hand that feeds you.'

Right, as per usual, thought Lando.

'So, what's up?' said Uncle Stanley, taking a metal pot of tea from the sideboard, pouring it into a cup and topping it up with whiskey.

'Why do you think something's up?' said Lando, between mouthfuls.

'I've known you for twenty-seven years, and I can tell a mile away when you're out of kilter.'

'Fine,' said Lando, knowing there was no point holding back.

'You haven't been right since before you went to Paris and then you came back fooling us all with this French escapade.'

'It's not an escapade.'

'What is it then?'

Lando pushed the bag of chips to one side and wiped his hands on a paper napkin.

'I don't know.'

Uncle Stanley was the best listener. Lando wanted to explain how he felt partly responsible for his father's death, even though he'd only been five hours old when he'd died, but he still couldn't say it out loud.

'I try to visualise my father here, strolling around the various departments, hoping it will give me a sense of place or purpose, but I just can't grasp it.'

'Maybe you're trying too hard,' said Uncle Stanley, leaning back in his chair. 'There are ideas in that head of yours that want to come out, so just let them.'

'I want to contribute,' said Lando, 'that's one thing I'm sure of because I'm fed up just floating about.'

'Calm yourself; now tell me what's going on.'

Lando had been scribbling on the back of old envelopes for months, writing down ideas on how he could give the business a boost, but he hadn't even attempted to mention them to his mum.

'I have one idea but it's far too late to do anything about it even if it was interesting.'

'Let me be the judge if it's a good idea, and if it is, we can decide if it's too late – and take off that woolly hat,' said Uncle Stanley. 'It might let the ideas come out faster from that head of yours.'

At least with Uncle Stanley, Lando would quickly know if his idea was any good.

'I want to make a Christmas ad,' said Lando, taking a sip of Coca-Cola.

'In a newspaper?'

'A film.'

'A television ad?'

'That sort of thing,' said Lando, 'but we'd put it online and post it across Shillington's socials.'

'Like the SuperValu ad? It had us all weeping with the little girl chasing the deer. That was a fine bit of storytelling.'

'Yes, that's the style I'm thinking of.'

'What's the hold-up?'

'I have no idea how to fund it.'

Uncle Stanley rubbed his chin. 'Do you know who you want to make the ad and are they available?'

'There's an agency called White Fangs on Camden Street, and they produce short films for an amazingly low budget.'

'I used to have my own white teeth once upon a time, now there's a story for you,' said Uncle Stanley, with a cackle. 'But no, you go ahead, leave the financing to me.'

'Are you serious?'

'Where there's money, there's time. I got lucky on a horse a month or two ago.'

'What was the horse's name?' said Lando.

'You won't believe me, but Heaven Scent.'

'Then this is heaven sent,' said Lando.

'And as we're dealing with high places, I think we'll call up my friend Jimmy, who knows a lad from a big, top-notch ad firm.'

'Are you sure, Uncle Stanley?' Lando felt motivated for the first time in a long time.

'I am. What is it your mother loves to say?'

'No tat. Which is why we want to create something worthy of Santa's approval.'

Chapter Twenty-Six

The central heating button flashed nineteen degrees on the screen, but the basement felt sub-zero. It had snowed overnight, leaving tiny, frosted crystals bundled up around the iron railings.

'Are you going out, darling?' said Delia, arriving in the kitchen in her dressing gown.

'No, I'm wearing my coat because it's freezing in here,' said Lando, tucking into a poached egg on toast. 'Fancy an egg?'

'Do keep your voice down, darling,' she said, sitting down at the table. 'I had a brandy before bed, and it's given me a real throbber.'

Lando poured a glass of orange juice and passed it to her.

'How was dinner?'

'Not very successful,' said Delia. 'De Croix called to say he had a headache and was going to have room service in the Merrion instead.'

'Lucky escape, judging by the duck,' he said, taking a mouthful of silky egg yolk on sourdough.

'Very funny,' she said. 'Make me a coffee, would you? And please turn on Lyric fm. *Marty in the Morning* is often the saving grace of my mornings.'

Lando got up from the table and took a Kilner jar of coffee from the cupboard. 'I actually have some news for you.'

'You do?' Delia's eyes brightened.

'Business related,' he said. 'We're going to film a Christmas ad for Shillington's.'

'Honestly, Lando, darling,' she said, quickly dismissing his idea. 'Apart from the fact we can't afford it, there is no time.'

'A day to shoot, another day to edit,' said Lando, 'add the music and it can be live on social media within hours.'

'And what about de Croix?'

'What about de Croix?'

'You'll need his approval.'

'I need your approval, Mum, you and I own Shillington's.'

'Fine,' she said. 'Now, if you'll excuse me, I'd better get dressed; I'm meant to be reviewing the Christmas-themed bedroom display with Martin.'

★

Under the guise of marketing expenses, Celine insisted on flying in the Head of Hair and Make-up from Le Marché Cher for Snow Ball preparations.

'Why not?' she told Immy. 'I'm a believer in doing things to a high standard, which is why we are going to turn you into the most beautiful girl Shillington's has ever had under its roof.'

Floor-to-ceiling mirrors had been installed in the fitting room at PS Headquarters, which meant no matter where Immy turned, she could see her reflection. She felt so nervous about her date with Flynn, she couldn't think of anything sensible to say.

'I have thirteen mirrors in my tiny one-bedroom flat in Paris,' said Vole, the make-up artist. 'I caught sight of myself in one of them the other day and I had to yell into my pillow. The party season is showing on my face and it's only the first week of December.'

Vole took Immy's hand and led her to the executive make-up chair, which Janette had sent up from her beauty department. Celine was insistent that Janette should witness Vole at work, particularly with her interest in contouring as his master class went viral on YouTube.

'Some might call me vain,' said Vole, studying Immy's face and holding out tendrils of her wavy hair as if they were tentacles from an octopus, 'but I believe a mirror should be more than just something we glance at once or twice a day to check ourselves.' He stood back from Immy and took a photo of her with his iPhone. 'I love to have a before and after shot,' he said.

'You know Vole has his own range of products?' said Celine, who asked him to take a picture of her posing in a little black dress with sheer red tights next to Janette, who held make-up brushes over her head as if she were a Martian.

'*Voila!* All vegan and cruelty-free,' said Vole, wiggling a comb between his fingers like a drummer with drumsticks, 'and thanks to sales on social media, I can pick and choose my make-up jobs.'

'Your posts are like chocolate sauce,' said Celine, 'we cannot get enough.'

'Show me an eye,' he said, staring at Immy's reflection, 'and I say, how smoky do you want it?'

Immy was going to answer and then realised it was a rhetorical question.

'It's all about being contemporary,' said Vole, dropping the comb and tying back Immy's wavy hair, 'but the smoky eye is timeless. It is the equivalent of the 1997 convertible Mercedes Benz. In Prague, my mother could transform herself from a housewife by day to a vixen by night. She would fling her apron to one side, apply eyeliner and lipstick, and a little blusher, tousle her hair and you wouldn't believe how she looked.'

'And you've been following in her footsteps, Vole,' said Celine. 'You have wowed us all at Le Marché Cher.'

'You are too kind,' he said, blushing without blusher, 'and now we focus on this pretty lady in the mirror.'

'As natural as possible please,' said Immy, trying to relax. A huge part of her longed for someone to boss her into experimenting with her looks but facing her reflection with so many onlookers seemed to go against her instincts.

'You have no worries,' said Vole. 'First, we are going to sculpt the features and you'll find immediately your eyes and lashes will look sumptuous.

'I'm not really into over-the-top make-up,' said Immy,

who longed to run to the loo but didn't dare disturb Vole, who was deeply focused.

'Sweetie, a Christmas ball is the one time you can go all-out with your beauty,' he said.

'In Paris, we like over-the-top drama,' said Celine, taking snipes of Moët & Chandon from the fridge. 'Christmas is the time you can wear all the sequins, satin or lamé you want, or even all of them together.' She twisted open the champagne top and popped a gold flute into the mouth of the bottle. 'For you, Immy, and Janette, of course.'

'*Vive la France*,' said Janette, taking a sip.'

'I do urge my clients to be sustainable,' said Vole, declining champagne in favour of Perrier. 'And I don't believe in flashing wealth about either.'

'You mean the champagne?' said Celine. 'I thought bubbles to get Immy in the mood would be fun.'

'I get it,' said Vole, 'but you must understand in Prague, we will literally discuss anything, sex, your *babička*'s skin condition, literally anything but wealth – it is taboo.'

Vole began applying base creams to Immy's face, which felt incredibly cold as she raised her chin, like a dog being massaged by its owner.

'Celine, *zlatíčko*, before you get smashed and I get focused on this doll's face and hair, have you got her gown?'

'I do,' said Celine, signalling to Janette to bring the dress over to Immy. Celine didn't take her eyes off Immy. 'I want to see your reaction to the dress I have chosen for you, Immy.'

The dress was breathtaking. Navy silk, floor-sweeping and embellished with sparkling beads and a halter neck. 'This is a classic investment gown that will not go out of date,' said Celine. 'You can be sure of this.'

'Not like my Scary Spice Debs dress,' said Janette. 'I spent a bloody fortune on it and it's still sitting in the closet of my dad's spare room.'

Chapter Twenty-Seven

A dozen long-stemmed red roses were delivered to PS Headquarters with a card that read, *Roses can't compete with your beauty. See you at 6.30 p.m., Flynn x.*

Immy stared at her reflection in the mirror while Vole looked like a near surgeon at work, he was using so many tools on her hair. She couldn't work out how she felt about the flowers. They were immaculate and certainly generous, but she'd have preferred a posey of celandine or daisies. Celine, Janette, and Vole made a big deal of the note, calling Flynn, 'The Poetic Politician.'

'No one has ever sent me flowers,' said Janette. 'Mind you, I've never sent flowers to anyone either.'

'In Paris, we send a single rose,' said Celine, filling a jug with water in the sink.

'That sounds more like it,' said Janette. 'That bouquet must have cost an arm and a leg, but then again, your man's a politician so he's loaded, isn't he, Immy?'

Immy was feeling under pressure and wished she'd

never agreed to go to the stupid ball. It didn't help that the hairspray was making her feel nauseous.

'Forget the glass slipper,' said Vole, 'tonight we go for glass hair, so I'm going to blow out your curls and then we'll use the flat iron to straighten your hair.'

'But I never straighten my hair.'

'Then maybe this is a good time to start? And we'll finish the look with an anti-frizz hairspray. *Voilà*, hair so shiny we won't need a mirror but your hair to see our complexions.'

Janette clapped her hands in excitement and knelt next to Immy's chair.

'Any chance I can stay in your flat tonight?' said Janette, quietly. 'I've got a Botox appointment at nine a.m. and I'd have to drag myself out of bed at an ungodly hour to catch the bus.'

'Fine,' said Immy, who was dreading having her hair straightened. 'The keys are on my desk.'

'Deadly,' said Janette, springing up to retrieve the keys. 'You won't even know I'm there and I hardly snore.'

Immy was about to give Janette directions as to where to find blankets for the sofa in her flat, when there was a knock at the door.

'Could it be more flowers for her ladyship?' said Janette, spinning the keys between her fingers as she opened the door. 'Sorry to disturb,' came a high-pitched voice. It could only be Leslie.

'Hey Leslie,' said Immy, who didn't dare move from her chair in case Vole flipped a lid. 'It's so lovely to see you, and you look amazing, I love your hair.'

'Thank you,' she said, unbuttoning her coat. 'I took your advice and took myself off to the good hairdresser's, who thought shoulder length was better, and for me to wear it down.'

'You look very glamourous,' said Celine.

Immy introduced the women and told Leslie that praise from Celine was high praise indeed.

'I've always wanted to go to Paris,' said Leslie. 'Maybe I'll suggest it to Bill, and on that note—' she handed a red heart-shaped tin to Immy '— shortbread for you, made by me and Bill.'

'You and Bill? Oh, Leslie, I must get up and give you a hug.' Without smudging her make-up, Immy carefully embraced Leslie and quickly sat back down. She'd promised Vole she wouldn't put on the dress until he had returned from having an emergency double cappuccino.

'We both wanted to thank you,' said Leslie. 'If it wasn't for you, neither of us would have been here and we may not have met.'

'But of course you would have,' said Immy.

'No, you see, Immy, it was the mindset you gave us.' Leslie opened her coat and did a perfect curtsey. 'And the style.'

Celine and Janette both whistled and clapped.

'Seriously, Immy, we are very grateful, and it wasn't as if we spent much time with you, but it was something in the way you encouraged us that made the difference.'

'Really?' said Immy.

'Bill and I have discussed it thoroughly, as you can

imagine,' said Leslie, blushing. 'We both agree, you are the one that brought us together and so please accept both the biscuits and the praise.'

★

As had always been the case at Shillington's, customers were cleared from the building by 6 p.m. It was a tradition Old Mr Shillington put into place during the 1920s so employees could accompany their families to Mass. From accountants to suppliers, the idiocy of the timing was pointed out that Shillington's should move with the times, as all their competitors now worked to late-night openings, but Delia was determined to hold on to tradition.

Celine called her father to arrange a welcome party for Immy's date, particularly as Flynn was a TD. De Croix wore a white rose in his lapel for the occasion, Lando didn't say much, and Stanley topped up his hip flask in case Immy needed a little Dutch courage.

'Ready?' said Celine, peering down from the gallery, two flights up.

'We are,' said Uncle Stanley. 'I'll just let in the politician. I can see him standing on the other side of the window like a cinnamon stick.'

Flynn, dressed in black tie, was hollering on the phone to someone and mouthed, 'Just one sec.' Stanley wasn't going to wait around while some kind of political pitch was taking place. He was about to walk away when he saw Flynn's whitened teeth smile from the other side of the glass.

'Come on in,' said Stanley, accepting the politician's handshake.

'Good to see you,' said Flynn, in his well-practised greeting. 'It's getting nippy out there.'

'I don't give a damn about the weather,' said Stanley, closing the front door behind them, 'but I do about Immy, so you be sure to treat her right or you'll have me to deal with.'

'Right you are, sir,' said Flynn, looking taken aback, which pleased Stanley. He knew things were tense between Lando and Immy, and decided a little jealousy would do Lando no harm, which he must have felt as she descended the staircase.

Janette led the procession as if she were a maid of honour, with gold tinsel tied around her high ponytail. She was followed by Celine, looking glorious as ever in a cream cashmere dress. But when Immy came into view, the men were momentarily silenced by her beauty.

Sweet as always, Immy shyly smiled and fidgeted with the strap of her dress.

'Aren't you a picture?' said Stanley, taking Immy's hand to steady her. He wondered how often she'd worn heels as high as those. He had an eagle eye when it came to ladies' shoes, having spent some years filling staffing gaps in the women's footwear department.

'This is the first time I've picked up a date in a department store,' said Flynn.

Stanley was going to say something smart but then decided to keep quiet.

'The beautiful swan,' said de Croix, as if he was assessing a fashion model. 'Lovely work, Celine.'

'It's easy to polish a diamond,' said Stanley, noticing that Lando didn't utter a word or take his eyes off Immy for a single second, just as Celine didn't take her eyes off Lando. This was some fine triangle, Stanley thought to himself, and it smelled like trouble.

Chapter Twenty-Eight

The Round Room of the Mansion House, filled with the 'who's who' and 'who's gonna be who' of Dublin, had been opulently decorated with sashes of red silk draped across the ceiling. Eager to maximise his networking opportunity, Flynn arrived with Immy fifteen minutes ahead of schedule and stepped forward at every opportunity, shaking hands, patting shoulders, and nodding enthusiastically. Periodically he turned to smile at Immy and may have considered introducing her to his many groupies of older-looking politicians, but rightly guessed she'd prefer to spectate.

Waiters with matching bands of silk around their waists circulated trays of champagne and miniature Yorkshire puddings with roast beef and horseradish sauce. Immy held a glass in one hand, a canapé in the other and watched the five-piece brass band begin their pre-dinner set. A solo trumpet played a rather moving rendition of 'Have Yourself a Merry Little Christmas', which Immy supposed could be possible until she looked to the door.

She was utterly gobsmacked to see Lando, so handsome in black tie that he made all the other men look like waiters in comparison. And there was Celine, dressed in an elegant black dress, her hair sleek and without any accessories other than red lipstick. Her slender arm was slipped into Lando's, and by far they were the most glamorous couple in the room. Immy felt like an over-iced cupcake in her dress, which she now thought was too low-cut and tight. She'd been swept away by Vole and his flattery, and Celine's total enthusiasm that she must go to the ball.

'Immy!' said Celine, spotting her like a hawk. She threw open her arms and trotted immaculately across the floor. 'Can you believe it?' She air-kissed with perfection.

Immy smiled and said, 'Not really.'

'Flynn got us tickets as a surprise for you,' said Celine.

Lando trailed behind and barely acknowledged Immy.

'Let's find a drink,' said Celine, taking Immy by the hand. 'Lando, you'll follow us to the bar, won't you?'

Immy didn't dare make eye contact with him. This was too ridiculous, and where was Flynn? So much for her date.

'This room is magnificent,' said Celine, looking up to the ceiling. 'There is enough silk up there to make a thousand dresses.' Immy felt complete envy for Celine's easy-going attitude, making every step seem like an adventure as she delighted in the details. 'Look at the table centres,' she said, 'a mini-Christmas village with glitter, isn't that beautiful?' Every word Celine uttered sounded even more fabulous due to her French accent.

'Good evening,' said Flynn, striding to the bar to shake Lando's hand. 'Good to see you.'

Lando didn't look overly thrilled to see him but was polite as always, whereas Celine gave Flynn a luxurious and lingering double kiss. 'You look so good,' she told him. 'You two are such a cute couple.'

Flynn looked thrilled to hear this whilst Immy wanted to crawl beneath the Christmas tree next to them.

'There's a chap over there I'd better say hello to,' said Flynn. 'I won't be long, Imogen.'

Why was he calling her Imogen?

'Darling, how long have you been here?' A woman with tightly cut red hair darted in front of Celine, with an ostrich feather branching out from a gold sequence strap across her forehead.

'Gilda,' said Celine, 'you look magnificent.'

'Of course, darling, and aren't you sweet to bring a little Parisian elegance to our Dublin festive.'

Celine turned to Immy. She was so well practised in making people feel included.

'Gilda Winterbottom, may I present Immy Brooks.'

'Aren't you a darling,' said Gilda to Immy. 'Are you French?'

'Irish,' said Immy, recognising Gilda as the PR who famously got the president to eat popcorn on stage at a literary festival and snack sales went sky-high. The company then brought out a special edition called 'The President's Popcorn Selection'.

'Oh, well, can't win them all,' said Gilda. 'You're not in fashion, are you?'

'I guess I am,' said Immy. 'I haven't had much practice as yet in telling people what I do.'

'Immy is the exclusive personal shopper for Shillington's,' said Celine. 'She is doing the most fabulous job and even my father is very happy with her.'

'Oh darling de Croix, is he here?' said Gilda, looking over their shoulders as she spoke.

'He's working tonight,' said Celine. 'You know how Papa is.'

'Sweet,' said Gilda, brilliantly condescending. 'Then I must fly and speak with that dreadful woman from Hedge & Hog.'

'A new client?' said Celine.

'Not yet, but I'm working on it,' said Gilda, flinging her feather boa over her shoulder. 'She's most likely on her third cosmopolitan, even though those things should have gone out of fashion by now.'

'How is your daughter? Did she have her baby?' said Celine.

'Well, there's a story,' said Gilda, raising her empty glass at a passing waiter. 'In short, my daughter's had the baby and my son-in-law has had the nanny.' She landed her glass on the waiter's tray. 'Another martini, there's a good chap.'

Immy had to stop herself from smiling. This woman was outrageous.

'I knew it from the moment I met the nanny, parading

around the house half-naked, and the next thing you know, she's snogging my son-in-law in the laundry.'

'Whoops,' said Celine.

'That nanny is nothing but a home-wrecker and that son-in-law is no better. My daughter is utterly traumatised and has talked me into interviewing nannies and choosing one that is fit to look after sweet little Otto without running off with his father.'

'I have a friend who often employs nannies when she's staying at her family home in Ireland,' said Celine. 'She has exquisite taste; I'll call her for you.'

'Who's that, darling?' said Gilda, who began scrolling on her phone.

'Elodie Gold. She is a painter; you must have heard of her?' said Celine.

'I read about her,' said Gilda, looking up from her phone, 'but was more interested in her outrageously handsome husband, one of those tall, well-educated Americans. You know, there really is nothing like a tall, well-educated American.'

'So you say,' said Celine, laughing at Gilda's clear obsession.

'I saw that he ... what's his name? Luke? He was in *Harper's* last week.' Gilda looked like she was going to go on a soliloquy about Elodie's husband, when a man drifted towards them, dressed in a green velvet smoking jacket.

'What are beauties like yourselves standing here gossiping for? Won't you spread the love instead?' As he spoke, a piece of canapé came flying from his mouth and rested on Immy's top lip. She had to stop herself from retching as she swatted the piece of food away.

'We're on our way to find our table,' said Immy, 'but I'm sure Gilda would adore discussing her latest PR campaign, wouldn't you Gilda?' Anything to avoid smoked salmon breath.

'Damn shame,' he said, stuffing the second half of his canapé into his mouth, 'thought I could have you lovelies to myself.'

'You'll have to make do with me,' said Gilda, 'and your timing is excellent.'

'Why is that?' he said.

'Because I want you to write me a big fat cheque to put Wi-Fi into every nursing home in Ireland.'

'Why on earth would I do that?' he said, wiping his mouth.

'Because they are bored as hell and I am setting up the perfect site for them to spend their money online, including minibars.'

'And what spurred this on?'

'We'll all be old one day,' said Gilda, patting her face. 'I can't rely on my daughter to take me in when I reach my dotage and as I intend to enjoy myself, I want to make sure nursing homes are up to my standard.'

'If we find ourselves in the same lodging, I do hope we have adjoining rooms.'

'Don't get too excited, big boy,' said Gilda. 'I'm at least a decade younger than you are, though I'm pleased we share a mutual vision of what high standards are!'

Chapter Twenty-Nine

With enormous golden baubles overhead, Immy scanned the table plan for her name. She was on the 'Figgy Pudding' table, while Flynn was appropriately seated at the 'Snowflakes'. She'd last spotted him fawning over a man identical to Anthony Hopkins. She was the first to arrive at her table, with a plate of Parma ham and melon to greet her. Immy couldn't bear melon and had a flashback to Sunday lunches with her parents when she'd drop the pieces into her mother's handbag, which always swung on her chair even when at home. She picked up a fur cone wrapped in gold foil with her name extravagantly written in pink calligraphy.

'Hey stranger,' said Lando, pulling out his chair to sit next to her.

'What are you doing here?' she hissed, seeing a fur cone with Orlando, but no Shillington as it must have been too long to fit, 'and why on earth are you sitting next to me?'

'The party planner must have had a sixth sense that you and I need to talk,' said Lando.

'But they don't even know me.' Immy looked at all the interesting people sitting at the table, busy chatting away to each other.

'No, but they know Flynn,' he said. 'The Mansion House throw parties like this at least three times a year, and you can bet your bottom dollar that everyone here has been carefully considered.'

'Because there's no way they'd invite me otherwise, you mean?'

'No, Immy, I don't mean it like that,' he said. 'They like their parties to be full of beautiful, successful people, who will make huge charity donations.'

'You can be really condescending sometimes, do you know that?'

'The only reason I'm here is that my father went to school with Christoph Ricci and he most probably wants me to snog one of his daughters,' he said, 'and obviously I can't, as Celine's over there. She'd kill me.'

Immy just looked at him and couldn't find a word insulting enough to deliver. He was clearly incapable of being serious and seemed to think their friendship was like the old days when Immy would make a bet as to how long a date would last. There was nothing for it but for Immy to get focused. She was with Flynn and tonight she was going to make love to a man who was serious about her, or at least seemed to be when he wasn't beaming smiles at potential political donors.

'You come here often?' said the Italian man to Immy's

left, dressed in red velvet with peacock feathers fanning out from his breast pocket.

'Nice line,' she said.

'I like to save my best lines for beauties.' She noticed how his crooked teeth highlighted the beauty of his cheekbones and huge green eyes.

'Red or white wine, madame?' said the waiter.

'Both please,' she said. Tonight, this urban chick was going to fly.

'You aren't seriously considering a fling with the politician, are you?' said Lando, as the man with crooked teeth discussed vegetarian options on the menu with a waitress.

'What does it matter?' Immy forked up a piece of melon and thought seriously about dropping it into Lando's pocket. She took a large sip of white wine instead.

'And why are you ignoring me?' Lando said.

'What?'

'You're ignoring me.'

'I am not ignoring you.'

Immy smiled at a waitress who took her plate and noticed the girl had piercings the whole way up her ear. She must wear lots of earrings when off duty, leading a dual life, like Immy, and right now she was pretending to be a woman who had no issues or ties with Lando Shillington.

'Besides,' said Immy, 'aren't you busy being loved up?'

'That doesn't mean we can't still hang out.'

'Friends don't leave for months without only a couple of pathetic messages.'

'And like I've told you a million times, I still feel bad

about that.'

'I needed you to take what had happened seriously,' said Immy, draining her glass of white wine and moving on to the red. 'I was really upset afterwards.'

'I got swept up,' he said. 'Celine has a way of —'

'Really, Lando, I don't need to know.'

'You know she wants to be good friends with you.'

'And we are,' said Immy.

'Good, and you look lovely, by the way.'

'Shut up and thank you,' she said, trying not to smile.

'I'm being serious,' he said, picking up a piece of Parma ham with his fingers and eating it in a way that looked so elegant. How was that even possible? She looked away as he spoke. She couldn't bear to be near him and as she tried to work out what was going on with her, she felt a tickle at the back of her neck.

'Lando,' said Flynn, standing over them both and reaching out a hand. 'Good to see you taking good care of Immy.'

'All the wolves are out tonight,' said Lando.

'It's a lovely party,' said Immy, smiling up at Flynn.

'I'll see you after pudding,' he whispered into her ear.

'More wine, madam?' said a waiter.

'Yes, please,' said Immy.

'He seems keen,' said Lando.

'Who, the waiter?'

'The politician.'

'So?'

'Be careful, that's all.'

'I hardly think you're in a position to give me advice,' she said, when her toothy neighbour passed a shiny silver pen to her.

'You vape?' he said. 'I've been reduced to sucking on this piece of metal. The Imperial Tobacco founders must be turning in their graves.' He looked at Immy. 'Let's take a selfie.'

'What?' said Immy.

'I like to record special moments in Dublin, and you two are on my table and this is a special moment.'

Standing up, he held his phone out in front of them and popped his head between Immy and Lando.

'Say Camembert,' he said.

Immy stared at the screen and saw Lando's face next to her. She had to get away.

The jazz band on stage began to play.

'Let's dance?' said the man.

'I really don't dance,' she said.

'Yes, you do, Immy, go on,' said Lando. 'She was born to dance.'

Immy scowled at Lando, pushing back her chair.

'I'm going to the ladies,' she said, and standing up, she felt immediately unsteady on her heels, the straps cutting into her ankles. The dance floor filled quickly with a crowd-pleasing rendition of 'All I Want for Christmas is You'. Abandoning her venture to the ladies, Immy instead plunged herself into the centre of the dance floor and let her body sway to the music. She raised her arms and began to feel incredibly sexy in her long dress. She imagined people watching her as she danced and felt so in sync with the beat.

Chapter Thirty

Lando knew he and Immy were caught in a place neither of them recognised. Their friendship had somehow disintegrated into something that felt uncomfortable and yet he couldn't keep away from it. Celine wanted him to dance but he needed to splash water over his face and get a fresh perspective. The entire evening felt uncomfortable.

Lando could hear whoops from the dance floor as he made his way to the gents. Towards the end of the corridor, he saw a man who could only have been Immy's politician, standing with a woman, whose dark plaited hair reached far down her back. Her eyes were heavily lined with kohl, her lips were full, and she wore too much blusher.

Flynn didn't seem to notice Lando was standing within earshot.

'I've been sitting next to one of your colleagues, who insists on sucking up to me,' said the woman.

Flynn slid his hand around her waist. 'Why not suck up to me instead?' he said.

'You are a bold man,' said the woman, tapping his nose.

'I popped into the kitchen earlier and downed a few oysters.'

'Well then,' she said, opening a door next to them.

'It's a sports cupboard,' said Flynn, switching on the light. 'Look at the golf bags.'

Lando pressed his hand over his mouth and tried to fathom what he'd just heard. Whatever about golf bags, this man was a pure sleazebag.

'You know, I don't think I've had a good shag since—'

'Friday?' she said. 'In your shower.'

'The architect was right when he insisted on installing a large shower in my bathroom,' he said. 'You never quite know when an orgy might come on the agenda.'

Lando could not believe what he was hearing. This innocent man from Leitrim, who seemed so earnest.

'I found the twins got pretty jealous,' Lando heard her say before she pulled the door shut. 'Next time, only bring one.'

★

As the music ramped up, so did Immy, a slight sweat on her body, feeling so good, so free. She didn't feel at all shy, thanks to the wine coursing through her veins. Her lace underwear kept slipping down from her bottom, and every so often she'd hike it up, loving the lightweight feel of her silky dress. After each song, she'd think about dashing to the ladies to re-adjust her underwear, but she was having such a good time, feeling anonymous on the dance floor, she didn't want to leave. The next thing she knew, her black pants fell further down her thighs, to her knees and then to her ankles until they cuffed her ankles together like a three-legged race. Except there was no third leg; she was quite alone when she felt briefly airborne and landed heavily on the dance floor. She couldn't hear any gasps above the music, but closing her eyes she knew people were looking down, staring at her, feeling sorry for her, laughing at her. She'd have to open her eyes and get up. Her elbow hurt, and her cheek felt bruised. Just one more moment and then she'd face the music. Someone took hold of her waist and, taking her hand, gently lifted Immy onto her feet.

'That was a proper fall, Immy, are you OK?'

Her eyes met with Lando. He looked very concerned and his voice was so full of sympathy she couldn't hardly stand it. She was not OK and, dropping her head, she could feel her eyes stinging with tears. In the old days, she might have found it funny, she and Lando would have laughed it off, had a shot of vodka and partied on – but not now. She felt like a clown, like a goat in a silk dress. This wasn't a world she belonged to.

'Let's get some ice on your cheek, Immy,' said Lando, but she pulled away, ignoring his offer of help. Now beyond excruciating embarrassment, she pulled up her pants, took off her heels and carefully walked across the parquet floor. She'd find Flynn. He'd soothe her, understand her and they could laugh about her fall, return to her flat and spend the night together. Maybe she could rescue the situation, after all, she just needed to find him. Or maybe she was still drunk.

Immy stood in the corridor outside the Round Room. She wiped her fingers beneath her eyes and saw a sign for the ladies at the end of the corridor. First, she'd take off her underwear and then tidy up her make-up, though she'd left her clutch bag on the table, including her phone. She felt quite tipsy and made an instant decision to block out what had happened on the dance floor with Lando. It was just classic for her to find herself in that position, and Lando wouldn't have been surprised. At least now they could officially avoid each other, as she was beyond caring. Immy walked along the corridor when a woman in a black dress slid out from a side room, looking behind her as Flynn followed, wiping his mouth, his forehead glistening with sweat.

'Immy, there you are,' he said.

The woman stopped for a moment and looked at Immy. 'He's all yours now,' she said. 'I just hope I didn't wear him out.'

'What?' said Immy. 'Flynn?'

'Don't mind her,' he said, rubbing his hand down her cheek. 'She's had too much to drink, and I think the same could be said for you.'

He was right, Immy had had far too much to drink and just wanted to go home.

'You are gorgeous, aren't you?' he said, putting his hands on her shoulders.

Immy looked at him, lipstick staining the corner of his mouth. 'Get off me,' she screamed. 'Take your filthy hands off me.'

'There's no need for that,' he said, looking up and down the corridor and obviously relieved there was no one there. 'She's just an old friend, and we work together sometimes and get together other times.'

'You're disgusting,' yelled Immy. She tried taking off a shoe to throw at him, but the sandal was strapped on, and she didn't have the patience to unbuckle it. Flynn tried to reach out for her, but Immy screamed, 'Get away from me,' and he did just that, running down the corridor and disappearing through double doors.

Immy tried to slow down her breathing and then realised her underwear was slipping down her thighs again. How could the night be so cruel to her? She felt utterly humiliated, she had never in her life felt so out of control. For what seemed like a minute, but may have been longer, she stood still, trying to work out her next move. She'd have to take a taxi and ask if she could pay them tomorrow. There was no way she could go back into the Round Room, just in case he was there.

Immy pushed her hair back from her face and took a deep breath. Slowly, she walked down the corridor towards the exit, where a doorman looked at her so kindly.

'Can I get you a taxi, madam?'

'Please,' she said, trying to remember if she had even

brought a coat with her. The shock of everything had made the night unbelievably blurry.

'We've been looking for you,' said Celine.

Lando handed Immy's bag to her.

'Thank you,' said Immy. There was no point worrying about how she looked at this stage, a bruise on her face maybe, and smudged mascara most likely. All Immy could focus on was keeping her breathing calm and holding up her underwear. If it wasn't so awful it might have been funny, but Immy knew there was nothing at all funny about this night.

'Let's get a cab together,' said Celine, who turned to Lando. 'I really don't think she should be alone.'

'*She* is fine,' said Immy, making sure not to make eye contact with Lando, but accepting a hug from Celine, who must have known something was up. Immy wasn't even sure if Lando had told her about the fall on the dance floor.

Within seconds she climbed into a car and managed to give her address. 'Thirty Merrion Street,' she said.

'Only round the corner, love,' said the driver. 'Did you have a good night?'

Immy didn't respond and concentrated on finding a twenty-euro note she'd stashed in the inside pocket of her bag.

On the short drive home, she curled her knees to her mouth and felt like the greatest fool on earth.

Chapter Thirty-One

The crescent of the moon looked like it was trying with all its might to squeeze through the night sky as the taxi driver waited, like an angel, until she'd pushed the key into the door of number 30. She turned to signal an OK sign to him before closing the door. All she wanted to do was sink her face into her pillow and cry herself to sleep.

She padded up the stairs, holding the rail just as she held in her tears, until she reached the third-floor flat.

'Immy?' came a voice from the sitting room. She'd completely forgotten Janette was staying, which was why the door to the flat was already unlocked. Was she losing her mind? Immy just wanted to be alone and to freak out in royal style, maybe drink her head off or eat a box of cereal; she literally didn't know if she was coming or going.

Janette stood at the sitting room door in a green dressing gown and pink fluffy slippers. She must have read Immy's expression, as she took Immy into her arms and patted her back like a housemistress or kind hospital matron. It felt like the first time in years that Immy had cried properly. She cried for her mother, remembering her hand waving out the car window, her long fingers, wafting in the air as she drifted out of Immy's life, occasional phone calls turning into text messages and the occasional postcard from Spain written in an illegible scrawl.

Her fall on the dance floor had opened a box which had held her shame of having to make up stories in school about her parents, pretending all was well at home and never telling anyone about her father's decisions dictated by the bottle. Nothing in her life had been on her own terms, even the dress she was wearing.

'Why can't I break away from all of this?' said Immy, lifting her head, wiping her eyes with Janette's handkerchief.

'That handkerchief is Shillington's finest, I'll have you know,' said Janette, which made Immy laugh just a little. 'You poor girl, it looks like you've had a rotten evening.'

Janette brought Immy over to the sofa. 'Even if this is my bed for the night, I think you'd better sit down there while I make you some hot milk and honey,' said Janette, puffing up the sofa cushions.

Janette returned with a jar of honey, twisted open the lid and dipped in a teaspoon.

'Natural sugar,' she said, 'for the shock.'

'You think I'm in shock?' said Immy, putting the sweet honey into her mouth, making her think of a birthday cake when she was tiny. Three yellow ducks, creamy icing, sweet like honey. Another surge of tears came, her shoulders aching from the release.

'I'm no therapist,' said Janette, 'but it seems to me like you've had a tough time, kiddo.'

Even though Immy hadn't voiced what was going on in her mind, she felt relieved to be understood by someone other than Lando. He was the only person who knew the true ins and outs of her past.

'Now it's time for me to put my skills to work before you turn into a pumpkin,' said Janette, propping up a mirror on the side table in the sitting room and covering a tray with a towel, tubes of product and cotton pads. She studied Immy's face. 'We'll take off the make-up first, then I'm going to put some of my soothing cucumber balm around your eyes, they're very puffy.'

She took the Kirby grips out of Immy's hair and brushed out the long strands, releasing a scent of hairspray.

'We've all had hard times, haven't we?' said Janette. 'I think you'll look back on this night, Immy, as your turning point.'

'You think so?'

'I do,' said Janette. 'Now close your eyes, I'm going to apply some cleanser. This is a special Christmas edition; can you smell the cinnamon?'

Immy's bottom lip began to tremble again.

'It's just—'

'What is it, Immy?'

'I'm afraid to be like her,' she said, one eye open as Janette swept cotton beneath the other, taking away tear stains and mascara.

'Like who?' Janette spoke very gently.

'My mum,' said Immy.

'Immy, you are your own person—' Janette applied toner to Immy's forehead '—and as pure as the botanicals in this product; you are making your own way.'

'I'm not though, am I? I live under Shillington's roof.'

'And what's wrong with that? Why shouldn't they help you? You're Lando's best friend.'

'Was,' said Immy.

'Is or was, makes no difference.' Janette pressed the cotton pads on Immy's eyes, absorbing the tears. 'When I was doing my make-up courses I was living with my dad in his council flat and took over his bathroom with my concoctions. It made sense until I could have my own place.'

'But you've got a proper career,' said Immy, 'and you have proper training whereas I've got a ridiculous title and all I seem to do is give relationship advice when it's Celine who chooses all the clothes. She's the personal shopper, not me; I don't think my job is leading anywhere.'

'You may think that,' said Janette, 'but things are always leading somewhere, you just have to believe that you are on the right path, and I know more than anyone that it isn't always easy, but if I were to count the number of times I was about to give up, I'd have no fingers left.' Janette twisted the lid off another tube of lotion. 'My dad encouraged me to keep going with my training when I wanted to pack it in. We lived on baked beans and hard-boiled eggs for two years while he paid for my training, and you know what I'm going to do? I'm going to set up my own make-up range; I'm determined.'

Immy began to feel a little better.

'I had this dream, clear as crystal,' said Janette. 'I was sitting at a big round table on the top floor of a skyrise in Nantucket with big executive types. Not the kind of place you'd expect to find yourself with a suitcase full of serum and moisturiser, but it was the ingredients, you see. The suits said I had the right ingredients, and they weren't just talking about my product, either.'

'You were the ingredient?' said Immy.

'In the dream at least, yes, and they said I had the belief and the drive to bring it to market, I just needed the distribution. It was like an episode of *Dragons' Den*.' Janette massaged the lotion onto Immy's face, which still felt so tense. 'But you know what? Even though it was just a dream, I can remember the feeling of being like one of those businesswomen,' she said. 'If you can feel it, you can be it,' said Janette. 'Try to remember this if you can.'

They rode the four-minute taxi ride from the Mansion house to the Merrion Hotel in silence. The driver must have tuned in to the situation as he made no attempt to chat.

'Would you like to come up to my room?' Celine's voice sounded as tense as Lando felt. He was seriously worried about Immy. What the hell was the guy playing at? Lando wanted to punch Flynn to the floor and maybe it was just lucky he and Celine left when they did.

'I'm not sure,' he said. 'Sorry, I think I might just head home. It's been a weird night.'

'I think you should come upstairs with me.' Celine was definite, and there was a part of him that knew he needed to make a call on moving things forward with Celine or not.

Lando peeped his head through the bedroom curtains and found a garden view of box hedges, pretty pathways and a fountain lit up by tiny lights.

'Help yourself to a drink,' said Celine. 'I'll be back in a moment.'

Lando thought about opening the mini bar, but when Celine disappeared into the bathroom, he had an urge to leave. Maybe he could slip out the door and send an apologetic text message. He could fake a tummy bug or a headache. 'Not tonight, Josephine,' was what he wanted to say, but how could he? Celine had been consoling and supportive, as well as putting huge amounts of energy into improving Shillington's.

When the bathroom door opened, Lando looked up to find Celine dressed in a lace-adorned slip nightie, skimming just below her thighs. She didn't speak as she walked towards him and in response Lando moved to the bed, kicked off his shoes and undid his bow tie. Crawling slowly across the bed,

Celine reached up to Lando and, with both hands, lowered him flat on his back. She looked incredible, smoky eyes, plump lips and scent of woody orange blossom. He tried to fix his mind on her, knowing he was living an experience which could only be a dream for so many, and yet he found himself observing the soft blues and grey paint colours on the wall.

'I have spritzed scent in every area I want to be kissed,' she whispered, as she straddled him. 'Aren't you going to take off your pants?'

Lando looked up at her, this French goddess who was trying her darndest to seduce him, and yet he couldn't. It didn't feel right. He didn't feel right.

'I'm so sorry, Celine. I truly am.'

Chapter Thirty-Two

Carol singers sang in acapella at the top of Grafton Street. The weather was indeed crisp and even, and Delia was feeling slightly encouraged by Shillington's. De Croix's adjustments, though small, gave each department head a fresh purpose and sense of pride in what they were selling. Even Social Media Christian seemed to be making an impact, with a visit from a woman with hair practically down to her ankles and claiming to have an obscene number of followers. She requested a complimentary lunch in exchange for a photo and review of Shillington's tea rooms, but Christian was sceptical and recommended starting with hot chocolate and marshmallow fluff on the house, and once new followers were generated, they may progress to a freebie lunch.

What was it about this time of year that made Delia feel so much like a widow? It wasn't as if Gregory had been big into Christmas. He was more of a summertime lover, climbing mountains, swimming in rivers and fishing. The great outdoors, and even though he claimed to be happy to inherit Shillington's, she wondered how he would have fared long term. Delia felt almost sure they would have sold up a long time ago, and maybe Lando would have his own, wholly unrelated career. The curse of inheritance, she whispered to herself.

'Imogen,' she said, seeing her standing outside Butlers with a takeaway coffee.

'Hi there,' she said. Delia thought she looked rather peaky. 'Are you all right?'

'I'm OK,' she said, 'but thanks for asking.'

Immy drove Delia mad at times. She seemed frequently distracted, and Delia never understood why she insisted on wearing so much black when there are so many feminine colours available.

'I'd better get back,' said Immy. 'I've got a client arriving in fifteen minutes.'

Delia checked her watch and knew she didn't hide her disapproval at Immy's apparent lackadaisical approach to client preparation.

'Good idea,' said Delia, nodding and managing to smile before a group of students with yellow rucksacks swarmed in front of her. She noticed Imogen had dropped a folded piece of paper at her heel and she called after her, but it was pointless over the teenage din.

★

In the shower that morning, Immy had conditioned her hair twice before using shampoo and had added filter coffee straight into her mug rather than into the machine. Janette had been incredibly supportive. The hot milk and honey had helped Immy to sleep, despite the vast amounts of wine she'd drunk, but her hangover paled in comparison to the embarrassment she felt for being taken in by the grotesque Flynn. She felt so cross with herself and made a vow never to be fooled like that again.

Whatever about seeing Lando again, the encounter with Delia outside Butlers had been a nightmare and thank goodness they'd met in the open air. It would have been typical of Delia, with her razor-sharp senses, to bust Immy for smelling of alcohol. Immy just had to get through today and then she could go home and roll into a ball. That was her main goal of the day. To get home and see nobody.

Her afternoon client had booked a session to buy winter shoes. Footwear was something Immy felt she could handle. In a very quick research session, she learned that her client carried weight, and not just on his waistline. He was the owner of a haulage empire as well as an environmentalist, famously planting over 2,000 acres of reclaimed land on his Wicklow estate. But more than that, he was the man who had been in and out of Delia's life for at least the past decade. Immy hadn't been introduced to Gerhardt properly, but she knew Lando quite liked him and used to encourage his mother to take the relationship seriously until she'd told him in no uncertain terms to keep out of her romantic life, because 'it doesn't exist'. At least that was what Delia had said to him.

'I'm in haulage,' said Gerhardt Klune, sitting heavily on the sofa opposite Immy. 'I'm also eccentric, or so they tell me, and for my sins, I'm a hopeless romantic.'

'I like your braces,' said Immy.

'My late wife chose them,' he said, 'she was a fan of mallards, and so I have ties and socks, even pyjamas with ducks on them if you can imagine, though perhaps you'd better not.' He had a lovely sense of humour, and his white beard made him look like a younger version of Santa Claus. Immy decided he was handsome, and despite his pretty large size, he looked healthy.

'Has anyone said you look like Brian Cox?' said Immy.

'Hah, and I ask you, do you mean the actor or the professor?'

'Oh, definitely the actor, as in *Succession*.'

'I'd take both accusations as compliments, and though I've heard of *Succession* I don't watch any television, or Netflix, or YouTube, but I do read the *New York Times*, *The Irish Times*, *The Times* and the *Financial Times*; how about that for an old timer?'

'Pretty good,' said Immy, feeling brightened in his company. 'Then how about shoes, are you looking for smart or casual?'

'The whole shooting match,' he said. 'Every five years

I buy new shoes for everything, so I'm talking loafers, brogues, sneakers, slippers, Birkenstocks. If it has a sole and feels good, then I want it.

Immy excused herself and went over to her desk to send a WhatsApp to Celine. They had worked out a system, where Celine had a range of styles ready in the next-door room, and on Immy's signal she'd arrive with the correct sizing and very many options.

'You are a size nine?' said Immy, who already had this information, but wanted to double-check so as to appear efficient.

'That's right, in footwear, though in age I feel about twenty-one, far from my seventy-one years.'

'And do you have a spend in mind?' Immy liked to ask this question so as not to presume clients wanted to spend a fortune.

'I don't mind,' he said. 'As long as the quality is there, I'll pay anything for good shoes.'

Immy returned to her sofa and filled their glasses with kombucha.

'Like a mint?' he said, taking a small silver box from his pocket.

'Yes, please,' said Immy, thinking they could only help with her paranoia of alcohol fumes.

'And you like your job?'

'Actually, yes, I think I do.' She was surprised by her entirely honest reply. In the past, when clients had occasionally asked her that same question, she'd often just said yes and had changed the subject before they could accuse her of being insincere.

'Almost every woman I meet now claims to have a personal shopper,' he said. 'But not Delia. She insists on doing everything herself, even running this place.'

'She's quite a lady,' said Immy.

'And the only reason I've been shopping here.' Gerhardt was very animated and made lovely expressions with his eyes. 'You think I don't know about online shopping? And certainly, it would be much easier than trekking here from Wicklow, but I suppose I'm a stupid old lovesick fool.'

'And are you going to see her?' Immy wasn't quite sure what to say.

'No,' he said, 'she gave up on me a long time ago.' He placed the silver box of mints on the table. 'We went to the same school, and you know, I think I loved her from the very moment I saw her.'

'That's amazing,' said Immy, seeing the look in his eyes. 'And what happened?'

'We were only kids,' he said, laughing, 'and being older, I left school long before she did and we went our separate ways, but I always looked out for her, no matter where I was.'

'Did you know her husband?'

'I did, and he was a very fine man.'

Immy thought of Lando for the millionth time, and of the times they'd discussed what his father must have been like. Lando said Delia could hardly bear to have photographs of

Gregory in the house because it was too painful. Even in Shillington's when the staff had wanted to mount a portrait of him, with a memorial plaque, rather than a brass plaque announcing his title as chairman and CEO, she'd vetoed it.

Gerhardt stretched out his arms and yawned. 'Excuse me,' he said, 'I'm a widower and don't have a woman to remind me of my manners.'

'You're perfect as you are,' said Immy, who couldn't resist wondering if Delia could be ready for a new romance.

Chapter Thirty-Three

The Northeast Business Park on the outskirts of Dublin did not look like the most creative location for an ad agency, but once inside, the visuals were electric, literally. There were neon retro 1950s signs, murals of Irish rock legends, from U2 to Thin Lizzy, and a twenty-foot spiralling ladder covered in multicoloured lights.

'It's our sustainable version of a Christmas tree,' said a young account executive. 'Even our mince pies are vegan. Would you like to try them?'

'No, thanks,' said Lando, knowing Uncle Stanley would rather eat cardboard than touch 'fake meat', as he called it. He was equally disparaging about 'fake beer'.

'I'll go find Gilda,' said the account executive, 'and if you like—'

It sounded like they were about to be offered further vegan delights when a crashing sound came from across the hallway, followed by a shriek.

Lando and Uncle Stanley looked at each other.

Another bang came, prompting the account executive to excuse himself and speed-walk to the source of chaos.

'What's going on?' said Uncle Stanley, taking a hand-kerchief from his pocket and pressing it to his forehead. 'Any chance they'll offer us a *real* ham sandwich? It's very close to lunch.'

'It's ten-thirty a.m.,' said Lando, admiring Uncle Stanley's orange velvet suit.

'I was up early,' he said, picking up a leaflet on yoga. 'Shirley wanted to try out one of her smoothies on me, and if my lips look like they've been on the claret, you'd be sadly mistaken, as it's beetroot.'

'And it tasted good?'

'Like rocket fuel, actually,' he said. 'I think our Shirley's got rather a knack for making up her own recipes, as long as she stays away from the turkey and strawberry concoction; that was purely revolting.'

A vision of leopard print came bounding towards them.

'Darlings, there you are,' said Gilda Winterbottom. 'You are sweet to come.'

'Not at all,' said Uncle Stanley, clearly charmed by the redheaded chief executive. 'You were very good to turn the ad around so quickly.'

'Anything for Jimmy,' she said, patting the back of her short hair, 'he's a legend around here.' She turned to Lando. 'And are you gorgeous, or what?' she said. 'Though don't have me up for sexual harassment, will you?' And she burst into cackles of laughter.

'All OK,' said Lando. 'But we'd love to see the ad.'

'We actually loved your idea, Lando,' said Gilda, scrolling through her phone. 'And we're really pleased with the finished result. Let me just call Studio A and make sure we can access the screening room.'

'Good on you, Lando, for seeing this through,' said Uncle Stanley.

Lando was feeling nervous, particularly with this flighty creative in their midst. Gilda was the very definition of volatile. 'Fancy a sausage roll before tucking into the ad, Stanners, darling?'

'Is it real?' he said.

'Alas, we're very on trend around here, so it's fake sausies all the way,' she said, taking hot-pink spectacles from her pocket and putting them on. She looked vaguely intellectual in a sort of pop-star kind of way. 'I do have real champagne, though, how about that?'

'Wouldn't say no to a glass,' said Uncle Stanley. 'What about you, Landers?' He elbowed Lando and seemed to be loving Gilda's influence.

'You go ahead,' said Lando. 'I don't think Mum will thank me if I drink and drive her beloved Mercedes.'

'The relic, old as time,' said Uncle Stanley.

'Fabulous,' said Gilda, who took two snipes of champagne from the fridge. 'No corks, sadly,' she said. 'I do miss the pop, but I suppose a twist isn't so bad.' She opened both bottles and popped in the gold sip flutes into the neck. Her phone pinged.

'Green light, darlings,' she said. 'Onwards to the studio.'

And, turning around, she yelled at the account executive, 'Julien, bring me a refill for my vape, would you?'

To keep up with Gilda, Stanley had to walk double his usual pace, but it was worth it. The screen room was impressive, with eight spaced-out green velvet chairs and a small stage. Gold-frame posters of Jessie Buckley, Liam Cunningham, Jamie Dornan and Ruth Negga lined the walls, making it all feel very Hollywood.

A man with peppered hair and a tightly cut beard arrived in the room.

'How are you, fellas? I'm Bruce.' He raised his hands in a greeting to avoid the handshake, which suited Stanley fine. He was feeling pretty worn out.

'Anything to drink, guys? A kombucha or water?'

'We've got the bubbly, Bruce darling,' said Gilda, putting her feet up on the back of the chair in front of her, displaying fine slender ankles. 'Now, let's move it along, shall we?' Gilda knew how to give instructions.

Bruce held out a gadget towards the floor-to-ceiling screen. An image of a bleak back garden appeared. 'Before I press play, just so you know, this ad is purely to put Shillington's on the radar of those online,' said Bruce, 'thus reaching out to a new audience, which is both time-efficient and in tune with the spend available.'

'Grand,' said Uncle Stanley, rubbing his hands together as he settled back into the viewing chair.

Bruce clicked the button, and the ad began.

'Here comes the music,' said Bruce, as Christmas bells were followed by very sweet ukulele. 'A once beloved and simple kitchen table is looking wretched and unloved outside in rain and snow and storms,' he said.

'It's exactly as I imagined,' said Lando.

'And here is the little girl,' said Bruce, 'in the sitting room, looking at an old black and white photograph of the very same table with her grandfather as a boy, sitting around it and laughing with his family.'

'So good,' said Lando.

'And there she is, whispering to her old Grandpa, who's in bed,' said Bruce. 'And this part was inspired, Lando, there's Grandpa, as you described, seeing the photo and his eyes light up. Next up, tah-dah, the family have the table in their kitchen, it's dried out and decorated head to toe in crackers and whatnot, and here comes Grandpa, wheeled in and everyone cries and feels the spirit of Christmas.'

Stanley got to his feet, overcome with emotion, and began clapping. 'It's genius,' he said, 'pure genius.' He wiped his eyes and sat down again.

'Good work, Brucie,' said Gilda. 'Do make sure to increase the font of the Shillington's logo, and then send this baby out to cyberspace, and may it make the public weep, set their satnav to St Stephen's Green and prepare to spend their well-earned money in our very favourite department store.'

'Cheers to that,' said Stanley, who wondered if he could ever tame the red-headed vixen.

Chapter Thirty-Four

Leslie's love-heart-shaped tin of biscuits sat on Immy's desk like a trophy. The symbolism meant the world to her. Even if it was sheer chance that Leslie and Bill had arrived at PS Headquarters at the same time, they'd found each other, that was the main thing. She opened her notebook and drew a love heart and a tiny Christmas tree next to her notes on body language. She hadn't heard from David and Tanya but maybe Cupid existed after all. She was feeling quite heartened following her meeting with Gerhardt, and it was extraordinary to have such insights into Delia, which made her sound much more human. She hadn't really considered how hard it must have been for Delia when her husband died on the same day her baby was born. And how difficult it must have been for Lando to have grown up having never met his father whilst living in the shadow of his legacy. Immy was feeling both guilty about and estranged from Lando.

'Hello?' came a voice through the crack in the door. 'Immy, are you there?'

'Come on in, Delia.' Immy stood up at her desk, as Delia

would expect. 'Would you like to sit down?'

'Not at all, but thank you,' said Delia, handing a folded piece of paper to Immy. 'This dropped from your pocket this morning when we met on Grafton Street.'

'Thank you,' said Immy, opening the note. 'It's just a receipt from my coffee, which I'd folded up, but that's really kind.'

'Well, I'm not one to be too nosy, and I of course didn't open it.'

'Still, it's kind of you,' said Immy.

'I do love colour,' said Delia, running her hands along the rail of dresses. 'Aren't these dresses pretty?'

'Celine has been amazingly helpful,' said Immy.

'That's Paris for you,' said Delia. 'Elegance breeds elegance, that's what my mother always said.'

Immy thought of her own mother and realised if what Delia said was true, then there was little wonder why Immy didn't feel elegant.

'I always think of the dress Amal Clooney wore on the cover of *Hello!*, honey gold, in last week's magazine,' said Delia. 'That's the sort of colour you should be recommending to customers this coming spring, Immy.'

Immy wasn't sure what to say. Maybe she wouldn't be working at Shillington's in the spring. Maybe she could do a course, taking a leaf out of Janette's book. Perhaps the time had come for Immy to make a big effort with her family because it was, after all, the only one she had.

'Well,' said Delia, 'I'm glad I've reunited you with your note.'

'Thanks again,' she said.

'Bye then,' said Delia, turning for the door.

'Actually, Delia, speaking of clients, I hope you won't mind my mentioning this, but I had a gentleman here this afternoon who apparently knows you.'

'Sorry?'

'His name is Gerhardt.'

'Oh Lord,' she said, blushing slightly but firmly rooted on the spot. Immy wasn't quite sure if Delia wanted to talk, so she prodded very gently.

'He said you were in school together.'

Delia surprised Immy by walking to the sofa and sitting down.

'He was in upper sixth when I was in my first year,' she said. 'Almost seven years older than me.'

'He seems fond of you,' said Immy, who was feeling so tired at this point she knew her inhibitions were lower than usual.

Delia took a pillow, placed it on her lap and rested her hands on top as if she was about to receive Holy Communion. 'A couple of years following Gregory's death, people asked me if I was ready to date. Can you imagine?'

Immy shook her head.

'Their thinking was that I should have a man in the house for Lando, the father figure that people speak of, but my brain literally couldn't compute that Gregory wasn't coming back.' Delia hunched her shoulders and stared at the notebook on the table. 'Twenty-seven years later, I'm still not sure I understand it. He was taken from me so suddenly.'

'Does it help that your husband got to hold Lando?'

Delia nodded and said, 'Yes,' and laughed a little. 'If you could have seen how proud he was, thrilled that Lando looked just like him, and he really does, like father, like son, and it breaks my heart.' Her eyes filled with tears so incredibly quickly and Immy wasn't sure about moving over to the sofa to comfort her. Delia was usually so reserved. 'I suppose there is a part of me that is bitter and maybe after all this time I need to let go.' Delia burst into tears.

Immy took the plunge and sat next to Delia, attempting to put her arms around her.

'Oh no,' said Delia, pulling herself together, 'that won't be necessary.'

Instead, Immy reached for the box of tissues and passed them to Delia to deflect the rejection, which seemed to give them both something to focus on.

'Thank you for the tissue, Immy,' she said, pressing the Kleenex against her nose. 'You are a kind girl.'

Immy moved back to the opposite sofa.

'You won't say anything to Lando, will you?'

'No,' said Immy, though in truth she thought she may have to.

'But tell me, what did Gerhardt say?'

'You really want to know?' said Immy.

'I do.'

'He likes you,' said Immy. 'He thinks you're a real lady, intelligent, and he literally would love to take you to dinner.'

Delia looked flattered. Immy could hardly believe it, as

she was expecting the idea to be basted like a turkey on Christmas Day.

'Do you think I should, if he asked me?' said Delia.

Immy had never, ever imagined giving Delia advice on her love life. She had never asked Immy's opinion about as much as a clothes-hanger.

'Well, um, I think,' Immy stumbled, but then gathered herself. 'I would say, why not? He's a kind man, he's fun and I bet he can mix a good cocktail.'

'All true,' said Delia, 'all true.'

And that was the end of the conversation. Delia stood up and fanned out the pleats of her skirt.

'I've taken up far too much of your time, Imogen, I am sorry.'

'Not at all, any time you want to talk.'

Delia looked appalled at the suggestion that she and Immy would 'talk' and made it clear the previous conversation hadn't really happened.

'Where will you be for Christmas?' she said to Immy, returning to formal conversation.

'My parents have invited me to Spain.'

'How kind.'

'Well, I guess they are my parents.'

Delia didn't seem to register what Immy was saying, and visibly straightening her back, she reverted to her controlled self.

★

Delia descended the stairs to her office and breathed deeply to erase the embarrassing display in front of Immy. And she certainly wasn't going to enquire further when Imogen said she was going to spend Christmas with her parents. If Delia didn't approve of Immy, she approved of her parents even less. When Immy was a teenager, it wasn't uncommon for either of her parents to turn up half-drunk when collecting her. Delia didn't encourage any sort of relationship with the family, despite the friendship between their children. Certainly, a part of her felt guilty because she knew she was hard on Immy, but they were employing her, and she was renting number 30. That Lando was now fixated on Celine was a relief, and even de Croix as an in-law was preferable to what she was sure were horrific alternatives out there.

As for Gerhardt, she worried about getting serious with him. For starters, he was a great deal older than she, not to mention he lived in the wilds of County Wicklow. And why should love come to her table now? Before she could consider anything, a decision had to be made about Shillington's and she was giving herself a Christmas Eve deadline. There was no way she and Lando were going to spend another Christmas in limbo land. Sales figures would decide their fate.

Chapter Thirty-Five

Frustration was an understatement of how de Croix was feeling. There was still no answer from Julie's mobile phone, and their maid, whom de Croix suspected disapproved of him, was of little help. His wife was out shopping, apparently, and there had been no guests – not a single additional person in the house since de Croix had left. But should he believe it? This was the perfect opportunity for Julie to have her revenge on their marriage. She was a beautiful woman; there wasn't a man in Paris who wouldn't relish a night with her and her silk negligée. In the past year, the lovemaking in their marriage had turned to duty sex, which was something he'd sworn would never happen. De Croix was a man of standards, which included pleasing his wife. When had he stopped trying to please her?

'Oh, dear God, forgive me,' he whispered to himself in his suite at the Merrion. What an opportunity lost. Why had he not brought Julie with him? They could have ventured into the fresh streets of wintery Dublin together. She with her long, fabulous woollen coats, and he, dashing in a tweed flat cap, like the stylish Irishman Cillian Murphy. They had such fun during the early years, doting over Celine and the tidiness of their lives. But the magic had gone. His obsessive business interests were certainly to blame, but he knew all in all it was his mistresses that had broken it.

In the rare moments that Julie had crossed paths with one of de Croix's mistresses, he'd made sure they would always address her formally with '*vous*'. He'd reminded himself that Julie had stated from the outset that she had never expected total honesty from him. But now that Julie's own honesty was in doubt, de Croix could literally not bear it. His cousin, who lived around the corner from their apartment, claimed he saw a younger man entering the doorway to the de Croix's building, and that Julie, looking ill at ease, was there to greet him. The recipe was not working. He would wrap up his time early at Shillington's, bow out and upon his return to Paris he would walk to Les Invalides and ask Gregory for his forgiveness next to Napoleon's tomb.

. De Croix stood outside the door to PS Headquarters, which had a rustic Christmas wooden heart decoration on the handle.

'Immy, may I speak with you?' he said. 'It's de Croix.'

Immy opened the door and looked almost professional. Welcoming him in, she ushered him to a chair and then sat at her desk like an executive.

'How can I help?' she said, as if he was there to share secrets.

'I've been looking over the sales figures and things are not adding up.'

'I'm sorry to hear that,' she said.

'You have clients, that's clear,' he said, 'but for the amount of time you spend with them, I'm not seeing the return.'

'In what way?' said Immy. 'The clients I've met so far seem very satisfied.'

'But they aren't spending to my satisfaction,' he said. 'As I am overseeing the margins of Shillington's, I'm going to need you to pull your weight.'

'But I—'

He could feel his face turning red, which made him feel even more irate.

'I don't want excuses, Immy—' De Croix raised his voice; it slightly croaked '—I want you to sell more products, clothes, shoes, crockery. I don't care what you sell, but I want results.'

She remained silent, which was wise of her.

'I'm sorry for shouting,' he said, 'but I want to be completely clear with you.'

'It's fine,' she said. 'I grew up with my father yelling at me, so I'm used to it.'

De Croix felt genuinely sorry. Whether she sold ten or twenty designer dresses would be only a drop in the ocean for what Shillington's needed. He was procrastinating, struggling with his announcement to Delia that he was going home. 'Business is business,' he said, rising from his chair. 'We are not a charity. The sales are still down, and even though we've been busy, the targets are not being met.'

Immy got up from her desk and held the door open for

him. He felt like a rat at sea as he took out his phone to make a call.

'Louis, *c'est moi*, de Croix. You have been seeking to expand your holdings in Europe, and I know of a property that you can turn into six or seven hundred apartments. Email me and I'll send you details and advise on when to approach. The family business is tender, and I expect they will sell without big demands. This is, I believe, quite the opportunity for you.'

Undeniably, de Croix felt guilty, but Shillington's clearly wasn't going to make it – and besides, there was no one capable there to run it. The spark had gone. They were Gregory's family, and they were good people, but not businesspeople. It was better to give a private buyer the heads-up rather than putting the family through the humiliation of seeking a buyer, with the risk of public scrutiny, which may affect their asking price. But what more could he do on behalf of Gregory? He had trained the staff, created a Christmas window of supreme quality, and added baubles worthy of Le Marché Cher. But to no avail; the public just wasn't biting. They would never meet their targets – it would take a miracle.

★

In the social media hub of Shillington's, Stanley sat next to Christian in an office the size of a broom cupboard.

'Whose idea was it to have your office in here?' said Stanley. 'You'll pass out with the heat.'

'I quite like it, actually,' said Christian, wearing what looked like earplugs. 'It's the warmest place in the store and Shirley brings me hot chocolate on the house.'

'Not a bad gig then,' said Stanley, 'but these cramped conditions are not kind to my tweed three-piece, so let's keep this brief.'

'Shillington's Christmas ad is nostalgia at its best,' said Christian, staring straight ahead at a screen of statistics, though he did have a second screen at his elbow, on which a series appeared to be playing. What were the brains of these kids like? Stanley figured they were so hooked on multiple screens, they must have developed a second brain. 'The little girl,' Christian continued, 'manages to change the course of her family's Christmas by showing her grandfather a simple photo, which prompted them to upcycle the once ignored table, transforming it into a hub of family and joy.'

'If you say so,' said Stanley.

'This is the story of a simple table which, when given a little love, like the grandfather, can flourish,' said Christian, who seemed quite enthused. 'In fact, the table symbolises the gramps in the ad, as they are both ignored until the little girl comes along symbolising the innocence of youth, and the buzzword of the year, inclusion.'

'Excellent,' said Stanley, 'and even though I only understand twenty per cent of what you're saying, it sounds like you're going in the right direction.' But the same could not be said for de Croix's phone call earlier. Stanley, who had paused on the stairwell to adjust his cufflinks, had heard every word of that call to Louis. 'Now, Christian, my good fellow, can you send the wind up our competitors and create some good old noise online? We want to reach eighteen-to-twenty-one-year-olds; these are our future consumers.'

'Oh Captain, my Captain, I will.'

'Good lad,' said Stanley.

'That's a quote from Walt Whitman, in case you're wondering,' said Christian, as Stanley stood up and opened the door to find a relief of oxygen. 'My own gramps was American, and he read that same poem to me.'

'And that's why you like this ad, I'm guessing?' said Stanley.

'You bet.'

'Then, I'll tell Shirley to add a few extra marshmallows and a big squirt of caramel cream to your hot chocolate from now on,' said Stanley.

Chapter Thirty-Six

The beauty hall was still relatively quiet, though the 'True You' area Celine had created, featuring shelves stocked with organic, non-toxic and chemical-free products, had increased footfall a little, but it wasn't enough.

'Fancy a complimentary eyebrow stencil?' Janette called out.

'I'm not sure,' said Celine, slumping into the chair at Janette's beauty counter.

'You don't seem like your usual upbeat self,' said Janette. 'How about a sample of this incredible serum to cheer you up?'

'I don't think serum is the answer to my problem.' Celine pressed her chin into her hand.

'Go on then, spill the beans,' said Janette, laying a handful of make-up brushes one by one on the counter. 'A problem solved and all that, and if her ladyship comes along, or your father, I'll tell them we are carrying out quality control on these brushes.'

Janette was like a tonic. Her sense of humour and absence of vanity was something Celine admired, and she wished she could be more like that. The night with Lando hadn't come as a huge surprise. His heart, and body, were meant for Immy, she knew it, but another side of her was put out that her sex appeal had failed. She had purposely waited to sleep with him so they could add fabulous sex on top of their solid foundation of friendship, which was what her parents had done. Her mother, Julie, had always been open about her sex life and had told Celine that when she'd met de Croix, she liked him so much she hadn't wanted to ruin their connection with casual sex. She'd withheld for five months during their courtship, making their connection unbreakable. But history was not to repeat in the de Croix's case, as last night proved. Lando didn't even find her attractive enough to attempt a thrust, despite her position on top.

'You know what, Janette? I think I just got out of bed on the wrong side.'

'Not a problem I have,' said Janette, picking up a brush and tickling Celine's nose. 'I find getting out of bed on any side is tricky.'

Celine decided to lighten up. Here she was at Shillington's to be positive and boost the business into a state where Christmas shoppers could sparkle. There was no point moping about a man who didn't want to sleep with her, even though she was still so fond of him and strangely she didn't feel jealousy towards Immy. She and Lando were obviously made for each other, though it may take an angel to make them realise it.

'Once Shillington's sales pick up,' said Celine, 'I'm going to suggest bringing in a technology where a customer can have their face scanned and try on make-up on screen.'

'So you don't look like a clown after a make-up session?' said Janette.

'Exactly, and it's for all age groups, so clever.'

'I feel really sorry for women coming to me for anything to make or keep them looking like twenty-year-olds,' said Janette, whose eye lashes were not unlike a Jersey cow. 'And I'm like, ladies, you're gorgeous as you are; celebrate your age instead of trying to blot out the wisdom on your faces.'

'Ah, but there are tricks and ways,' said Celine. 'In Paris, a woman over forty would never wear mascara on her bottom lashes during the day and this avoids any smudges.'

Janette dived behind the counter and came up with a slender box between her fingers. 'Unless you apply this baby.'

'*Qu'est-ce que c'est?*' Celine giggled.

'Let me show you.' Janette opened the mascara, pressing the gold top to release the wand. 'Now, move towards me and look into my eyes.'

Celine did as instructed and noticed tiny flecks of green in Janette's brown eyes.

'I'm just applying a new waterproof and conditioning combination, which means you French ladies can doll up your lashes after breakfast with no worries about looking like pandas by lunchtime.'

'You are a very talented make-up artist,' said Celine,

feeling very relaxed. 'If I didn't have to keep my eyes open for you, I'd fall straight to sleep.'

'Siestas are very good for you,' said Janette. 'My brother-in-law pops under his desk for twenty minutes every afternoon and returns to the hot seat like a new man.'

'That sounds very nice.'

'I could do the same if I didn't have her ladyship scanning the halls, but then I've never had any trouble in nodding off and I do have lovely clean sheets to go home to.'

'You live alone?' Celine opened her eyes.

'With my dad,' said Janette, 'but he works night shifts, so as he says, we pass like ships. What about you? Are you a resident of the Chateau de Croix?'

'No,' said Celine. 'How would I get lucky?'

'Whoops,' said Janette, 'there's mascara on your eyelid. Close your eyes for a moment.'

Celine rested her eyes and felt a tiny touch from Janette, which then swept across her brow bone.

'All gone,' said Janette, holding up a mirror to Celine. 'What do you think?'

'I think I'll take you out for lunch and then you can judge if I have panda eyes or not.'

Chapter Thirty-Seven

The brass standing lamp peered over the desk as Delia sat quietly in wait of her audience. Celine arrived just a minute later. Any other girl might have reacted badly to his rejection, though he had never meant to be cruel. Lando had explained to Celine that his mind just wasn't in the right place. As he was so obviously embarrassed, she'd kissed his forehead and told him to go home.

'Nice lamp, Mum,' said Lando.

'De Croix chose it,' she said, quite dismissively. 'Why don't you both sit down?'

Celine sat on a chair in the corner of the room, while Lando sat opposite his mother and crossed his legs.

'Here we are,' said de Croix, marching in with a tray of champagne flutes.

'What are we celebrating, Papa?' Celine said, smiling at Delia.

'We always celebrate the good news with champagne,' said de Croix, passing a flute to Delia and to Celine.

'Lando, darling, close the door, won't you?' said Delia.

He refused a flute and then asked his mum seriously, 'What's going on?'

'Yes, what is it?' said Celine.

'Your father,' she then said, turning to Celine, 'is facilitating a sale, so that we Shillingtons can walk out with our heads held high. It's a generous offer and I've decided to take it.'

Lando could only hear a muffled sound in his ears. He looked at his mother but couldn't make out what she was saying. Was this what shock felt like?

'Sorry, what?' said Lando, standing up. 'Mum, sorry, but what are you saying?'

'Calm, Lando,' said de Croix, raising and lowering his hands like a conductor in an opera house. 'As I say, this is good news.' He opened a second bottle, letting the cork hiss rather than pop, as was correct in the school of etiquette though it took the fun out of the delivery.

'I am giving you the freedom you have been so obviously craving,' said Delia, remaining seated. She hadn't yet taken a sip of champagne.

'Who says?' said Lando.

'Now you can navigate your own career path,' said de Croix, 'and while you decide, there will be plenty of money to keep you going.'

'Lando, did you know?' Celine looked very upset.

'No, I knew nothing about this,' he said.

'Darling,' said Delia, 'I decided it was best.'

'You didn't even ask me? And what about Uncle Stanley?'

'With respect, Lando, your mother is the sole shareholder and is in total control of the company.'

'Darling, don't worry,' said Delia, 'we'll make sure Uncle Stanley has sufficient funds to get a place in town, and whilst I realise it may not be quite the location he's used to, it will do. Stanley's been very lucky up until now, living here rent-free.'

'Rent free? Mum, it's Uncle Stanley we're talking about here, he is part of our family.' Lando put his hands on his head, feeling like his brain might explode. 'What would Dad say?'

Delia turned to de Croix.

'I think he'd say, "quite right", most probably,' she said.

'Quite right,' said Lando, 'you really think so? Because I think he'd be disgusted.'

'What would you know?' said Delia, the tone of her voice rising.

'Because I heard him,' said Lando, trying to keep the emotion out of his voice. 'I heard him, Mum.' He spoke more softly now. 'I heard him talking about his vision for this place.'

'Don't be ridiculous,' she said.

'The radio interview with Dad from 1996, just before I was born,' said Lando. 'A producer played a recording of it for us when Uncle Stanley and I went to the media agency to view the ad.'

'I'd hardly call something you and Uncle Stanley stitched together "an ad".'

'Mum, why are you being like this? Uncle Stanley paid

for the ad out of his own funds, and by the way, the ad is amazing.'

De Croix made a second attempt in offering champagne to Lando but quickly retreated.

'I don't know what interview you're talking about,' said Delia.

He couldn't decide if she was lying or not. Mind you, she'd attempted to broker this sale without him; why wouldn't she cover up any knowledge of his dad's wishes for the future?

'Why not let your mother put you out of your misery, young man?' said de Croix.

'So you can tear this place down? Or flog it on to a vulture fund? No bloody way,' said Lando, and without looking at Celine, he left the room. He needed Immy; she was the only person he could trust. Celine was caught in the middle, and it wasn't fair to blast off about her father in front of her. He may have been livid, but he respected the relationship between children and their fathers, as it was something he had never had the chance to experience.

★

With one last client to go, Immy had never been so ready for the end of the day to come. The most sickeningly obnoxious bouquet of flowers had arrived that morning, along with a teddy bear and card, which read '*Sorry we didn't have a chance to dance x Flynn.*' Or sorry for being caught having sex with someone else at a party, more like. Immy binned the card and gave the flowers to Janette as a thank you for being so kind to her the other night.

On her way out, she'd arranged to collect organic bath oil, which she'd ordered from the beauty hall, and Janette promised to give her as many samples of face, body and foot creams as she could muster. The *pièce de résistance* would be takeout pizza from Milano's, a bottle of white wine from O'Briens and *Bridget Jones* for the forty-eight millionth time.

Without warning, the door opened and Lando walked in, then turned around and walked out again. He didn't make eye contact with her, but she noticed how pale he was.

'Lando?' she said loudly, thinking he must be in the corridor, but when she stepped outside, he wasn't there. She left the door open and returned to her desk. If he was coming to give her a lecture about drinking too much and making bad choices about men, then he needn't bother. She knew all too well about her mistakes, and if he said he wanted to deck Flynn, she'd say, 'not if I see him first'. But Lando didn't return, and after twenty minutes Immy welcomed a new client who wanted to buy a dinner service for her new daughter-in-law.

On the way out of her office, Immy's phone rang. It was Lando.

'Are you with a client?' he said.

Immy felt a rage rise within her. Receiving a 'holier than thou' lecture from Lando was all she needed to round off her day.

'I should probably lie and tell you I am with a client because then I could avoid having to listen to you criticise me about my drinking and dreadful taste in men when I've been the one who's been here for you since we were twelve years old.' Immy knew she was getting into her stride. 'I'm the one who's listened to your whining about all the pressure of inheriting a business, and your "poor me, what will I do, I'm so indecisive" attitude.'

No reply from Lando so far.

'Well, I've had it, Lando, so don't even bother trying to point out all my failures.'

'Is there anything else you'd like to add?' he said.

'Not that I can think of right now, but I'm sure there's more.'

'Then I'll say goodbye.' Lando hung up. She could have gone on and thrown further insults at him, but he'd saved her the bother. But there was no sense of relief following her outburst. She felt awful. The truth was, she wanted her best friend back. He used to be like her comfort blanket, and, somehow, she had turned him into a pin cushion.

Chapter Thirty-Eight

One of the sash windows in PS Headquarters had jammed open, but Immy didn't mind as she daydreamed and watched snowflakes fluttering in and melting on the white carpet. She had always loved snow, even though this morning's call from her dad should have put her off. Apparently, they'd been invited on a trip of a lifetime to Val d'Isère by friends of theirs for Christmas.

'And you and Mum are saying yes?'

'That's it,' he'd said, quite joyously as he'd figured Immy was making it easy for him to get off the hook, which was correct as she was past caring. Her parents didn't want a daughter mucking up their tidy retirement in Spain, which 'runs like clockwork. Golf at ten, Sangria at six'.

Recalling what she'd said to Lando on the phone had done nothing to improve her mood. Yes, she may have gone too far, but it had been necessary to get her point across. Not surprisingly, she hadn't seen or heard from him since.

A brief hammer on the door was followed by Janette, holding an iPad and what looked like a jam doughnut.

'Immy,' she said, quite out of breath, 'can you make room for a last-minute client?'

'That's easy,' she said, 'I've got the next three hours completely clear.'

'Good, because I've just had Elodie Gold on the phone and she'll be here in, I'd say, ten minutes max.'

'I definitely recognise the name.'

'You'll recognise her,' said Janette, sitting down on the chair opposite. 'She's a painter and influencer.' Janette swiped the screen of her iPad and held it up to show Immy. 'Thirteen million followers, how about that?'

'Not bad.'

'But it's her dish magnet of a husband who's the real draw,' said Janette. 'He's got a record label and signs all the biggies.'

Luke Hampton and Elodie Gold brought a sort of regal, arty, rock 'n' roll vibe with them. Elodie looked very natural in a camel-colour jumpsuit with blonde hair in a loose French plait. Luke was dark-eyed with a stubbly chin and looked like a gladiator in his brown suede jacket.

'We love the VIP lounge,' said Elodie. 'It's so different to any department store we've ever been in.'

'It's like Gramps's house,' said Luke.

'Though in much better condition,' said Elodie. She looked around PS Headquarters. 'Good call opening the window.'

'It's actually jammed open,' said Immy, showing Elodie and Luke to the sofa, 'and I may be building my own snowman if the maintenance man doesn't turn up soon.'

'It's healthy though,' said Elodie. 'Even on the most freezing days, Gramps kept his bedroom window open. He used to shop here, a long time ago.'

'That's so cool,' said Immy, trying to keep her eyes on Elodie rather than her husband.

'We miss Gramps,' he said, in a Boston accent. 'He was like a grandfather to me too, and a big part of the reason I got to set up my business, and El got her painting career up and running.'

'I have a complicated family,' said Elodie, taking lip balm from her bag and offering some to Luke before applying her own. 'But life's easier now.' She and Luke gazed at each other, and Immy couldn't help but feel envious. What a feeling that must be, to have completely requited love.

'Before we shop, or my wife shops, more accurately,' said Luke, winking at Elodie, 'is Stanley Shillington still here?'

'Uncle Stanley,' said Immy, 'yes, sixty-two years later, he's still here.'

'That's great,' said Luke, 'I have a client who did business with him some years ago, and he'd love to reconnect at some point, but if I could have a cell number, I'll get my people to sort it.'

'Of course,' said Immy, 'and are you Christmas shopping today?'

'I wish,' said Luke. 'The airline lost our luggage so we're here for the basics until it turns up.'

'Basics? I'm here for more than basics,' said Elodie.

'I'll contact my colleague Celine, and see what we can do,' said Immy, as frantic beeping came from the street.

'Don't tell me it's Ramor Z,' said Luke, striding over to the window.

'I thought you told him to wait?' said Elodie, rummaging through her bag.

'You try getting RZ to follow instructions,' said Luke. 'Oh Christ, he's being totally swamped by fans and paparazzi.'

'Once I find my phone, I'll call security for some back-up,' said Elodie. 'Immy, have you heard of Wildbird Records?'

'I think so,' she said, wondering if this celebrity moment could be the very antidote to de Croix's grumbling about her lack of sales.

Luke stepped in from the window, looking so handsome with snow on his dark hair.

'We signed Ramor Z last year,' he said, 'and he promised to keep a low profile until his new track drops tomorrow, but obviously that isn't happening.'

'He's our very own wild bird,' said Elodie.

'Can I take a look?' said Immy.

'Be my guest,' said Luke, 'I'm going to call Ramor Z's security detail and get a fast solution to this mess.'

Immy looked out to see an enormous black Mercedes people carrier, slowly turning white with snow. The sight of flashing cameras and what looked like hundreds of people taking selfies was something she had never seen before.

Immy brushed snowflakes from her forehead and turned to Elodie.

'Does Ramor Z like to shop?'

'Cars and watches mostly,' said Elodie, lazing elegantly on the sofa while Luke scrolled through his phone.

'Why not bring him into Shillington's?' said Immy. 'We can keep the cameras and fans out; he'll be totally safe.'

'Luke?' said Elodie, 'can you bring Ramor Z, and I can continue shopping up here with Immy?'

'Okay,' said Luke, 'let me make a call.'

'Of course Ramor Z had to bring the tractor, at least that's my nickname for it,' said Elodie. 'It's basically a very luxurious Mercedes van conversion, kitted out like a private jet. There's even a bed for the bodyguard.'

'And that's where Ramor Z will be staying tonight if we don't get this chaos sorted,' said Luke, dashing apologetically out of the room.

Chapter Thirty-Nine

The double doors to the hallway of Shillington's opened and three beefy men, dressed in long dark coats and sunglasses, arrived with hollers and hands waving like winter barley behind them.

Janette saw a flash of silver between the men, and then she looked again. A neat figure, dressed in metallic trousers, an oversized leather jacket and black Prada snow boots. He wore sunglasses and carried a little chihuahua in his arms. The cosmetic department put down their phones.

'Let's go see if we can find something good for Santa, shall we?' His voice was deep, American, luxurious, and instantly recognisable. Janette had listened to an entire podcast about Ramor Z, whose platinum album had broken all records for being the first rapper to stay at number one on the Billboard Charts for sixteen glorious weeks. She looked around the department and everyone seemed to freeze. The voice of de Croix, promising to sack anyone who treated a celebrity differently from a normal customer, must have been ringing in their ears. 'They choose our store, and we must provide the sanctuary they desire to shop in peace.'

Janette followed Ramor Z and his crew to the stairwell, where they climbed to the first floor like invaders from another planet. 'Love these,' said Ramor Z, picking up a pair of lobster-red cashmere socks. 'Don't these feel amazing?' he said, throwing a pair to one of his beefy sidekicks, who nodded in agreement.

'I'll take fifty pairs for my crew.'

The young man behind the counter, slightly choking, said, 'You know they cost a hundred and ninety euros per pair?'

'Sure,' said Ramor Z with a grin. 'In fact, make it sixty pairs.' He turned to Janette. 'You got some luggage, homie?'

'Are you speaking to me?' she whispered as he walked towards her.

'Hold it,' he said, putting his hand on Janette's shoulder. She had to use all her strength not to knee-wobble to the floor.

'*Thought I needed a filling done*,' rapped Ramor Z,
'*tried to find a willing someone,*
ended up at Shillington's,
toothache was killing mon,
I see a girl and take her for a whirl.'

'You captured that, Briggs?'

'Recorded, Ramor Z,' said one of the beefies.

'That was amazing,' said Janette through a tight smile as she tried not to fangirl him, when a tall, dark and handsome dish arrived.

'You never know when inspiration strikes, Luke my man.'

256

'And you never know when you're going to get mobbed,' said the dish, who must have been Elodie Gold's husband. Janette had watched a segment about them on *Entertain Daze*. 'I thought you were going to nap in the van,' said Luke.

Ramor Z held up his little chihuahua in the air. 'We got bored, and Ziggy Z needed a pee; isn't that right my little hero?'

'Haven't you heard of asking one of your guys to take Ziggy Z for a whizz on the sidewalk?'

'My boy Ziggy Z don't do sidewalks, Lukey.'

'Do you have to call me Lukey?'

'Do I have to keep writing Billboard classics and making you a goddamn fortune?'

'Fair enough,' said Luke, fist-bumping Ramor Z.

'I was just asking this lovely lady about luggage.' Ramor Z smiled at Janette, flashing a gold filling. 'And though my luggage didn't get lost like my man Luke's, I'm bored with my own set. Can you lead me to the land of plenty?'

Janette nodded and said, 'Follow me.' Thank goodness her iPhone was at her counter so she wouldn't be tempted to take a photo.

'Hold on,' said Ramor Z, walking over to the sunglasses section. 'I like those.' He picked up a pair of Prada sunglasses and put them on. 'Looking good, homie?' He turned to Janette.

'Very good,' she said, noticing that Luke looked impatient. Then a hissing from behind the men's braces.

'Janette,' said de Croix, 'come here.'

'All right, de Croix?'

'How long has that rapper been here?'

'About ten minutes,' said Janette.

'Fine,' and de Croix squealed under his breath as Ramor Z stood in front of a twenty-four-carat gold iPhone, which de Croix had put in place as a centrepiece for Christmas bling. 'Do you know what the margins are on those items he is buying? If word gets out that Shillington's is attracting this calibre of customer, it could skyrocket us higher than the Virgin jet.' Maybe they wouldn't have to sell after all?

Ramor Z took off his leather jacket to reveal a baggy T-shirt with a Turtle motif and proceeded to glide around the store, pointing at objects for his team to purchase. He took selfies with staff, who at this point had to think safety in numbers. De Croix could sack the entire department. Phones pinged, staff members squealed, and Ziggy Z was treated to Shillington's turkey and cranberry pie in a reindeer-shaped dish, delivered by Shirley.

'Wait,' said Ramor Z, 'I want a piece of bling for my boy Ziggy Z.'

'Are you serious?' said Luke. 'You know the word is spreading like wildfire and you are going to be swamped out there?'

'I got my boys, and I got you, Lukey,' said Ramor Z with a grin, patting Luke's cheek. 'Besides, you like me to invest my dollars, and some diamonds for my Ziggy Z is gonna be an investment piece.' Ramor Z looked like he was going to break into another spontaneous rap, when he looked to the door and took off his sunglasses and passed Ziggy Z to Luke.

'My man Stanley?'

'And look at you, young man, in your silver pants and snow boots, where are you off to, Mount Everest?' The men embraced. 'And that jacket's real leather I take it?'

'Italian, baby,' said Ramor Z. 'Only the best, like you taught me.'

'And you remember? Sure, you would have only been eighteen or nineteen.'

'Those were formative years, Stanley, and Pop kept telling me, "What would Stanley do?" And I'd say, my man Stanley would tell me to keep going.'

'Why didn't you tell me you were coming?'

'I wanted to surprise you, my man Stan, and I've got a sweet ride outside,' said Ramor Z. 'It's got the kitchen sink of features, man, leather upholstery, heating, cooling and even a twelve-point massage.'

'You had me at hello, Ramor Z,' said Stanley.

'And Stanley, I've got a minibar with crystal glasses, and the bathroom has a waterfall faucet; you're gonna love it.' Janette and de Croix looked at each other. This day was getting more and more surreal.

★

Six Theory cashmere jumpers, three Chanel dresses, two Christian Dior skirts and a Miu Miu coat later, Immy felt like she'd been part of a real-life 'Twelve days of Christmas Fashion' with Elodie and Celine. When Elodie said she was looking for 'more than the basics', she hadn't been joking.

She'd arrived into complete mayhem on the second floor, Shillington's bags were being packed with tissue and mountains of shopping. Ramor Z was sitting on a sofa flanked by Janette and Uncle Stanley, while Ziggy Z cocked his leg on a cardboard cut-out of Brad Pitt promoting aftershave.

'My boy Foliey told me his grandma gave him an old shirt,' said Ramor Z to his tight audience of Shillington's staff. 'It was dirty around the collar, and he put it at the bottom of a pile of stuff, thinking to himself, "I'm never going to wear that." But, hey, I told him, it's the thought that counts.'

'I love Foliey,' said Janette, who looked in her element next to the hottest thing in the music industry, 'he's the next best rapper to you, Ramor Z.'

'Immy,' called Uncle Stanley, 'come and meet Ramor.'

'Z—' he paused for effect ' — the name is Ramor Z.'

'Ah, you've become soft since I last saw you, Ramor's a fine name.'

'These days, I like a little extra,' said Ramor Z, looking like he was enjoying the banter.

Immy couldn't decide whether to put out her hand to the glamourous star rapper and thought she'd wait for his signal, but it didn't come so she ended up doing a sort of awkward wave.

'I spent a winter with Ramor Z's family in Queens,' said Uncle Stanley.

'He educated us,' said Ramor Z. 'My pop first thought about sending me and my sibs to a Swiss finishing school but when he heard about my man, Stan, we were put through the ringer, watching our Ps and Qs, teaching us some good, right-on social manners.'

'Not a word of a lie,' said Stanley. 'Your father just wanted a little Irish influence over the lot of you, and a fine bunch you were and sure, look at you now.'

Immy looked around for Lando but there was no sign.

'Isn't that something?' said de Croix, most likely looking interested in case any further purchases could be tempted. 'I pride myself on my Irish roots.'

'You French, my homie?'

'With a drop of Irish whiskey in my blood, I like to think,' said de Croix. Immy had never heard such humour from de Croix. 'And this little puppy is yours?' Ziggy Z began humping de Croix's leg.

'He's something, isn't he?'

'Indeed,' said de Croix.

'I've got Netflix making a documentary about Ziggy Z, and they're calling it a dog-umentary. Isn't that keepin' it real?'

De Croix clearly saw an opening. 'I hear your doggie would like a Christmas bauble from our jewellery department.'

Ramor Z looked interested. 'No,' he said, 'I'm looking for diamonds, baby, a necklace for my Ziggy Z.'

'Well, I wasn't thinking specifically,' said de Croix, his eyeballs dilating, as Ramor Z got to his feet.

'You know, Mr Frenchman, I'm into it.' He nodded at one of his entourage and the tallest man in the long coat gently scooped up Ziggy Z.

'Want to go shopping, my precious?' said Ramor Z in a baby voice, and Ziggy Z began to bark.

Delia crossed the beauty hall like a bee ready to land on a flower full of pollen.

'Welcome to Shillington's,' she said, looking smart in a white shirt and string of pearls. 'A little bird told me we had the honour of music royalty.' There was no way Delia had any clue who Ramor Z was, but Immy admired her approach. 'I'm Delia Shillington, owner of this fine department store.'

'Pretty lady,' said Ramor Z. 'My man Stanley didn't tell me his relations were hotties.'

Delia blushed and was about to respond when a golden retriever covered in soap suds came galloping around the corner, zig-zagging through counters and staff, with André red-faced and soaking as he gave chase.

'Lollipop,' he called, 'come back here.'

But Lollipop the golden retriever did quite the opposite and flew in the air, floored Delia and galloped up the stairs, followed by Ziggy Z.

'Mum?' shouted Lando, who had arrived with his mother but stood to one side to let André chase the dog.

'Get my baby back,' yelled Ramor Z, and his three long-coated men hammered up the stairs.

'Mum?' Lando knelt next to her and looked up at Immy, who dialled 999. It looked like more than a fall. 'Mum?' Lando pressed his hand on Delia's cheek, but there was no reaction.

Chapter Forty

DUBLIN HERALD

THRILLS AT SHILLINGTON'S

AS RAMOR Z CAUSES MAYHEM

The 34-year-old was spotted leaving Shillington's on St Stephen's Green on Friday evening with designer shopping bags and his entourage, including the adorable chihuahua Ziggy Z. The Billboard Top 100 singer and rap artist stopped briefly for selfies as hordes of fans gathered outside the store. Making a peace sign before climbing into his Senzati Luxury Mercedes VIP V Class People Carrier, the star's vehicle whisked away with a garda escort, which had been on standby.

★

Lando sat on the floor next to Delia, who remained unconscious. De Croix and Celine had cleared the area, leaving Stanley and Immy alone with Lando as they waited for the ambulance to arrive. The mood was sombre, and the only sound was of a staff member mopping the floor on the landing, still wet from the dog chase.

When the ambulance arrived, Immy stayed glued to Lando's side, trying to reassure him that his mum would be OK. He insisted on travelling in the ambulance. Immy stayed behind with Celine and Janette, who had now become part of the inner workings. Shillington's was to close for the remainder of the day. What began with such a bang of stardom, ended with despair. On top of the worry about Delia, Immy desperately wanted to apologise to Lando for what she'd said. She had spoken so badly out of turn, and she wished more than anything to take her words back.

★

The paramedics assured Lando that his mum was reacting well to treatment following her mild heart attack, but it didn't ease his mind. Lando prepared himself to face his mum's death and accept the blame. The strain and uncertainty around running Shillington's had to be the root cause, and if Lando had stopped his selfishness and took the lead as he knew his mum wanted him to, she wouldn't be lying motionless with an oxygen mask.

When they reached the Mater Private, Delia was brought to the coronary care unit, where a series of electro-cardiograms and blood tests were performed. Lando answered a multitude of questions but still couldn't believe his mum was going to make it through. His mind raced through his future. Could he keep Shillington's, given the shame he felt for letting his mum down? And surely everyone would blame him, including Immy who had already made animosity towards him clear. Lando had never felt so alone and couldn't even be sure that he'd have Uncle Stanley's support.

★

Delia woke up and stared at the ceiling, having had the most vivid dream. She had been lying in bed next to a snoring Gregory, and she'd slipped her hand beneath his pillow, gently stirring him. He'd said, 'sorry, my love,' and had turned over and gone back to sleep. She'd felt happy to see him sleeping so soundly as if he hadn't a care in the world but then she'd looked down at her pregnant tummy, which had swelled and then gone flat, as if her baby had never existed.

'Mum, it's me.'

She turned her head and there was Lando. 'Thank God,' she said, crying in relief to see him.

'You're going to be fine,' he said. 'I'm right, here, Mum; it's all OK.'

'Where am I?' Delia saw two small tubes taped across her hand, which ran up to bags hanging at the side of the bed like handbags on a display rail in the women's department. She thought back to Ramor Z warmly shaking her hand, and to happy faces at Shillington's.

'You've had a mild heart attack,' said Lando, 'more of a warning shot, the consultant said.'

'But I'd been so good with my low-cal butter,' Delia said, smiling, 'though it tastes revolting.' She felt relief to find her humour, thank God for it and for Lando. 'Darling, I'm bowing out, I've decided.'

'No, Mum, you're going to be fine; the medical team, they all say so, you're going to make a one hundred per cent recovery.'

She could hear the panic in his voice. 'Not of life, darling,' she said, feeling weak but determined to unpack her thoughts. 'I want to retire.' All she wanted to do now was sleep. 'And Lando?'

'Yes, Mum?'

'Can you let Gerhardt know?'

★

The VIP room may have been an eclectic space for customers, but for Lando it was full of ghosts. He looked up at photographs of his grandparents posing next to Peter O'Toole and Paul Newman, sports cars parked at the arched doorway, staff members dressed in brown coats diligently attending to customers, and his father proudly cutting a ribbon when the stained-glass window in the hallway had been renovated in 1980. A glorious gallery of Shillington's past success, which de Croix had tried to fast-track to the incinerator by persuading his mother to sell up without a fight.

De Croix appeared at the door and closed it quietly behind him.

'Thank you for your message, Lando,' he said. 'It is good to know your mother will make a full recovery; we have all been praying for her.'

'Why did you come here?' Lando leaned on his grandmother's printing press for strength.

'Because you asked me to meet you. In a text message about an hour ago, I believe?'

'To Ireland,' said Lando. 'Why did you come here and try to get Mum to sell?'

'I don't know what you mean,' said de Croix. 'You asked for my help.'

'Yes, but I didn't ask you to punch a hole in my family's dreams.'

'You came to Paris; I gave you every possible training, along with my wife.' De Croix seemed to have to gather himself at the mention of Julie. 'It was supposed that my daughter and I could assist.'

'Assist?' said Lando, squeezing his eyes together. 'You put on a show, lured us into thinking we could save the business and then told my mother you had a buyer who would put Shillington's out of its misery.'

'I did not word it in such a grotesque way.'

'Fine,' said Lando, 'but as far as I can tell, you came to spectate on the slow death of my family's business.'

De Croix looked shocked. 'That is what you really think?'

Lando didn't respond.

It must have been over a minute before de Croix spoke

again, and during that time Lando realised he may have gone too far with his accusations. He had invited himself to Paris as another stopgap to avoid making a call on his future, and when he'd arrived there, all he could think about was his fear that he had fallen in love with his best friend. And within days of being with the de Croix family, he'd somehow replaced Immy with Celine.

'I came here,' said de Croix, speaking slowly and carefully, 'because I feel desperately sad for what happened to your father, and though your mother has done the most incredible job, she can't go on forever.'

De Croix took Lando's elbow and led him to the sofa. 'Your father, for all his easy-going traits, was organised, do you see?' He rubbed his hands as he spoke. 'He knew exactly what he was doing in making me your godfather, Lando –' De Croix's voice choked ' – just in case something happened, it was almost as if he knew.' He paused. 'It was almost as if he knew he wasn't going to make it.'

Lando knew de Croix was being sincere.

'I have gone over and over your father's death,' said de Croix, 'and though it is twenty-seven years ago, sometimes it feels like yesterday. I remember when Gregory called to say your mother was going into labour, I was –' De Croix bit his lip and shook his head ' – I was in the middle of a deal, and I cut him short on the phone.' Tears streamed down his face as he spoke. 'To this day, I wish so much –'

Lando put his hand on de Croix's shoulder. 'It's OK,' he said. 'I didn't realise how you felt.'

'I would have lost Le Marché Cher if I hadn't focused on

the deal because I had made so many mistakes, the bank was about to take it from me.'

'And the deal, you made it?'

'I made it,' said de Croix, 'and yet your father didn't. I suppose I have survivor's guilt.'

Lando put his arm around de Croix as they sat side by side. He knew, in his entire being, that nothing could have stopped the lorry that night. The roads were icy, the street was narrow, and there was nowhere his father could have gone, but up.

'Even though I never knew him, I know for certain he would have wanted you to make the deal to keep Le Marché Cher.'

De Croix turned to look at him. 'And what a godfather I've been,' said de Croix. 'Presenting the easy way out when you needed me to show you the way. I am sorry, Lando, I truly am.'

'You have shown me the way,' said Lando. 'I want you to stop the deal and I want to fulfil Mum's request,' he said, feeling freedom for the first time in his life. 'She wants to retire, she really does,' said Lando. 'It's time for me to take the wheel.'

The men embraced and then shook hands.

'I'm proud of you, just as your father would be,' said de Croix, getting to his feet. 'Now, let's see if we can make a last-minute sprint to the finish line of Christmas Eve with a profit.'

Chapter Forty-One

Like a gentle bear, Gerhardt stood at the door and signed for a food delivery from Le Cave. It was like an alternate reality. Delia was at her home, with a man she'd known for as many years as her husband, and yet only now did she feel ready to consider companionship.

'Aren't you meant to be resting?' said Gerhardt, turning to Delia. 'I've ordered your favourite.'

'Carbonara?'

'Of course,' he said, handing what must have been a generous tip to the delivery man judging by the smile on his face. 'Now how about we get you back into bed before lunch.'

'You are truly kind to come to my house and play the butler for the day, Gerhardt, but please don't take it to extremes. I was only in hospital for five days.'

'Five important days,' he said, raising his eyebrows, 'and not to be taken lightly.'

'I really don't know why Lando called you; such a fuss over nothing.'

Next to Lando, Delia knew Gerhardt was the one person she could rely on. They had known each other for so many years, they were like ham and eggs, even if she couldn't admit it. 'Lando called me because he knows I'll take good care of you,' said Gerhardt, 'and that's just what I intend to do. And by the way, I don't for one minute think I'm your butler, but in saying that, I'd better announce that lunch will be served in fifteen minutes.'

'And pudding too?'

'But of course, my sweet,' he said, theatrically flinging a tea towel over his shoulder and doing a shimmy across the kitchen. 'I may not be up to Jagger's speed, but I'm not bad for an old guy from the Wicklow hills.'

Delia had to stop herself from blowing him a kiss. But perhaps, in due course.

★

Shillington's tea rooms sweetly made shepherd's pie for Stanley so he could invite Lando over for supper. The boy needed scaffolding around him, and Stanley had a plan.

The steaming hot dish sat next to Stanley's kitchen sink, while he found the corkscrew and took two wine glasses down from a cupboard.

'I want you to get that Ramor Z lad to send on his email,' was Stanley's first instruction to Lando, 'and then find Christian in his techy broom cupboard and ask him to purchase a huge flat screen to put next to the stained-glass window.'

'And what's going on this screen?' said Lando, who was looking better than Stanley had expected. He'd been at the hospital every day with his mother, and, with Gerhardt's help, they had the basement flat tidy for Delia's return, just as she would have expected.

'Our Christmas ad is going on the screen,' said Uncle Stanley, 'and no sound needed. The look on Grandpa's face when he sees the table all dolled up for Christmas lunch will be enough to get the punters sobbing into their hankies.' Stanley shoved a serving spoon into the pie and put a huge dollop onto a plate and passed it to Lando. 'We want people watching the ad outside Shillington's, and to then gallop inside and shop like the last of the world's Christmas puddings are going on sale.'

★

'This is the moment we've been waiting for,' said de Croix, holding a football-sized gold star in his hands. 'It is lucky December thirteenth, and we have got forty-eight hours to prepare Shillington's for our grand opening of the Twelve Days "Off" Christmas event to give Dublin a never-before-seen shopping experience that *cannot* be found online. Are we ready?'

'Yes, chef,' called out a salesperson from the tech department, quickly correcting himself. 'Sorry, Mr de Croix, I've got a second job as a sous chef, and I get confused.'

De Croix, despite the cold shoulder from his wife Julie in Paris, was determined to stay buoyant and make up for lost time with his godson in the best way he knew how: *delegation*.

Floor by floor, de Croix, with daughter in tow, walked through departments at speed, shooting out instructions and corrections.

'We are opening features that cannot be experienced online,' he told Delia over the phone, who was at Pipestock Castle, happily sipping a cup of tea with Gerhardt.

'I didn't realise life could be so good,' she told de Croix.

'Then I feel only happiness for you, my dear,' he said, wondering if he would ever enjoy the good life with Julie again. He had considered booking himself into the world-class Auralia Clinic in Dublin for a dermal filler. He was looking tired, he thought, and wanted to smooth away lines and furrows before returning to Paris. How else was he to compete with his wife's young lover?

'Let's start at the beginning of this Christmas shopping experience,' he said to Celine. 'You've met André, our salon specialist for the puppies?'

'Good to see you in Ireland,' said Celine. 'What is the Christmas theme for Doggie Hairdos?'

'This season,' said André, waving a brush in one hand and silver ribbon in the other, 'I am creating "The Scent of a Canine" for each of my clients.' He guided the de Croix to a row of glass bottles with traditional raised perfume lids. 'This fragrance is called Cinnamon Paw.' De Croix took a sniff and thought it wasn't bad. 'And this is Fluffy Tail Tarragon.'

'It smells like my housekeeper's cooking,' said de Croix. 'Which is not a bad thing,' he added, to reassure André.

'Following the warm bath in eggnog shampoo and conditioning oil made from spicy tea, the sweet doggie will be treated to Bow Tie, Blow Dry, resulting in a beautiful ribbon around the head or the neck, depending on the doggie's orientation.'

'I love it,' said Celine, 'it makes me want to have my own puppy.'

'And all my customers receive a home-baked, organic biscuit, shaped like a cat,' said André.

'A cat?' said de Croix.

'Of course,' said André, 'we all know dogs love to chase cats.'

The beauty department had a huge table at its centre, with gold placemats and silver cutlery, borrowed from the all-new 'luxury furniture & design' department. Janette had laid the table with food-inspired beauty products: cardamon latte smooth body lotion, coffee-scented face masks, sweet & salty nail polish, fruity lip gloss, doughnut-shaped bronzers and eye shadow shaped like chocolate bars.

'We're creating a "Beauty Feast on Christmas Eve",' said Janette.

'Go on,' said de Croix, as he studied the girls' sales technique.

'Be nice, Papa,' said Celine, who looked more like an assistant to Janette as she held up the products while Janette introduced each one.

'We all want to look good for Santy, don't we?' said Janette, 'or should I say, *Père Noël*.' Celine appeared to find this hysterical, though de Croix didn't really see why. 'We are here to show those seeking Christmas glamour how to prepare a feast for the eyes, the lips, the cheeks, the decollete.' Celine again found this hilarious.

'Sorry, Celine, what is so funny?'

'Janette is learning French, Papa; isn't she doing well?'

Chapter Forty-Two

Delia sat in the passenger seat, taking in the sight of Pipestock Castle, which looked as old as its distinguished neighbours across the snowy Wicklow Valley, though she knew it was no fairy-tale structure from centuries ago but a new-build conceived by Gerhardt himself.

'I might as well tell you before we arrive, Lando.'

'Yes?' he said, driving up a bumpy avenue of icy potholes.

'Yet again, as he does every year, Gerhardt has asked me to live with him.'

Lando didn't respond.

'And this time, I've decided to accept,' she said, undoing her seatbelt. 'I don't want to be like a gatekeeper in the basement of our house and for you to think I'm spying on you.'

'I'd never think that, Mum.' Lando turned off the engine. 'But Gerhardt is a good guy; I think this is a good move for you.' It was the oddest thing that he felt like crying at that moment. A fully grown man, feeling like a little boy.

★

Gerhardt stood at the front door with a huge tweed rug over his shoulders. He watched as Delia and Lando got out of the car.

'You made it here alive, at least,' said Gerhardt, shaking Lando's hand. 'This old Mercedes of yours, Delia,' he said, knowing it would instantly get up her nose.

'What about my car?' she said.

'Wouldn't you like an electric car? All you have to do is point the steering wheel in the right direction.'

'This car has been parked outside Fitzwilliam Square for thirty years, and isn't used to potholes of the country, or roads that aren't salted.'

'Let me buy you a new car.' Gerhardt loved to spoil the ones he loved, though he knew this one would be a harder nut to crack.

'I don't want a new one, I like mine just as it is.'

Gerhardt winked at Lando. 'Just as well,' he said. 'You know what an old dog I am, and you know what they say about old dogs. Shall I help you up the stairs?' He put out his hand to Delia.

'No, thank you,' she said, hiking up her long green Liberty print dress. 'I do Pilates twice a week, and I've been told my pelvic floor is much younger than my age.'

'I'm sure you're right,' he said.

Lando didn't have to say much. It was like being in the middle of an episode of *The Odd Couple* except deep down he guessed these two were in love.

In the hall, they stood on the stone paving looking up at carvings beneath the hammer-beamed roof.

'It was my late wife's suggestion,' said Gerhardt. 'You know this chimneypiece alone has thirteen thousand bricks.'

'Ever been tempted to put alligators in the moat?' said Lando, looking out the window at the drawbridge. 'No need for a burglar alarm in this place, I guess?'

'Very astute of you,' he said. 'The drawbridge was put in for that very reason.'

Delia was looking impatient as Gerhardt went on to talk about his late wife, who had bought him a three-tonne digger for his sixtieth birthday.

'Like me, she believed this land deserved to have something beautiful built on it,' said Gerhardt, 'and reproducing a building that will one day be historic was and is, my intention.'

'I'd say you've succeeded,' said Lando.

'I lost myself in building this place when she passed away,' he said, and Delia's eyes seemed to soften. 'She always knew what was good for me, and this place makes me happy. It's my lifelong project, along with shopping,' he said, winking at Delia.

'Easily done when you have the funds,' she said.

'Which reminds me –' he took a small box from his pocket and passed it to Delia ' – my latest gadget. At the touch of a button, I have geothermal underfloor heating and solar panels for electricity.'

'And that reminds *me*,' said Delia, 'Lando, did you ask Frank and Bob to turn down the radiators on each floor?'

'They said they'd do it, but that doesn't mean much,' said Lando, 'especially as they are paid to be doormen rather than maintenance men.'

'I can send in my man,' said Gerhardt. 'He could be with you in the morning.'

'No need,' she said. 'De Croix and Lando have things under control at Shillington's, don't you, darling?'

'We do,' said Lando, who could only think of catching Frank and Bob cracking into a bottle from de Croix's stash of Château Mouton over lunch, claiming that cheap wine gave them heartburn.

'On that note, to the kitchen,' said Gerhardt, 'it's time for a pre-lunch drink.'

'Your choice of art is questionable,' said Delia, as they walked past an oil painting of a naked woman and a pussy cat over her crotch.

'That painting means a lot to me,' he said. 'It was the first proper investment piece following my uncle's generosity.'

'A will windfall?' said Delia.

'No, he was alive and gave my brother and me a cheque for one thousand Deutsche marks each. Ulrich, of course, lodged the cheque and spent it in days on frivolous things. But I –'

'You invested,' said Delia, 'and of that, I approve.'

'Yes, but not in the traditional sense. I bought a field, and in that field I planted a crop of plums. They were rare at the time in Frankfurt, and I knew the soil was perfect for them.'

'You made jam?' said Lando.

'I made schnapps with the plums, which was then bottled and sold as a limited edition.'

'I'd love to taste,' said Lando.

'And with my earnings, I bought more paintings and land, I grew more plums, made more schnapps. Do you see what I'm saying, Lando?'

'Must you go on and on about how rich you are?' said Delia, though Gerhardt suspected she was delighted.

'You know I love to talk about money,' he said, picking up a bottle of pink gin from the drinks table. 'I wish that you'd take my advice on board rather than struggling on at Shillington's, sticky-taping over the cracks that instead require sound investment. I could turn that place around for you.'

'Out of the question,' said Delia, accepting a glass of gin, 'the decision has been made.'

Gerhardt felt very sorry for Lando and didn't like this approach. 'The business your family has been running for generations, you would really throw in the towel without any kind of battle?'

Delia placed her glass on the kitchen table with a tap loud enough to warn him off. 'If you knew what you were talking about, Gerhardt, you'd find Lando and I have been battling on for some time.'

'That's OK, don't take me too seriously,' he said sincerely

to them both. 'I've always been a jester, though usually there is truth in what I say.'

Delia held up her glass to the light. 'Lando, you'd better drive home; this is going straight to my head.'

'That's good for you,' said Gerhardt. 'I think you need to unwind every now and then, Delia, wouldn't you agree?'

'Definitely,' said Lando.

'And you too, young man. It isn't right for either of you to feel the stress.'

Gerhardt knew he had the right people to help them if only they'd let him bypass de Croix, whose heart, he knew, was in the right place. He'd always been fond of the French, partly due to his beautiful nanny from Bordeaux, but as a German he knew he could do it better. He held up the artisan beer bottle.

'I've drunk the finest wine in the world, on yachts, in hotels, on balconies, even in my bathtub—'

'Do keep it above board, Gerhardt,' said Delia.

'And I don't think I'll ever find a better wine, so I go on a mission to find the best beer in the world.'

'You're extreme,' said Delia.

'You think so? I remember a house in my childhood, and they used to serve cats instead of chicken,' said Gerhardt.

'Ouch,' said Lando.

'And instead of pineapple, they'd serve pickled turnip. No one knew what the fruit tasted like, so what difference?' 'You see this large roof overhang?' he continued. 'It offers protection from the sun, but in the winter, when the sun is lower in the sky, it lets the light in.'

'Thanks to a very expensive architect,' said Delia.

'Expensive, yes,' he said, 'but I wanted to bring the outdoors indoors, and have natural light flooding into the room.'

'You are besotted,' said Delia.

'It is with you I am besotted,' he said, collecting their glasses for refills.

'Lando, what about this stubborn mother of yours,' he said. 'She won't give me an answer. Even underfloor heating. How many castles will you find in this country with underfloor heating.'

'Haven't you heard of putting on an extra sweater?' said Delia, clearly embarrassed by the attention.

'I think you're going to love it here,' he said, putting his hands in the air.

Delia looked at him with a smile and he felt hopeful for the first time in a long time.

★

That night, the door to Lando's bedroom was barely open but Delia had to speak with him. She used the torch on her iPhone to find her way across the room to his bed. He was lightly snoring, as he had always done since he was a little boy.

Delia swept her hand gently across his forehead.

'It's been the two of us for so long,' she said, as he opened his eyes, 'and there's such a part of me that just can't bear to let you go.'

Lando reached for her hand. 'Mum,' he said, sitting up. She could still see the sleepy eyes of her little boy.

He took a moment to take in what she had said. 'You know you are amazing, Mum? Raising me single-handedly, having lost Dad and taking on the department store.' Lando smiled. 'Even saying it out loud makes it sound too huge for words, and yet you did it.' He looked at her with the kindest eyes a mother could ever see. 'You climbed the most enormous mountain, Mum, and now you deserve to rest. I'm ready.'

Delia cried with relief. She hadn't realised these were the words she had been wanting to hear from Lando for a long, long time.

'You're sure?' said Delia, holding his hand tightly.

'I'm ready, Mum; I know I can make Shillington's work.'

'But how?'

'I'll find a way,' he said. 'Now you sleep easy, and we're going to move you into that cushy castle with the underfloor heating, OK?'

With light coming into Lando's bedroom from the hallway, Delia could see the outline of Gregory's portrait hanging over the chest of drawers, and that night she slept properly for the first time in years.

Chapter Forty-Three

On the third floor, Lando could not have felt prouder for all they had accomplished in the lead-up to the opening of Shillington's for the Christmas countdown. Yes, there had been mayhem, with dogs on the loose from Doggie Hairdos devouring cakes in the tea rooms, to the Christmas cracker ice sculpture splitting in two and smashing on the footpath outside the store. But the team had come together for the sake of the past, present and future.

Lando hadn't realised how much he'd learned from the de Croix's over the past five months. As a father and daughter team, their attention to detail and high standards made for an atmosphere where failure was not an option, and problems were there to be solved. One issue he had yet to crack was his relationship with both Immy and Celine. He and Immy had not met in private since she'd told him what she thought of him over the phone. Action, he figured, was the best response. Let her look around the store and see what an impact he was making and then she could review her judgement. As for Celine, though always friendly, they hadn't been out together for days. He had wanted to sleep with her again or at least try to sleep with her, just to see if there was chemistry, though he knew even asking the question was a sure enough sign that it simply wasn't there.

Mimicking the style of de Croix, Lando leant over the gallery and clapped his hands.

'Hi everyone, can I have your attention please?'

From the ground floor up, Shillington's staff, dressed in aprons by the aptly named Enrich & Endure, embodied the most beautiful colours chosen by Celine. De Croix had suggested that colour-coding each floor would foster unity and it seemed to have worked. Privately, Lando's favourite twist of all was the addition of the new logo, which he'd devised with the apron-makers in about five minutes flat. A simple silhouette of Shillington's arched doorway with the doormen, next to '*Shillington's, not just for Christmas*'. For Lando, this was a statement of intent, which he swore to his late father he would carry out, and yes, it all cost money they didn't have right now, but Lando took a leaf out of Uncle Stanley's book and decided to take an educated bet.

He looked up and down at the faces gathering to hear the speech he had practised over and over to rouse the departments and make them feel that every smile, kind word and sale this Christmas would make all their futures more secure. Taking a breath, he was about to launch into his opening line when he saw Immy, looking up at him from the second floor. That face, his best friend, the missing piece of his jigsaw. 'I'm sorry,' she mouthed, and he understood immediately.

'Thank you for being here this evening,' said Lando, thrown by his brief moment with Immy. He'd have to cut to the key messages and talk about the Christmas lights, which was a line he could remember clearly. 'In ten minutes, and counting –' he checked his watch ' – at six p.m. in addition to the mass of recycled gold foil wrapped around Shillington's portico, the front of our magnificent building will light up like a glorious Christmas tree.' Everyone cheered. 'And this signals blast-off for our Twelve Days "Off" Christmas campaign, cleverly devised by Mr de Croix to make Christmas shopping more joyful by having the New Year sales, well, before New Year!'

'Do the sales apply to staff too?' said Shirley, who appeared to be sucking on a straw of one of her famed Christmas pudding smoothies, rumoured to have been enjoyed by Ramor Z according to gossip.ie, though who started the rumour was unknown.

'Shall I answer this for you, Lando?' said Delia, from the ground floor.

'Please do,' he said.

'No,' said Delia, 'the Christmas sales won't apply to staff members.'

A groan came from high and low.

'Because you will all receive an additional twenty per cent off products already on sale.'

Whoops and cheers reverberated around Shillington's.

Now that's how to motivate staff, Lando thought

to himself, even if it was going to cut into their profits – just in case this really was their last Christmas running Shillington's, though he didn't even want to consider it. But at the very least, the staff could remember the family with good feelings.

'The lights, Lando,' said de Croix, from across the floor, tapping on his Cartier watch.

'Got it,' he said. 'OK, everyone into your positions, and the lights will light up in six minutes.' At that very moment, the power went. Bang. Just like that.

'Lando?' It was Immy. 'The fuse box, it's in Uncle Stanley's apartment. Meet you at the top.'

The torch from Immy's iPhone lit up red suede pumps as she climbed the stairs. Celine loved to dress Immy as if she was a cut-out doll, laying out her clothes each morning in PS Headquarters. The feel of beautiful clothes made Immy feel more confident and together. Any kind of help felt like a relief, as she didn't have a clue where she would be this time next year, or maybe even next month. Lando's determination to keep Shillington's had spread like wildfire, creating a movement of goodwill between staff, but until Immy heard Lando's intentions from his own lips, she couldn't quite believe it. How could a person change so dramatically? It was as if he was 'playing shop', walking around departments, taking notes, and even wearing a jacket and tie. Was this really Lando and could he sustain the facade?

'Immy?' said Lando. 'We don't even have the key to Uncle Stanley's room.'

'He never locks the door,' she said.

'OK, that makes sense; of course he doesn't.' He seemed quite apprehensive around her, even though she was the one who badly needed to apologise.

'We have four minutes,' he said, meeting her face-to-face outside Uncle Stanley's door. 'Do you think we can sort it out?'

She wished he was talking about them, as she longed to sort them out.

'Yes, I think so.' If there was one thing in life Immy was sure of, it was how to make sense of a fuse board. Her mother was deeply impractical, could barely peel a potato and was dreadful at city parking. On rare occasions when the lights went out, she'd pick up the telephone, light a cigarette and gossip to a friend, instructing Immy to open the cupboard beneath the stairs and sort it out.

'Can you smell the turf?' said Lando, pushing open the door and guiding Immy. 'I don't know where his supply comes from, but he seems to light the fire all year round.'

'I guess it reminds him of growing up in Roscommon,' said Immy, shining her phone on the walls to find the fuse box. 'Here,' she said, locating it outside the miniature kitchen. 'No wonder Uncle Stanley doesn't cook with the size of that kitchen.'

'He's been on the tea-rooms diet for years now,' said Lando.

'Can I have a chair?'

'Sure,' he said, lifting a wooden chair from behind a desk. He put out his hands to steady her as she climbed up.

'Thanks,' she said.

'You're welcome.'

'How many minutes left, and how can you be so calm?'

'Three and a half minutes,' he said, 'and I'm calm because I'm with you.'

Immy didn't reply. How was she meant to reply?

'And thank you for apologising.'

'Well, I meant it.' She looked down briefly, her iPhone shining on his silky hair. There was the trip switch that held the entire electrical system of Shillington's to ransom. Lando steadied her when she wobbled on the chair, his hands holding her waist. She felt her heart speed up, just like that, in the silence and the dark except for the torchlight. She wanted to place her hands on his, but instead she remained still and closed her eyes. Even though every second that ticked by drew them closer to light and interrupted this moment, which felt so good, she had to push up the switch.

The lights came on, and she looked down at Lando, and just as he looked up at her the impatient voice of de Croix resounded. 'Let there be light,' he bellowed.

Immy jumped down from the chair and tucked her curls behind her ears.

'I guess the public is waiting,' she said, and she ran out.

Chapter Forty-Four

The following morning, at her flat in Swords, Janette hung her head upside down to apply a conditioning treatment to her towel-dried hair. She thought about getting the kitchen scissors to trim off dead ends but instead sat up and grabbed the remote on her bedside table. *The Sunrise Show* on HBO in America was Janette's favourite. She recorded it every afternoon, so she could wake up to Lola and Joanie. What a duo, one of them always ending up in emotional tears during a celebrity interview. They loved nothing more than rags-to-riches stories.

The phone pinged with a message from Celine.

> Good morning, I'll bring you a cinnamon Danish for breakfast after all your creating last night at your beauty table. See you at 8 a.m. X

Janette wondered if Celine had stayed the night with Lando. It was hard to know what was going on with them, but Janette chose to continue focusing on the positive and she might try out a few more words of French today, thanks to her new Duolingo app, which would kick the ass off her old French teacher. She'd told Janette she'd amount to nothing and should prepare for a life of rubber gloves and Fairy Liquid. What an old bat; if she could see Janette's Diploma of Beauty Therapy and the distinction she got in the Make-Up Marathon, where Janette did the make-up of ten models in thirteen minutes, she'd eat her words. Mind you, Janette's own daily marathon was no joke. Cleanser, eye cream, vitamin C and now serum, followed by moisturiser and SPF, and that was before the make-up went on. The routine was exhausting but as her beauty mentor at the Dublin academy told her, 'Your future self will thank you.'

On TV, Lola and Joanie were running through their favourite on/off celebrity love affairs, and their favourite 'PDAs for the paparazzi'. The odd snog or bum squeeze in public never bothered Janette. If you're with someone, and you're good together, why not show the world? Unravelling a pair of tights, caught up with underwear in the dressing table drawer, she was sure she heard Lola or Joanie say Shillington's. *The Sunrise Show* was America's biggest morning chat show. It wasn't going to name-check a Dublin department store, but looking up at the small flatscreen she felt her eyes pop at the sight of Shillington's facade in all its Georgian glory, along with Frank and Bob flanking the arched doorway.

'And now at the top of Billboard's Hot 100 chart,' said Lola, sitting on a swivel chair, next to Joanie, 'we have, TINA, the hottest woman in pop, to tell us more about the inspiration behind her latest smash hit, "No More Lonely Boy This Christmas".'

Janette picked up her phone and sent a panicked WhatsApp to Celine to turn on HBO. She then tried to call Immy, but no answer.

'You've collaborated with the R&B singer Ramor Z on the single "No More Lonely Boy This Christmas",' said Lola.

Someone in the audience wolf-whistled, TINA began clapping and the audience followed.

'How does it feel?' asked Joanie.

'Surreal,' TINA said, dressed in a red jumpsuit and grinning from ear to ear, 'but you know, it's taken years to get here; it didn't just happen.'

'And your story is a special one,' said Lola. 'Tell us about the inspiration behind the song.'

The camera closed in on TINA's face. 'I left home on my eighteenth birthday, and I knew where I was going. I'd saved enough to get me from Monaghan to Dublin and straight into JFK, baby.' The audience whooped and clapped again. 'I hitched a ride to Queens, where I crashed with a cousin, and then began my graft in the music business.'

'Was it the luck of the Irish?' said Lola.

'I make my own luck,' said TINA, coolly, 'except when it comes to "No More Lonely Boy". This is all thanks to Shillington's.'

'Shillington's, what's that?' said Joanie.

'It's not a what,' said TINA, 'it's a department store.'

'I have to admit,' said Lola, turning to the audience, 'we're all a little confused.'

'Shillington's is a beautiful department store in Dublin city. I had my team schedule an appointment for my little brother with the personal shopper,' said TINA, holding her hands in prayer. 'I wanted to spoil him a little and asked for him to be kitted out in a knock-your-socks-off suit for the GRAMMY Awards.'

'Wait, you're bringing your brother to the GRAMMYs in the spring?' said Lola. 'And by the way, congratulations on the nomination.'

'Thanks,' said TINA. 'My boyfriend's touring in the spring, and Bill is the only other man I'd have by my side.'

'You and your brother are close?' said Lola.

Janette could sense the show was tiptoeing towards the tear-jerking sentimentality.

'I've never quite forgiven myself for leaving him behind on the farm; he begged me to take him.'

'What about your parents?' said Joanie, bottom lip starting to tremble. 'They aren't —'

'No,' said TINA, 'it's just they were from another era, religious and strict on us, but especially my brother as he was the boy.'

Lola pressed her earpiece and Janette guessed she was being told by the producer to move the interview onto a more exciting level.

'Tell us what happened with the personal shopper in Dublin,' said Lola.

'She listened to my brother, spent time with him, boosted his confidence, found him the most fabulous suit, and he met the love of his life.'

'You're kidding,' said Joanie. 'Was it a set-up?'

'It was serendipity,' said TINA. 'There was an overlap of appointments, and the moment Bill saw her —'

'Who is she?' said Lola.

'I'll just give you her first name, which is Leslie,' said TINA.

'I like it,' said Joanie and Lola in unison, smiling at each other.

'I could hear the love in his voice before he even told me,' said TINA. 'You know, my brother has been lonely since I left him; he was only eleven, and the guilt has gripped me ever since, and to know Bill has a girlfriend means everything to me.'

'Have you met her?'

'Leslie? Not yet, but I'm coming home for Christmas.'

'Home to —?'

'To Monaghan, home to Clones Lace, the Lipton's shopping emporium and the famous country house, Hilton Park, where I'm going to marry that man of mine as soon as he takes five from his world tour.'

'Love really is in the air for you this Christmas,' said Joanie. 'Are you ready to sing live on air?'

'You bet.'

'And here's to the Love Department at Shillington's,' said Joanie, who began to clap with Lola, while TINA made her way to the live stage.

'*No more lonely boy this Christmas,*' she sang.

'*He's had his thrills and his spills, but love lured*
him to Dublin City and he's sitting pretty with his love.
No more lonely boy this Christmas.'

Chapter Forty-Five

Immy woke up to aching tension. She'd thought that once her apology had been made to Lando she'd feel better, but if anything, she was more confused about him than ever. The phone charging at the end of her bed kept pinging and ringing, but she was too exhausted to crawl over to it. She hit the snooze button again and decided to stay in bed until the very last second to leave for Shillington's. When she finally managed to scramble out of bed, she pulled on yesterday's clothes, scraped back her hair and found her eyes were bloodshot. That was all she needed. She thought about the article she'd read by Marian Keyes, who said 'the kindest thing you can do for yourself is to take off your make-up before going to sleep'. Immy had pretty much accepted that she wasn't ever going to be very kind to herself.

Pulling the front door of number 30 closed, the phone rang again, and this time she answered.

'Slow down, Janette, and no, I haven't checked my messages or voicemails,' said Immy. 'Yes, I'm on my way, and no, I'm not wearing a hat. Why should I?'

★

Janette didn't have time to answer Immy's question about the hat, though the answer would have been a definite, 'Yes.' A *Star Plus* news anchor was reporting outside Shillington's following TINA's interview on *The Sunrise Show*. This was so satisfying for Janette, as nobody at Shillington's seemed to have had time to hear about the extraordinary interview she'd witnessed on TV.

De Croix paraded through the store, announcing that the Twelve Days 'Off' Christmas campaign was already a success, as crowds were gathering outside. It was only a matter of time before they'd come in to shop. However, Janette knew the shoppers were there to gawk at the TV cameras.

★

Immy walked along Merrion Row and put a five-euro note into a busker's guitar case. He sang a jazz version of 'Merry Xmas Everybody', reminding her of watching a marathon of films with Lando last year, camping out on a mattress in front of the TV at number 30.

Up ahead, she saw a large white van parked on the footpath outside Shillington's. Surely not another deluxe camper van for a pop star. She thought back to Ramor Z, and considered the creative spirit that had overtaken Shillington's, including Shirley's 'School for Lazy Cooks at Christmas', teaching clever recipes requiring little preparation yet looked like hours had been spent in the kitchen.

'Excuse me, miss?' said a woman, pushing a furry micro-phone towards Immy as she approached the arched doorway. 'Do you know anything about the personal shopper at Shillington's?'

Without hesitation, Immy said, 'No, and excuse me, I'm late for work.'

'What about TINA? Do you know she credits the personal shopper at Shillington's for her hit single currently topping the Billboard charts?'

'Sorry, what?' said Immy, 'TINA who?'

'TINA,' said the reporter, looking shocked that Immy hadn't heard of the name before. 'She's the hottest female artist in the States right now.'

Immy pulled up the collar of her coat and focused on getting to PS Headquarters. She had to clear her head before her first client. 'This place is turning into Rodeo Drive with all the celebrity buzz,' said Frank to Bob, both of whom were beside themselves with excitement and beamed smiles at Immy as they held the door for her.

The Christmas music was in full swing at Shillington's, with Martin of the soft furnishings and bedding department lining up the tunes from his Dazzling DJ counter, which de Croix and Lando had reluctantly signed off on. Lando's main concern was that Martin would fall asleep on the job, but he assured them that music was the one thing in life that kept him buzzing, particularly as Delia had gifted him a Snoreeze watch for his missus, and it seemed to be doing the trick! Jànette waved at Immy from her counter, and it looked as if she was in the middle of talking a group of customers through the *Beauty Feast on Christmas Eve.*

Immy finally made it to her desk, and thank goodness there was no sign of Lando. She opened her laptop to check her schedule for the day, and then her notebook. She had thirty minutes before her first client, and Celine had already been briefed to put a rail of evening dresses together for a size twelve, with a generous bosom, although she was discovering that the sizes customers supplied over the phone were often optimistic.

And then she did it. She couldn't resist but type 'personal shopper, Shillington's' into Google, and lo and behold, a picture of the most glamourous woman called TINA appeared, with the caption:

TINA dedicates her number 1 Billboard chart hit 'No More Lonely Boy This Christmas' to her younger brother, rekindled with the love of his life, all thanks to the personal shopper at Shillington's, Dublin, Ireland.

This was followed by an interview on Twitter, with Bill. That can't be Bill, and Leslie? What? Immy must be going mad. This was more than surreal.

'Bill O'Brien and Leslie McAdoo, thank you so much for taking the time to speak with us,' said the well-groomed blonde broadcasting live from *E Entertainment.'*

'That's right,' said Leslie, 'and she and this beautiful French lady helped me to choose the most gorgeous dresses.'

'Leslie, will you be going to the GRAMMYs with your new boyfriend?'

She smiled shyly. 'I'm not sure just yet,' she said.

'I'm mad about her,' said Bill, throwing his arms around Leslie. They looked so in love. Immy couldn't believe what she was seeing.

★

Christian, with his gorgeous wavy hair, arrived at PS Headquarters with Celine, who bear-hugged Immy.

'Social media is going wild, Immy,' said Celine.

'Truly wild,' said Christian. 'And the ad has had over six thousand shares already.'

'Are you serious?' said Immy, feeling overwhelmed.

'May I sit down?' asked Christian.

'You must,' said Celine.

'On Instagram,' said Christian, 'TINA has called out for influencers to "get their behinds to Shillington's and celebrate the heart of retail".'

'She's American?' said Celine.

'Irish,' said Christian, 'from Monaghan. And what's more, Gen Z is loving the #oldschool vibes of Shillington's.'

As snow fell early the next morning, the media huddled together with their cameras and microphones outside Shillington's. Immy couldn't believe the media would be so interested, and quickly put on a pair of sunglasses. She felt like some kind of accidental celebrity from a reality TV show and felt such relief to see Lando rushing towards her.

'Come with me,' he said to Immy, taking her hand while politely declining to engage with the reporters. Frank and Bill opened the doors, from the inside.

'Glad to be inside,' said Frank, 'away from the rabble out there.'

'Though my missus said the paparazzi got a fine shot of me yesterday,' said Bill, locking the doors, as soon as Lando and Immy were in the hallway. 'I'm in *The Herald* online apparently.'

'You'll have to up his wages, Lando,' said Frank, 'with a celeb like that manning the doors.'

'We'll see,' said Lando, patting Bill on the back, and bringing Immy to what had always been his mum's office, and then de Croix's office, and now it was his office.

Lando offered Immy a chair on the opposite side of his desk. If he hadn't looked so concerned, it would have felt like a job interview.

'De Croix says it's a dream come true,' said Lando after a long silence.

Immy didn't respond.

'And yet you look like it's the end of the world,' he said. 'What's going on with you, Im?'

'I'm not who they think I am,' she said. 'Tanya was searching for an older man, who didn't want to go clubbing, and David wanted someone to have supper with, to watch films with, it's all simple stuff, and so yes, I did overlap their schedule, and I probably shouldn't have but I figured to myself, if I can bring people together and make them happy, then why not?'

'And Bill and Leslie?'

'It was just timing,' said Immy, noticing how tired Lando looked, with violet shadows beneath his eyes. 'They knew each other already, and then Bill happened to arrive at PS Headquarters ahead of schedule and that was it, they clicked.' She looked up at Lando. 'I'd never seen anything like it in my life.'

'But Immy, this is all so good, and whether you like it or not, you made all of this happen.' Lando picked up a pen and weaved it through his fingers as he spoke. 'I've been reading the comments online, and what you're doing is really special.'

'I can't be responsible for people's love lives,' she said. 'It's too much. What if they get hurt and go through breakups, or even worse: what if they get rejected.'

'You know what? I think it's my turn to lecture you.'

Lando's nostrils were flaring, which Immy had read about during her body language research, except this time it really wasn't a fit. She remembered that if a man flares his nostrils it's to take in more air and more of the potential partner's scent.

'Why are you smiling?' he asked. 'I mean I'm happy to see you smile, but I'm serious in what I'm saying to you.'

'Sorry,' she said, 'continue with the lecture.' At least her weird observations lightened her mood.

'I think you've got to stop feeling sorry for yourself,' he said. 'There, I've said it.'

'You think I'm feeling sorry for myself?' she said. 'Really?'

'This is a real opportunity for you, and I don't want you to waste it.'

'And what about Celine? Is she *your* real opportunity?' Immy just blurted it out and immediately regretted it. 'Lando, I didn't mean to say that; just forget it,' she said, standing up.

'I'm not just going to *forget* it, Immy,' but she left the room and before he could say anymore, she closed the door behind her.

Chapter Forty-Six

Standing on the roof tower, Gerhardt saw Delia's Mercedes driving up the avenue. She was an hour late, though he had been waiting his entire life for her to join him.

'Thank you, John,' he said, as his butler held up an emerald-green cloak.

'A gentle colour for the lady; I don't want to scare her off on her first day here.'

'Everything is in place,' said John.

'A Christmas wreath on the door to Delia's bedroom?'

'Indeed.'

'And turbot on the menu for dinner?'

'As requested,' said John, nodding in agreement.

'Though we have a way to go before that, don't we? We first need the lady to arrive.'

★

Following much deliberation, Delia sat in her car, wondering if she was doing the right thing. She watched as Gerhardt stood patiently by the front door and, knowing him, he'd wait all afternoon if she asked him to, even in the freezing cold.

She slipped her feet out of her driving shoes and pushed into a pair of heels. She was damned if she was going to start out life at Pipestock Castle in flats and, getting out of the car, she stood without the aid of her stick.

'You've come,' he said, walking towards her, his eyes soft with affection despite his tone.

'As you see,' said Delia, checking that her pearls were in place around her neck. 'And as friends,' she added. 'A purely platonic arrangement as agreed.'

'As you wish.'

'I do,' she said.

'Then a man can only dream, and I'll be delighted to have you living with me.'

'And don't expect me to drink that poisonous schnapps,' she said, taking his arm.

'Certainly not, but you will let me spoil you a little, won't you?'

Delia felt a mist of tears in her eyes. The thought of someone taking care of her, really looking after her ... it had been a long time.

'A little would be lovely,' she said, and together they walked towards the castle. 'Thank you, Gerhardt,' she whispered.

'What was that?' he said, pausing for a moment.

'Nothing,' she said, 'but a cup of tea would be lovely.'

'Then a cup of tea you shall have, my dear Delia,' he said.

'One other thing, Gerhardt: must you wear those cloaks on a daily basis?'

He turned to Delia and, taking her left hand, he kissed her gently on the ring finger. 'As Burt Reynolds once said, "You can only hold your stomach in for so many years".'

★

The bust of Constance Markievicz was surrounded by seagulls, clawing the snow. Celine was happy to be standing there with Lando at that moment, pale-pink clouds hiding behind leafless trees. It was how she had imagined Dublin at Christmas. Lando, with his hands in his pockets and she, searching for freedom, which she felt she may have found.

'The countess was a woman who stood up for what she believed in,' said Celine, 'and I admire that.'

'You learned about her through history in school?' said Lando.

'No, but I knew about her from talking with friends at the Académie, where she met her husband.'

'I liked being in Paris,' he said.

'And now?' Celine linked her arm in his.

'I like it here, in Dublin.'

'I'm glad, because so do I.'

He turned to face her, gently adjusting the collar of her coat.

'I think we're quite similar, aren't we?' he said.

'You're right, and sooner or later we are going to have to let those we love know how we feel.'

★

'Shillington's looks incredible,' said Celine, as they waited for the pedestrian lights to turn green. She laughed at a little car, honking its horn with a Rudolph the Reindeer nose on its bonnet. 'It looks like there are a million stars shining from the bricks, and Papa's gold foil makes the doorway look like Aladdin's lamp.'

'I'd love to know what Dad would think of it,' said Lando, 'and even my grandparents, and all of the Shillington ancestors.'

'They would say, well done,' she said, 'and I say the same.'

Lando looked to the arched doorway as they crossed the street, and blinked when he saw the huge, shiny, black Mercedes van roll up on the footpath.

'You're kidding,' he said. 'Ramor Z is back?'

'Did he even enquire for Stanley after he left?' said Celine.

'I'm not sure,' said Lando. 'I haven't heard from him; I don't think anyone has.'

The driver stepped out of the van and pulled back the sliding door to reveal Uncle Stanley, posing in a deluxe-looking fur coat.

'Don't worry,' he yelled, stepping out of the van with an elegant stick to keep him steady, 'this fur is faux, ho-ho-ho.'

'Uncle Stanley, wonders never cease,' said Lando, striding towards him.

'Watch my threads, now,' he said, putting on a New York accent, and embracing Lando, and then Celine.

'You look as amazing as the lights on the building,' said Celine.

'You're very kind,' said Uncle Stanley, 'but I'm not a patch on Ramor Z and TINA filming a music video together on Ha'penny Bridge. You should see what they're wearing. I've just been there and talk about gyrating hips.'

'Uncle Stanley, wonders never cease,' said Lando.

'And I could say the same about you, my boy,' he said. 'I had a rather fortuitous meeting with Ramor Z yesterday, and I know I'm drenched in faux fur, but it's bloody well freezing out here.'

'Let's get inside,' said Lando, signalling to Frank and Bob.

'Grand,' said Uncle Stanley, 'and over one of Shirley's plum pudding smoothies, which I've been dreaming about ever since she mentioned them to me last week, I'll give you the run down on where we're at.'

★

Stanley sat behind the mahogany desk in the office at Shillington's. It was the very first time in his sixty-two years working there that he'd ever been in this position.

'Am I feeling like the cat who got the cream or what?' he said. 'Is that you, Immy, standing by the doorway? Come in, would you; there's no need to be shy around us, is there, de Croix?'

'Certainly not,' said de Croix. 'In fact, Immy, you must have my chair, and I will stand.'

'I'm fine,' she said.

'You must,' he said. 'You've earned it, I can tell you.'

After Delia's heart attack, Stanley realised that seeing things from a distance is one of life's gifts. De Croix seemed more grounded than before, and the same could be said for his daughter. It was as if each one of the de Croix family had found their sense of direction. Shillington's as a department store was surely humming with business, but more than that, the building was alive again. Stanley could taste the hunger in the air to buy and sell, a chemistry which had existed since the beginning of time. As for Immy, despite the immense praise bestowed upon her across the media, and right up to TINA, the Irish woman who made it BIG in the USA, he could see that that wasn't what she needed to find peace in her heart.

Stanley lifted his Christmas pudding smoothie cup and tapped it on the table like a judge might bring a court to order, though all present were more than peaceful.

'It might come as a surprise to you,' said Stanley, 'but for some time I've been a silent partner in7 Wildbird Records.'

'Luke Hampton's label?' said Immy.

'The very one,' said Stanley. 'Now, I ran this by Lando before you all arrived, and I've also discussed this with Delia —'

'What are you telling us, Stanley?' said de Croix. 'You've been investing all this time?'

'Sure, what else would I have been spending sixty-two years of wages on?' he said. 'I've been eating in the tearoom, living rent-free and receiving my cost price.'

'When you put it like that, I can see where the savings would come in.'

'Ramor Z called me with an opportunity in 2018 when he was being signed by an independent label, which had limited financial backing.'

'And you were the backer?' said de Croix.

'I was, and the rest, as they say, is history. Ramor Z is on Planet Rapper, and he's bringing home the bacon to his Uncle Stanley.'

'You old dog,' said de Croix, who looked flabbergasted.

'Therefore, with Lando and Delia's blessing, I've become an official shareholder of Shillington's,' said Stanley, 'with Lando being the majority.'

Celine began to clap, and de Croix and Lando joined in, along with Immy, who smiled at Stanley but hadn't uttered a single word.

'There are plenty of details to run through in due course,' said Stanley, 'but the main announcement I'd like to make – before I hand over this comfortable chair to Lando, who is the head honcho now – is that TINA is going to run a mentoring scheme for kids in the city and get them playing music. Similar to what those boys in U2 did.'

'I think it's marvellous,' said de Croix, 'and makes me wonder if Le Marché Cher can run a similar programme to give back to society.'

'I like it, Papa,' said Celine.

'And what about you, de Croix?' said Stanley. 'Would you like to stay on as an advisor? You've done a serious amount for this place.'

'I am returning to Paris and what will become of me, who knows, but that is not important,' said de Croix, getting to his feet. 'I couldn't be prouder of you, Stanley, and of my godson, Orlando, and you can be sure you'll always have the support of Le Marché Cher, and we can share promotions, share socials, ambassadors, the works.'

'And where's Christian?' said Stanley. 'I asked him to wait outside while we attended to business.'

Lando got up to open the door, and Christian stepped in shyly.

'Well done, Christian, take a bow, because thanks to your techy know-how, along with all the media hype, Shillington's Christmas ad has gone viral.'

'It has?' said Lando. 'I'm sorry, Christian, I've barely been online to view the stats.'

'Don't worry about being online, Lando; the stars have aligned for you at last, and it's been a long time coming,' said Stanley.

'You think Dad has something to do with it?'

'I do,' said Stanley. 'I do very much think that.'

★

'Immy, could I have a word?' said Stanley, once de Croix and Lando left the office.

'Of course,' she said, 'and huge congratulations.'

'Have I ever told you about the nun?' he said.

'What about the nun?'

'I'll save it for a rainy day,' he said with a wink. 'But what I do want to say to you is plain and simple.'

'I'm listening,' said Immy.

'It wouldn't take a genius to work out that you two are meant to be together.'

'You two, meaning?'

'Well, I'm hardly talking about the unspeakable creature you went to the Snow Ball with, am I? I'm talking about Lando.'

'I think it's too late for that,' said Immy, 'but thank you for suggesting it.'

'I don't think it's ever too late,' he said. 'Just look at me. I'm taking Gilda Winterbottom to Christmas dinner with Ramor Z in the Oak Room at Adare Manor.'

'Go you, Uncle Stanley.'

'All I'm saying is, it's never too late.' And with that, Stanley blew a kiss to Immy and hoped to God she'd see sense.

Chapter Forty-Seven

'Twas the Sale Before
Christmas at Shillington's

Long before the appointed time of 10 a.m. on the morning of the informal opening of Shillington's Christmas sale, unexpected numbers of people crowded around the entrance, and when the doors were opened, the rush was like the perfect melody of 'Jingle Bells' in de Croix's ears. Even though he was feeling low about his marriage, and the thought of returning to Paris to face Julie's probable admittance of a 'toy boy', he chose to channel his positive energies into what could define his godson's future. He owed this to Gregory. Within minutes, hundreds of customers and inquisitive spectators swarmed like honeybees around the building, lining every counter.

At first, the women's department received the most

attention, but when they got wind of the incredible sale in menswear they scattered to buy ties and jumpers, pyjamas and multicoloured socks, which Delia had ordered when she'd found herself in a particularly good mood. The store ran like clockwork. Everyone knew why they were there, including Uncle Stanley in his velvet mustard three-piece suit, directing customers to their desired department, along with several temporary staff members enlisted to assist at the sale. Stanley felt like a golden Labrador, there were so many people reaching out to feel the texture of his threads.

All day, hundreds visited Shillington's, and the staff were so in sync, the air of pleasure from both staff members and customers was almost tangible.

The media referred to the sale as being the largest in Christmas history.

'LAST-MINUTE SHOPPING PAYS OFF AS SHILLINGTON'S PRE-CHRISTMAS SALE PIPS NEW YEAR TO THE POST,' said the *Sunday Independent*, 'LONG BEFORE THE POST,' describing how the public 'dived in to get their money's worth. Everything was arranged beautifully on the shelves, and staff looked festive in their bespoke Shillington's aprons.'

'The Twelve Days 'Off' Christmas' had been such a hit, shops across Ireland began bringing their New Year's sale forward. Hordes of people arrived at Shillington's, many booking themselves in for the personal shopping service, in what had become unofficially known as the Love Department.

Lando coordinated staff as they welcomed customers to the store and distributed satin memorabilia wristbands. Though he was busy greeting shoppers, he managed to stop for a couple of interviews with *Entertainment Weekly* and KCLR FM. Every department was flat out. Even Martin – whose wife's snoring had practically disappeared since she'd started wearing the Snoreeze watch – was enthused as he discussed the ratings of duvet togs and the spring-ability of mattresses with those searching for the best sleep, and more. Gerhardt had come along to spectate, with Lando's mum, who really did look very content. Country life was suiting her, he was sure of it, and Shillington's was only a short hop away, even if she insisted on driving her petrol-guzzling Mercedes.

'Mum,' said Lando, pushing a smart green wheelbarrow towards her, 'this is for you.'

'Is this for wine bottles or compost?' she said.

'It is for whatever you wish, Mum,' he said, parking the barrow next to Gerhardt. 'I think Shillington's has dominated your life for long enough, and now it's time for you to exchange the department store for the garden.'

'You know, I've just started watching *Real Housewives*,' said Delia. 'So watch out, I may be back as one of your extravagant customers.'

'Nothing would give me more pleasure, Mum.'

'And darling,' she said, looking at Gerhardt, 'I've also decided to change my name.'

'No way?' said Lando, hugging them both. 'I'm thrilled, really I am.'

'Are you really, darling?' said Delia, taking his face in her hands.

'Of course I am, Mum. But I'd better go back before this place turns into a riot.'

★

De Croix watched Celine wading through the crowds towards him.

'Can you believe it?' she said. 'This signals success for sure.'

'The spirit of Shillington's has always been strong,' he said, noticing that his daughter looked rather coy. 'You have something to tell me, my sweet?'

'I tried with Lando, Papa,' she said, 'I really did. But it's a girl that I love.'

'Why not?' he said. 'It's all love, isn't it?'

De Croix felt surprised that he wasn't more surprised.

Celine hugged him tightly. 'Thank you, Papa.'

'And before you tell me who the lucky woman is, who will tell your mama?'

'Let's see who sees her first,' said Celine, who didn't seem vaguely concerned about the state of her parents' marriage.

'One more night in the master suite alone for me,' said de Croix. 'You know I fly to Paris tomorrow morning?'

'Papa, you worry too much,' said Celine, twirling into Janette's arms. 'Look to the door, Papa, somebody has invited Santa Claus.'

'It wasn't me,' said Janette, kissing Celine. 'My Christmas wish has already come true.'

De Croix did not look to the door but at his daughter, who was flushed with happiness. He had never seen her smile like that with any boy. Contentment for his daughter was all any father wanted. As for his own life, he'd have to return to Paris and start again. Maybe take a flat on rue Saint Dominique; at least that way he would be within walking distance of Napoleon, who these days would be his only confidant. However, in the corner of his eye, he noticed a red figure.

'*Joyeux Noël mon chéri*,' came a voice from beneath the red Santa hat.

'*Père Noël*?' said de Croix, and pushing back the red hood, Julie gazed at him.

'You thought I'd forgotten our anniversary?' she said.

De Croix got to his knees and hugged her waist. 'It's really you, my love? You're not some kind of ghost of Christmas past?'

Julie knelt down to meet him. 'I am your present, and your future, my love.'

'Truly?' said de Croix, who could not believe his eyes.

'The time apart has been good,' she said. 'I've been running with my personal trainer, who has a boyfriend almost better-looking than you.'

'Ah, *ma chérie*,' said de Croix, 'and what I was thinking you don't even want to know.'

'It's a wake-up call for us,' said Julie, 'that's all. We are OK.'

The reassuring voice of his wife meant more than all the shelves in Le Marché Cher, and all the baubles on its forty-foot Christmas tree.

'I've missed you so,' he said, knowing he would never ever consider a *cinq à sept* again. '*Seras-vous à moi 365 jours par an, pour toujours?*'

'*Oui*, my love,' said Julie, 'and you won't believe how fit I've become.'

'And I've never been more in love with you, Madame Noël.'

Julie kissed his lips with a tenderness he hadn't felt for years. 'Are you surprised about our daughter?' she said.

'You already know? I was going to tell you over a glass of red wine.'

'I think I've always known,' she said, 'but I had to wait for Celine to find out for herself, and now she has.'

'You are even more perfect than I could imagine,' said de Croix.

'Christmas is all about love, isn't it?'

'Especially when I have a suite in the Merrion Hotel,' said de Croix, rising to his feet. 'Shall we?'

'I thought you'd never ask; saddle up the reindeer and let's go, *mon amour*.'

★

The clock in the hallway of Shillington's struck midnight, which Immy could hear from her desk in PS Headquarters. She picked up her brown leather book and flicked through her clients and research notes. She had learned so much, and yet, here she was, sitting alone on December 23rd, while her parents headed off skiing. In a big way she was relieved. What would they have talked about? DNA was all they had in common now, and Immy realised that was just the way it had to be. She couldn't spend her life trying to work them out; it was time for her to make her own plans, to suit herself and maybe even take the personal shopping role seriously. Though she knew it had little to do with the clothes, and everything to do with her listening ear and ability to impart the fruits of her research on body language.

'Time for one more client before Christmas Eve strikes?'

'Lando?' She picked up her notebook and held it between her palms like a prayer book. 'I'm sorry about Celine,' she said quickly, to get it out of the way. 'They came up to tell me just a little while ago.'

'We were never really more than friends,' he said, 'which is more than can be said for your love matches; I mean, Immy, I had no idea.'

'I guess it's like *Sliding Doors*,' she said, 'all about timing.'

'I've been doing some research of my own,' he said, taking a little Moleskine notebook out of his jacket pocket. 'Will you join me on the sofa?'

Immy left her notebook on her desk for a change and sat down.

'OK,' he said, sitting opposite her, 'when Matt Damon met the love of his life, he said —' Lando squinted his eyes to read the page ' — oh God, I may need to think about glasses, but in the meantime, Matt Damon said, "I literally saw her across a crowded room and eight years and four kids later, that's my life".'

Immy smiled and said, 'Nice timing for them.'

'When Anne Hathaway found the love of her life, she told her best friend, "I knew from the second I met him that he was the love of my life".' Lando ran his hand across the page as he read, which looked so adorable.

'Sweet,' said Immy.

'And finally, Eddie Redmayne and his now wife started out as friends. According to the article I read, Eddie said, "She was very beautiful and very funny and ... so we became friends", and they went on to fall in love.'

Immy glanced at the coffee table, empty without the notebook.

'Did you ever think of adding me to your book?' he said.

'Lando, I—'

He moved towards her.

'I hadn't realised how I felt until I saw you at the Snow Ball, and I was so caught up in trying to save this place, I somehow managed to delude myself from thinking about what could happen.'

Immy tried to speak but he kept going.

'I've been afraid to save Shillington's. Somehow, I thought it was better just to let things slide, and the sooner the store went, the sooner Mum and I could get through the pain of losing it, and at least if we got out, Mum could have security.'

'But, Lando—'

'And when I saw how focused you had become up here, I started to see the business differently.'

He spoke so quickly, Immy had to catch her breath as she worked out what he was saying.

'Lando, what's going on?'

'I think there was one match you forgot to strike,' he said, curling a strand of hair behind her ear. 'The thing is, and I really hope this doesn't mess things up, but—'

'Yes?' she said.

'I'm madly in love with you, Immy.'

She couldn't speak for a moment.

'Lando, don't you realise *I've* been madly in love with you all along?'

Lando reached for Immy's hands, and he was smiling, truly smiling. And now his lips were slightly open as he leaned in, closer, and closer until he kissed her, making every inch of her body tingle and her breath almost disappear as they melted into each other. Closing her eyes, Immy wondered if this was some kind of Christmas Eve dream, but it was real and it felt like love.

Have yourself a Merry Little Christmas – you deserve it.

Acknowledgements

In 1928, my grandfather, George Moore began working for 'the real' Shillington's store in Portadown, County Armagh. He was sixteen years old and rode ten miles on his bicycle to and from work each day, dealing with hardware. Grandpa stayed at Shillington's for sixty-two years and went from an apprenticeship to co-managing director. For as long as I can remember, he wore a tweed suit every day of his life, with a pencil in his jacket pocket in case a measurement was required.

The Shillington's in my imagination, however, is a luxurious department store filled with clothes, jewellery, and beauty products, along with every gorgeous thing you can dream of. Though it may be different style and location to the store of Grandpa's time, I feel the spirit of Shillington's would be similar: resilient and brimming with strong family values.

I'd like to begin my acknowledgements by thanking Grandpa for being the kind and loyal gentleman that he was and my thanks to the Shillington family for your guiding light.

I draw my inspiration far and wide and the generosity I receive brings good vibrations to the fore. I am hugely grateful to the following people for spurring me along as I wrote *The Love Department*:

Ben and Jessica Rathdonnell, Andrea Frank Thorslund, Daisy Jacquier, Charlie Fowler, Adam Goodwin, Alex Price, Charlotte, Ed and Émilie Capel Cure, Mary Claire Grealy, Rachael Comiskey, Donna Sherwood, Lessie Forde, Brian Kingham, Alexander Durdin Robertson, 'the Charleston Avenue beauties: Iona, Lucy and Tiffers,' Mike Casey, Jay Cashman, Dede Gold, Johnny and Lucy Madden, Lu Thornely, Anna Baker, Jenny Pringle, George Fasenfeld, Sally Gibbs, Cilla Patton, Amanda Morris, Ali Tyndale and Tara Egan Langley, Mathew Forde, Sebastian and Ali Barry, Emma Ramsden, Jono and Sheana Forrest, Ned Kelly, Megan Comiskey, Jo Patton, Bono, Bernard Doyle, Annabel Butler, Dermot Cantillon, Mark Boobyer, Alex Blackwell, Justin and Jenny Green, John Brogan, Gillian Keegan, Jen Page, Anthony Farrell, Stephen Mannix, Yoly Smith, Freddie Durdin Robertson, Andy Cairns, Anne Bowe, Jamie Drummond, Dita Von Teese, Keith Barry, Jo Fennell, Nat Nicholson, Patsey Lawlor, Anna Rose McMahon, Trevor White, The Little Museum of Dublin, Rebecca Flanagan, Finley Gallagher, Dr Samir Ali, Brendan, Hendy and Deirdre Joyce, Brendan Comiskey, Alanna and Sophie Fasenfeld, Jago Butler, Bex Shelford, Etta Crowe, Gillian Stafford, Super Car Snapper and Jellystone, Maca Deroda, Annalu Sanminatelli, Ava Lowe, Bill Power, Don Hawthorn, Aidan O'Sullivan, Eamonn McEvoy, Patsey

Lawlor, Ed Galvin, Amanda Butler, St. Columba's College, Suzie Shorten, Martina D'arcy, Vanessa van Edwards, Margaret Keenan, Dessie Hynes and Paul Hynes, Eugenia Garcia Mingo, Cliff Reid, Nuala Reilly, Linda Maher, John O'Donnell, Immy Benson, Declan Broderick, Lola Campillo, Lisa van der Pump, Sharon Lector, Fred and Joanna Madden, Robin Kwyoski, Jeremy and Nicola Perrin, Seamus, Emma and Jessie Raben, Anna McHugh of An Post and Suzy Webb, the loveliest lollipop Lady.

Thank you to Keith Hunt for being our wonderful landlord of Number 30, which played witness to romance in real life. Thanks to Ann Tully, the most stylish lady in the travel business, and to Gesa for Båstad inspiration and for reminding me to write beneath a tree on a summer's day. I bow to the Merrion Hotel for meeting the supremely high standards of Charles and Celine de Croix and I am continually grateful to Daria for my New York beginnings.

Many thanks to Emma O'Carroll and Maria McEnery for introducing me to the Volvo XC40, energising in every way (and 100% electric) with adjustable seats as comfortable as the perfect office chair. Thank you, Hugo, for the Festival of Writing and Ideas, and Richard Forde, huge thanks for making those who want to write feel like they're in with a shot.

Kudos to John Shillito, founder of the world's largest department store, which opened in Cincinnati in 1878. Thank you, Ross for the Night before Christmas and thanks Claudia for dressing Ramor Z in Prada snow boots. Thank you, Guy Trebay, for your brilliant article in *The New York Times* on quiet luxury. *Chicagology*, I loved reading about the Potter Palmers of Chicago, thank you so much, and admiration to John Van Osdel for such amazing architecture.

For making my department store research a divine experience, huge thanks to Brown Thomas, Harrods, Liberty, Fenwicks, Selfridges and Harvey Nichols.

Larry, thank you for raising my intellect by introducing me to Emile Zola, and Bernard de Croix for being a good friend with the best name.

Thank you, *Harper's Bazaar*, for insights into 'Clean Beauty' and Jack Brophy, thanks for your skincare wisdom. Alexander Maksik, many thanks for sharing 'My Father's Voice' in *The New Yorker* and thank you Sam Taggard, for sales advice. And Jacqui Doyle, thank you for urging me to follow my path.

Gigantic thanks to Hachette Ireland for publishing *The Love Department*. Ciara Doorley, thank you very much for your patience and goodwill, and many thanks to Joanna Smyth and Stephen Riordan, along with Elaine Egan. Claire Pelly for being a lovely editor, with an excellent sense of humour, thanks to Donna Hillyer and huge thanks to Mark Walsh for your high-powered skills.

When I'm in the flow of creating and stumble upon a question, I sometimes pick up a magazine and often find the answer I was looking for and for this, I'm especially grateful to *The Week*.

Thank you, Joan Millar, Liza Patton and Louise

Knatchbull, Aficionados of Retail, and muchas gracias to
Alfie and Ollie for taking care of Oldfort and Queen Dilly.
Thanks to Noelle for keeping our house in order, and for
your positive and upbeat presence. And Alma, huge thanks
for your brilliant support. Mary McManus, thank you
for being a bright shining star at Bishopscourt, and John
McDermot, a beacon of light. Huge thanks to Sir Richard
and Diana for the most incredible time at Villa Torre to rest
our writing limbs and thank you Andrew and Nicola for
your sparkle from afar. Lizzie, 'Lizzie of London,' thank
you for being so wonderful (and the finest advocate for
tea) and for tremendous encouragement, huge thanks to
Konrad and Katherine.

This is by no means a regular occurrence, but there are
times when I feel like magic happens – when I feel like I'm
doing what I was born to do. It is one of the most satisfying
feelings. And my thanks to Herbie, the true Master of the
Universe, and Jacquie, for guiding me along.

To the finest artist *merci beaucoup*, John Schwatschke.
Shane M. Byrne and Roly Ramsden, thank you for
reminding me to aim high, thanks to Elizabeth Hamilton
for making me feel like it's all worthwhile, and Coibhe,
thank you for Hermes and stylish correspondence.
Multiple thanks to Amelia's Garden Flowers, Plunkett
Press, Auralia, Johnson's Tailors of Tullow, the Lismore
Biscuit Company, Rathcon (luxurious) Christmas Trees,
Enrich and Endure Aprons, SAMAYA Ayurvedic Beauty
and Jenning's Opticians.

My thanks also to the Lord Mayor of Dublin for the Oak

Room, and grazie to Marty in the Morning on Lyric FM for putting a spring in my step.

Dom, *le succès à Paris vous attend, vous et votre magnifique famille*, and thank you William and Emily for our blissful wonder-field #organic at Oldfort. Huge thanks to my agent, Ger Nichol, who has the patience of a saint and best determination. Thank you, Aunty Helen for your wisdom and best sense of humour, and Aunty Virginia, Paris loves you.

To the kindest of men, thank you Ahmed for reminding me that slowly and surely, the egg will walk. Valery, Queen of Elegance, thank you for knowing what to say and when to say it, good timing is always stylish. Thank you Tom and Sasha for reminding me that there is a gorgeous, big wide world out there. Nicola, thank you for helping me to find answers I would never have found if it hadn't been for you, and for glorious days in Number 30, and Alice, thank you for the finest scone/scon marathon, beach walk philosophies and Chippendale adventures. Thank you, Liz and Gilly, with special thanks to Finner's for a doily-free supply of zany names. And darling Jemima, thank you for serenading me on the piano as I wrote this book, and *muchas gracias* Bay for exquisite cooking and to both gorgeous daughters for making sure I got sufficient writing done before diving into *Gossip Girl*. Thank you, dearest Mum, for being consistently brilliant and wonderful in multiple ways, including the best holiday adventures (even on the 12th floor!) Thank you, Clare, golden star #ICAVIP. Sarah Beth, you are a bright shining diamond, and speaking of

precious, Turtle, love is still the answer and thank you
Rupert and Sophia for reaffirming our belief. Lastly, very
special thanks to Rosie O'Neill, Queen of Chicago, whose
fabulous artwork kept me company as I wrote this book,
to Eve Fasenfeld for her kindness and beauty, and to Jilly
Cooper, who sparked my imagination in the first place.